J.C.FIELDS

A STORM DOES THIS WAY COME

VINCI
BOOKS

For Mikey, Chloe, Alice and Peyton.

Vinci Books

vinci-books.com

Published by Vinci Books Ltd in 2026

1

A CIP catalogue record for this book is available from the British Library.
Paperback ISBN: 9781036706579

The EU GPSR authorised representative is Logos Europe, 9 rue Nicolas Poussion, 17000 La Rochelle, France
contact@logoseurope.eu

By J.C. Fields

Dakota Storm

A Storm Does This Way Come

The Sean Kruger Series

The Fugitive's Trail
The Assassin's Trail
The Imposter's Trail
The Cold Trail
The Money Trail
The Dark Trail
The Virtual Trail
The Ominous Trail
The Manchurian's Trail

Foreword

The novel you hold in your hand began as a humble short story penned sometime in late 2017. I've changed computers since then, so the date stamp is questionable. Most short stories I write, once completed, are set aside and for lack of a better word, abandoned.

Not this one.

The title began as *The Rescue* and I wrote it as an entry to a short story contest sponsored by one of the local writer's groups. If I remember correctly, it came in third. That short story is now Chapter 1 of this novel. However, the text has undergone extensive editing since 2017.

I kept going back to the story, because it begged to be expanded into a more complete narrative. Finally in the fall of 2022, I submitted the revision to Paul McSorley's YouTube Podcast, *Fear From the Heartland*. The first seven chapters can be heard on the podcast. The audience response confirmed I needed to finally write the whole story.

The title comes from a discarded manuscript started

during the summer of 2013. I loved the title, but the story, not so much.

So, here it is, a new novel titled, *A Storm Does This Way Come*. At this time, I really don't know if I will write a follow up. My gut tells me I will, but when, is a different matter. When you get to the end, you'll see there is a lot of wiggle room for a second book featuring Dakota Storm and Apollo. Sometimes, I can't help myself.

I hope you enjoy this tale, as much as I enjoyed writing it.

J.C. Fields, Summer 2023

Part I

Chapter One

East Missouri

Fog shrouded the creaky old footbridge, reducing visibility to twenty feet in any direction. The effect magnified the isolation Dakota Storm already felt. The muffled sound of water rushing over rocks and boulders seventy-five feet below the bridge added a surreal aspect to his surroundings.

His heart pounded as he stared at the narrow-suspended bridge whose length disappeared into the mist. His determination, amassed since the accident, waned as he approached the steel cabling securing the bridge's expanse. Doubts about his decision suddenly crept into his conscience.

Is this what I really want?

Pain and guilt consumed his every waking moment. He needed an escape. But was this the coward's way out? The answer eluded him. All he knew was his wife and three-year-old son were gone forever. Killed in a senseless car accident caused by a drunk driver. The thought of spending another Christmas without them produced a painful hollow feeling.

The image of his wife on their wedding day came to him as he closed his eyes. Her white dress and the crown of white statice and lavender remained as vivid in his memory as the day she wore them. But now, two years since the incident, the image resembled a picture rather than a real person. He could only remember his son's face if he focused on a photograph. His guilt deepened as his memories faded.

Grasping the steel cable, he stood still for what seemed like forever. The wooden planks under his feet darkened as dusk settled over the park. He put one foot on the bridge and heard it creak.

Through the gloom created by the fog, he heard a whimper. Standing still, he tilted his head toward the sound and concentrated. It grew in intensity. As an ex-military dog handler, he knew the tone of an injured canine. On instinct, he yelled, "Where are you, boy?"

From the depths of the mist surrounding the bridge came a series of desperate barks. His original purpose for being at the bridge vanished as he rushed toward the sound of a wounded animal.

Halfway across the creaky, swaying bridge, he discerned the shape of a medium-size dog tied to one of the bridge planks. As he approached, the dog barked then bared its teeth in a snarl.

Storm steadied himself, holding on to the top cable of the bridge as it swayed from his movement. "What's wrong, boy?" His voice remained calm and soothing as he walked slowly toward the animal. "Are you caught?"

Staring at the approaching man, the canine stopped barking, dipped its head, and whimpered. Storm kneeled a foot away from the dog's closest reach and spoke in a gentle voice. "You're a pretty one." As he spoke, he searched for the spot where the dog was tied. It appeared to be a leash or rope entangled amongst the wooden planks of the bridge.

The trapped border collie displayed the standard black-and-white coat. Its bright eyes revealed the full intelligence of the breed. He sat in front of the dog, crossed his legs, and talked to the animal. What he said mattered not, using a calm, soothing voice did. From its appearance, the dog had been trapped for a while. The hair was soaked and matted, but the ears pointed up while the tail wagged with anticipation. Storm could see a choker collar, used for training, attached to the leash. On closer inspection, it appeared to be adjusted to keep the animal from escaping.

As darkness descended, he made an attempt to touch the dog. To his surprise, it allowed him to pat its head. The more he talked, the calmer the canine grew. Taking a leap of faith, he untangled the leash. "Let's get off this bridge and get you something to eat." Without hesitation, it followed.

Four hours later, Storm had the animal fed, watered, and bathed.

Clumps of matted hair littered the bottom of the bath tub after trimming and brushing the dog's coat. The canine now slept on a blanket next to his bed as he searched several local websites for any notifications of a missing border collie. The search proved fruitless. Sitting back against the headboard, he watched the dog's chest rise and fall. "Maybe it's best I don't find who left you on the bridge to starve. Not sure I want to return you to the person who would abandon such a beautiful creature."

The border collie raised his head and watched him, his tail occasionally thumping the floor. He knew the canine was incapable of smiling, but it sure appeared to be one. "What am I going to call you, boy?"

The collie's tail thumped the floor harder.

"What about Apollo, the Greek god of light and healing?"

The speed of the thumping increased twofold.

"Then, Apollo it is." A new thought came to him. "Maybe, while I was rescuing you, you were rescuing me as well." He kept his gaze on his new companion. "God works in mysterious ways sometimes, buddy."

Chapter Two

St. Louis County, Missouri

December - Three Years Later

Dakota Storm and Apollo entered the St. Louis County Sheriff's locker room thirty minutes before the start of their shift. As he placed his civilian clothes in his locker, someone behind him yelled.

"Hey, Storm, Cap wants to see you in his office."

Turning, Storm saw his shift commander, Brad Garrett, at the end of the locker row with his hands on his hips.

"Why?"

Garrett shrugged. "Don't know. Above my paygrade. All he said was for you to report as soon as you arrive."

"Got it. Thanks, Sarge."

As he moved through the crowded room, Apollo stayed on his left side in perfect step as they approached Captain

Guy McBride's office. After knocking on the frame, he remained outside the open door.

McBride waved him in. "Shut the door, please."

Storm's first thought was, *Uh, oh. What have I done now?* He stood at parade rest in front of the desk, waiting for whatever chewing out might follow.

"Relax, Storm. Have a seat."

He lowered himself into one of the two wooden chairs in front of the ancient gray metal desk.

McBride smiled, gathered the paperwork, tapped it on the surface to make a neat stack, and placed it in his out-basket. He glanced at Apollo sitting to the left of Storm. The border collie panted, it's eyes on the him while it sat ramrod straight. "Is that dog always by your side?"

"His name is Apollo, sir."

"Yes, I know. You didn't answer the question."

"You wanted to see me, Captain?"

McBride chuckled. "Like I said earlier, take it easy. You're not in trouble. The reason you're here is because I got an odd email this morning."

Storm's posture relaxed slightly, but he kept his guard up. "I take it the email concerned me?"

The captain nodded. "The message also concerned Judy and your son."

At the mention of their names, Storm tensed.

"I'm sorry you were the first responder at the accident site, Dakota."

The deputy inhaled deeply and pursed his lips.

"I know it's still difficult for you to think about the accident, but you need to hear this."

Blinking back tears, Storm steeled himself and asked, "What about them?"

"The email was not specific, but there's an inmate at the

Jefferson City Correction Center who is dying. His last wish is to talk to you."

"Who is he? Someone I arrested?"

A nod from McBride confirmed his statement.

"What's his name, Captain?"

"Eli Burns. Do you remember him?"

"Vaguely. Wasn't he part of a stolen car, chop-shop gang?"

"Yeah, that's him. You were undercover and helped convict him. He's in the JCCC infirmary, dying from cancer. Reportedly, he only has a few days to live and wants to meet with you."

Storm blinked several times. "Not sure I want to talk to him."

"Don't blame you, but, according to the warden's email this morning, he said he has information you need to know."

"I'm on duty for the next five days, sir."

"Not anymore. I want you to change out of your uniform and head to Jeff City when we're done."

"Am I on special assignment?"

"As of five minutes ago."

"What do you think this is about, Captain?"

"Don't know. Hopefully you'll know by the end of the day."

JCCC rules did not allow canines into the facility, so Apollo stayed in the pickup. Being late in the fall, with temperatures hovering in the mid-fifties, he was safe and comfortable in Storm's old Ford F-150. After showing identification as a St. Louis County deputy, he was escorted to the infirmary and a small room with one bed. The individual residing there appeared emaciated and barely alive. A male nurse attending to various tubes attached to the inmate's body looked up as Storm entered the room.

"Are you Deputy Dakota Storm?"

"Yeah."

The nursed touched the patient's shoulder. "Eli?"

The man's eyes fluttered, and he stared unfocused at the figure above him.

"Eli, the deputy you wanted to speak to is here."

The man turned his head toward the door where Storm stood. Dark circles under the dull blue-gray eyes contrasted with the translucent skin and hairless head. The fluorescent light above the bed gave the man a ghostly appearance. He croaked, "You Storm?"

"Yes."

He raised a shaking hand and waved the deputy closer.

Approaching the man's bedside, Storm observed a small tear trickle down the inmate's face.

In a voice barely above a whisper, he said, "As you can probably tell, I'm dying."

Storm folded his arms.

"You already know that, so I'll be brief. The death of your wife and son wasn't an accident. They were murdered."

Tilting his head, Storm remained silent.

"The guy wasn't supposed to be drunk. He was paid to make it look like a one-car accident."

The world spun as Storm steadied himself with a hand on the wall next to him. "What do you mean, he was paid?"

A series of hacking coughs racked the inmate's frail body.

The shock of the revelation gave Storm pause. He

waited for the patient's spasms to settle down. When they did, he leaned over the bed. "What do you mean he was paid?" he asked again.

The infirm man blinked rapidly for several seconds. "I was the guy they told to steal a car for him to use. The plan was for him to run your wife's vehicle off the road. Make it look like a hit-and-run. But he'd had a few too many drinks and fucked up. He was headed in the wrong direction when he hit her car head-on."

"Why are you telling me this?"

Through gritted teeth, he said, "Because you need to know the truth, and I can die in peace. I'm not a murderer, Storm."

"Right."

"There's a reason she was killed."

"I'm listening."

"It had to do with who she was."

"What are you talking about? She was Judy Storm."

Burns shook his head. "Her name wasn't Judy…" The man stiffened and looked at his caregiver. "The morphine is wearing off—please."

The nurse inserted a syringe into the tube attached to the patient's left arm. As the chemicals flowed into the inmate's body, his demeanor changed, and he relaxed. "That's better." He glanced again at Storm. "I didn't know who she was, either, until I got here."

"Burns, you're not making any sense. Her name was Judy Thorn, and I met her at a friend's birthday party."

"Her name wasn't Judy Thorn."

"What was it?"

The man shook his head. "Don't know."

"Whose idea was it to kill her?"

"I knew him as Gimpy."

"What kind of a name is that?"

"Nickname. No one used their real names in the group. He walked with a slight limp."

"Why was she targeted?"

"Because she escaped…" Another coughing fit racked the man's body. His eyes closed and he gasped for breath.

Storm turned toward the nurse.

"It's the drugs. I have to use more each time to control his pain. Eventually, either the morphine or the cancer will kill him."

Burns' eyes closed.

Storm watched the man for several seconds. He was out cold. "How long before he's conscious enough to talk again?"

"Couple of hours, maybe more."

Storm returned four hours later and was once again escorted to the infirmary room where two orderlies were cleaning. When he knocked on the doorframe, one turned. "Deputy Storm?"

"Yes, where's Burns?"

"Passed away about thirty minutes ago."

Chapter Three

Central Missouri

Storm took the scenic route back to his home in Chesterfield, Missouri. The two-hour drive from Jefferson City gave him time to think and talk with Apollo. His conversations with the dog were more thinking-out-loud sessions than true discussions. Since finding the border collie three years earlier, it had never offered an opinion, just unwavering loyalty.

Thirty minutes into the drive, Storm glanced at the canine strapped into a dog safety harness in the passenger seat. Its keen eyes focused on the road ahead. "What do you think, Apollo?"

The dog turned its head, its gaze now fixed on his handler.

"Yeah, that's what I think, too. I don't know if I should believe the guy or not."

Apollo kept its gaze on Storm, tongue out and panting.

He displayed the same expression he did the night Storm and he first met, the appearance of a smile.

Storm continued, "Why would someone I vaguely remember drag me to Jeff City to tell me Judy was really someone else?"

Apollo tilted his head slightly, but, as was his habit, did not answer the question.

"That's just silly. When we were dating, she showed me the house she grew up in, and we drove by the elementary school she attended. I saw her high school yearbook with all the notes her friends wrote in it. She even talked about her days in college and the guys she dated." He watched the road and lapsed into silence. Ten minutes later, he said, "She never talked about her parents because they died when she was young. She lived with her aunt."

He stopped. "You know, Apollo, she and I never visited the aunt. I wonder if she's still alive. If she is, maybe we could find her?"

Apollo shifted his position on the seat and closed his eyes.

After a quick glance at his canine partner, Storm returned his attention to the road. "I've never been through her personal papers. I just couldn't make myself do it. I wonder if she left any information there that could help me find the aunt."

Glancing at Apollo again, his companion kept one eye open, looking at him. "Thanks for the talk, buddy. I'm not sure I buy the old man's fantasy."

The canine raised his head, yawned, shifted position, and closed both eyes.

Storm chuckled. "Leave it to you to remind me to get back to reality."

Two Weeks Before Christmas

With five years having passed since his wife and son's untimely death, Storm finally felt the desire to decorate the home for the holidays. Bringing the decorations into the house from the attic helped with his need to accept the fact they were gone.

When he opened the first plastic tote, he almost stopped and took all of them back to the garage. Judy's favorite decorations were on the top. One of them was a music box depicting the manger scene. As tears formed in his eyes, he straightened and took a deep breath. He exhaled slowly.

With renewed determination, he arranged the items from the container around the house. To the best of his memory, he replicated how she decorated the rooms. In another storage box, he found the Christmas tree bulbs. As he rummaged around, he noticed a strange ornate jewelry container on the left side. Judy had insisted each year that she, and she alone, would decorate the tree. Now, he found something in the container he had never seen before.

With trepidation, Storm lifted the box out and examined it. Apollo appeared by his side, having awoken from his morning nap. Looking up at his master, he panted at his normal rate. Storm turned his attention to the dog. "Should I open the box, buddy?"

A small whimper came from the animal.

"Yeah, I think I should, too." Storm studied the wooden box with intricate carvings on the top and sides. He found a latch and flipped it open. The contents amounted to a leather-bound journal. After a moment of hesitation, he lifted the book and opened it. His late-wife's eloquent handwriting greeted him on the first page.

My dearest Dakota,

If you have found this journal, my past has caught up with me. For that, I am sorry. I did not mean to fall in love with you, but I did. You have made me happier than I ever thought possible. Plus, I was almost able to forget where I came from. I am currently pregnant with our son and hope the three of us can live in peace forever. But sometimes the gods do not allow past transgressions to go unpunished.

Within the pages of this journal, I have recorded information you will need to keep yourself and our son safe.

I know I should have told you the truth from the beginning, but if you had known the facts, you would have walked away. Call it selfish, but I could not take the chance of losing you.

Take care of yourself and our son, knowing my love for you will never die.

Judy

Storm read the passage with disbelief the first time and grudging acceptance by the third. He sat cross-legged on the floor next to the plastic tote. As he looked up from the journal, Apollo laid his head on the deputy's knee. His eyes seemed filled with sorrow, reflecting his owner's feelings. Placing a hand on the dog's head, he whispered, "Holy shit, Apollo."

Storm rapped on Shift Commander Garrett's doorframe.

Garrett waved him in. "What's on your mind, Storm?"

The deputy handed the man the journal. "I found this in some of Judy's personal things I had not been through."

The sergeant hesitated to accept the book. "Uh…not sure that's any of my business, Dakota."

"In reality, it is, Sergeant. It outlines the structure of a criminal enterprise working out of both St. Louis and Memphis. The connections stretch all the way to Biloxi, Mississippi and New Orleans on the coast."

Taking the journal in his hand, Garrett thumbed through the pages. "Drugs?"

"Yes, plus illegal guns and sex trafficking."

Focusing on Storm, Garrett asked, "Was Judy…"

"No, sir. According to the journal, she escaped their clutches in her late teens and managed to start a new life."

Setting the book down, Garrett said, "Was she killed because she escaped?"

Storm shrugged. "I don't know. But that's my assumption."

Folding his arms, the sergeant tilted his head. "Let me guess. You want to investigate all of this?"

"No, sir."

"Then why bring it to me?"

"I'm requesting vacation time."

"To investigate it?"

"No. I need to understand how she got involved with them."

"Same thing."

"Not really." He paused. "Besides, I haven't used much vacation since the accident. I've got over six weeks built up and believe it's time to take it."

Garrett remained quiet after he picked up the journal again and thumbed through the pages. He turned his attention back to the deputy. "All right, Storm. Vacation granted."

"Thank you." The deputy retrieved the journal and turned to go.

Just before he exited the office, Garrett said, "Dakota, if you run into trouble, call me."

Turning, Storm gave the man a sad smile. "Thanks, Sergeant."

Chapter Four

Memphis, Tennessee

Two Days Later

Christmas lights lit the night skyline of Memphis as Storm drove through the downtown area. Apollo sat next to him, tongue out, panting and his head swiveling as they passed the decorations. The industrial part of town between the airport and the Burlington Northern Santa Fe railyards north of East Shelby Drive being their destination. According to Judy's journal, the warehouse he sought could be found on Malone Drive.

Storm wore black jeans, a long-sleeved black layered insulated shirt, black New Balance athletic shoes, and a rolled-up black balaclava. The white sections of Apollo's coat were dyed black with a canine-safe coloring dye. The two would be invisible in the darkened recesses of the area the deputy guided them toward.

After consulting the GPS unit on his phone, the vacationing law enforcement officer drove by the location looking for any signs of guards or security cameras. He saw no indication of physical sentries, but he did note the presence of multiple surveillance devices.

After parking his Ford F-150 half a mile from the warehouse, Storm rolled down his balaclava. Face covered, he grabbed his black backpack and exited the truck with Apollo hot on his heels. Keeping to the shadows far from the lights of the area, it took them twenty minutes to reach the rear entrance of the building. Once there, he extracted a paintball gun from his backpack and aimed it at the security camera covering the rear entrance to the warehouse.

The red liquid-filled projectile splattered on the lens, effectively blinding it. He adjusted his aim and fired at another one. With both cameras disabled, he ran to the back door. Testing the knob, he determined it would be faster to use a crowbar. Not subtle but effective. Extracting the device from his backpack, he inserted it into the space between the lockset and the doorjamb. With two strong pulls on the bar, the door swung open. This accomplished, he and Apollo entered the dimly lit interior.

Kneeling beside the dog, he made a circling motion with his index finger and the canine took off into the interior of the structure. Visibility within the building came from numerous security lights. Before Storm could start his search, Apollo yelped once.

Rushing in the direction of the sound. He found the dog sniffing at a door that appeared to be the entrance to a separate section of the warehouse. Placing his ear against the entrance, the sound of female voices pleading for help emanated from within.

By means of the same crowbar used on the back

entrance, he jimmied the door open and was greeted by the sight of ten young girls. All appeared in their teens, each hugging themselves, tears flowing down their cheeks, and trembling.

One brave soul asked, "Who are you?"

"Are you all okay?"

The same woman said, "Do we look okay? We're in a warehouse in the middle of who-knows-where with no food or water. How do you think we are?"

Storm abandoned his plans to search the warehouse. "If you want out, ask your questions later. Right now, follow me."

He turned and guided the ten girls out of the building.

———

Thirty minutes later, police cars, ambulances, and fire trucks gathered around the warehouse. Female police officers attended to the young girls, runaways from Mississippi and Louisiana ranging in age from fourteen to eighteen.

A Memphis police department sergeant stood in front of Storm. "While we appreciate your help with finding and freeing these young ladies, what the hell were you doing in there?"

"Following a tip." He showed the officer his St. Louis County deputy sheriff ID.

"You could have come to us first."

"I could have, but I didn't."

"I don't need to remind you about the number of laws you broke with your illegal entry into the building."

"No, you don't. But you're missing the fact that ten underage females were being held against their will inside. Do you also fail to recognize that they are probably part of a sex-trafficking ring that extends from New Orleans to St. Louis?"

The tall officer offered his hand. "George Stevens."

Storm shook it. "Dakota Storm." He pointed to the border collie sitting next to him. "That's Apollo. He's a certified K9 officer."

"Okay, Storm. How did you learn about this?"

"From an informant, before they killed her. I have her notes."

Stevens sighed. "We knew something was off about this warehouse but never could obtain enough evidence to get a search warrant."

Storm did not answer.

Another Memphis police officer walked up to Stevens and whispered in his ear. The sergeant's eyebrows rose immediately and he said, "You're not free to go yet, Storm. Stay put. I have something I need to tend to." He hurried away, following the other policeman.

Storm scratched Apollo's head and said, "Good find, buddy."

The dog looked up, his tongue out, panting and seemed to give the deputy a smile.

After a few minutes, Storm lowered the tailgate on his pickup and sat with his legs dangling. Apollo jumped up and lay next to him.

The young woman who had spoken to him earlier walked up, a blanket wrapped around her shoulders. "They tell me you're a police officer."

Storm said, "My name's Dakota. What's yours?"

The young woman tilted her head and hesitated for a moment. "They call me Angel."

"Yeah, but what's your real name?"

She did not answer right away. After a few moments she said, "Isabelle."

"Well, Isabelle, it's nice to meet you."

"I wanted to thank you for getting us out of there."

Storm shrugged. "Glad I could help."

She clutched the blanket tighter around herself. "We're not the only ones, you know."

The deputy raised an eyebrow.

"This place is an overnight stop for us girls. We would have been moved again in the morning."

"How do you know that?"

"That's what we were told. Those shitheads didn't even give us food or water."

After shaking his head slightly, Storm asked, "Who brought you here?"

The girl took a deep breath and blew it out. "Tall, bald guy. Said his name was Billy. I didn't believe him. Who would use their real name in this kind of a situation?" She took another breath. "Before he locked us in the room, he said he'd be right back with bottled water and burgers. Asshole never returned."

"Did you know where you were headed?"

"No."

"Who are these girls?"

"Mostly runaways. Two of us aged out of the foster care system with nowhere to go."

"What about relatives?"

"Most of us don't have any, or they've disowned us."

"How old are you, Isabelle?"

"Old enough."

Storm folded his arms and focused on the young woman. The silence lasted for an unusual length of time.

Finally, she said, "Eighteen."

"What happened to your parents?"

"I've never met my father. My mother's in prison somewhere in Louisiana."

"I'm sorry."

She shrugged. "Not your fault."

"What about your last foster care parents?"

After a chuckle, she said, "They didn't give a shit. Once the state stopped paying them, they kicked me out."

Stevens returned to the pickup. "Well, Storm, you've uncovered a hornet's nest here."

"How so?"

"There're enough stolen guns in there to arm a division. We also found a body."

Raising an eyebrow, Storm remained silent.

"It appears someone killed him execution style. Bullet to the back of the head, and he's face down on the concrete floor."

Isabelle asked, "What's he look like?"

"Bald and tall is all I can tell you at the moment."

"Now I know why he never came back with our burgers."

Stevens frowned at the girl and then Storm.

The St. Louis County deputy said, "She just told me someone matching your victim's description brought them here. He was also supposed to bring them food and water."

Folding his arms, the police sergeant turned his attention to her for a few moments. "Can you identify him?"

"Yeah, if you want me to."

"Follow me." He pointed a finger at Storm. "You stay here. Don't leave."

Midmorning, Storm and Apollo were still waiting by the Ford F-150 for Stevens to release them. Noting he wasn't under arrest kept him from being too worried. Apollo, after consuming the contents of Storm's last water bottle, lay next to him on the truck tailgate.

The girls were on their way to a clinic. Those under eighteen would be transferred to a facility for homeless children. Isabelle and another eighteen-year-old girl would then be taken to a shelter for battered females.

Apollo raised his head and stared at the approaching Memphis police sergeant.

"You're free to go, Storm."

Sliding off the tailgate, the deputy asked, "What changed your mind?"

"I talked to your commanding officer."

Storm remained quiet.

"He informed me you are one hell of a good deputy and were in St. Louis yesterday until six p.m." With a slight pause, Stevens smiled. "The medical examiner thinks the bald guy died around six thirty last night."

With a nod, Storm asked, "What will happen to the girls?"

"They'll be fine." Stevens gestured toward the warehouse and continued, "There are signs throughout the building this is a regular stop for human trafficking. While we knew about it, it's been off our radar for a few months. We appreciate you exposing it for what it was."

"Any idea who owns the place?"

"A local investment company. They use a property management firm to handle the leasing agreements. That company told us a manufacturer out of New Orleans pays the rent." He chuckled. "The outfit in New Orleans has no record of leasing the building."

"How's the rent paid?"

"Whoever rented the building paid cash up front for a year."

"In other words, a dead end."

"Appears that way." He paused, stroked his chin, and then took a breath. "Uh, we found some disturbing evidence in another section of the warehouse."

"Let me guess. Drugs?"

Stevens shook his head. "Blood on the floor of a different storage room. We aren't sure what it means, but the forensic guys are telling me it's from five different individuals."

"Damn."

"I not supposed to tell you this, but thanks for helping expose this place, Dakota."

With a grim nod, Storm shook the man's hand and returned to his pickup.

As he sat in the driver's seat preparing to leave, he closed his eyes. The image of the ten girls in the room intruded on his thoughts. He would never forget their look of sheer terror.

Chapter Five

Memphis

At fifteen minutes before nine p.m., Storm and Apollo occupied a motel room on the city's south side. While he studied his wife's journal, Apollo slept on the floor next to him. Without warning, the border collie's head snapped erect, and his ears straightened.

A low growl emanated from the dog's throat. The deputy reached over to the bed and extracted his personal automatic pistol, a Sig Sauer P226, from his backpack.

Apollo stood and approached the door, sniffing the sill. He then started barking furiously. Stepping over to a wall next to the window, Storm moved the curtain so he could peek out. Two men stood there holding pistols pointed at the door. In the split second he saw them, both faces were burned into his memory.

He whistled, and Apollo ran to his side just as the two men started firing into the door of his hotel room. The larger of the two raised his foot and slammed it against the door. It crashed against the wall.

As the first intruder rushed in, Storm fired his Sig Sauer twice. The man collapsed on the floor, blood seeping into the carpet.

Heavy footfalls receded off into the darkened hotel parking lot.

———

Memphis police sergeant George Stevens knelt to examine the body lying in the hotel room doorway. He stood and turned to Storm. "I know this guy. He's been the topic of many conversations during our morning briefings. I can guarantee nobody's gonna miss him." Stevens then examined the bullet holes in the door. "Looks like they were pointing down."

Storm nodded. "Apollo was at the door barking."

"Glad they missed."

"So am I."

"Okay, Storm, why did they come after you?"

"I have no clue, Sergeant." He folded his arms. "My question is, how did they know where to find me? I didn't even make the decision to stay here until I saw the sign for the place."

"Apparently, they figured out you're the one who found the girls. Probably followed you here from the warehouse." He stood back as the medical examiner technicians loaded the dead man onto a gurney. "We have a positive ID on the body we found there."

"Who was he?"

"William Mallard."

"Isabelle told me he wanted to be called Billy."

"There you go. He's from New Orleans, and one of the NOPD detectives told me he was knee-deep in the smuggling trade down there. He also expressed relief he was now my problem."

Storm tilted his head. "Why are you telling me all of this, Sergeant?"

"Because we didn't know any of this until you showed up twenty-four hours ago. Now, I've got two dead thugs and ten homeless teenage girls."

"Better than ten dead ones."

Stevens looked over his glasses at Storm. "There is that." He paused. "Why is it, all this doesn't happen until you start snooping around?"

Walking over to the desk in the hotel room, Storm picked up the journal and tossed it to Stevens. "Because I found that."

Catching the object, Stevens flipped through it. "It's a diary. So?"

"Are you going to arrest me?"

The sergeant chuckled. "No, Storm. You seem to know more about this situation than anyone. I'd like to get your help."

Pointing at the book, the deputy said, "My wife and son were killed in a head-on collision five years ago." He then told Stevens about the prisoner who confessed on his death bed to orchestrating the accident. "I found the journal with some Christmas ornaments I hadn't touched for years. It outlines the criminal organization William Mallard belonged to. The sex trafficking has been going on for at least a decade or longer. It tells how my wife escaped and started a new life. These guys chose to punish her because they thought she'd talk. She never told anyone about her experiences. Except in the journal. I would like to think her words could help shut these assholes down."

Stevens skimmed over several pages, shut the book, and handed it back to Storm. "Like I said, my department is requesting your help."

"I'd have to clear it with my commander."

"That's already in the works. My boss will be talking to yours sometime today."

The ringing of Storm's cell phone interrupted the discussion. "Just a second, Sergeant." Pressing the accept call icon, the deputy said, "This is Storm."

"Dakota, it's Carter."

"What's all the commotion in the background, Carter?"

"That's why I'm calling, man. We got a call about a fire. It's your house. I'm at the scene and those are the sounds of firemen trying to put it out."

Silence filled the hotel room as Storm stared at a wall. "How bad?"

"It appears to be fully engulfed, but then, I'm just a county deputy, not a firefighter."

Glancing at his watch, Storm did the math in his head. "I'm four hours away. I'll leave right now." After ending the call, he turned to Stevens. "My house is on fire. I'm going back to St. Louis. Give me your cell phone number, and I'll talk to my commander while I'm there."

"Dakota, you're probably guessing this gang set it on fire."

"Yeah. I wouldn't want to bet against it."

———

Going on close to thirty hours without sleep, except for a quick nap during the afternoon, Storm headed north on I-

55. The time approached two a.m. as he passed the last exit for Sikeston, Missouri. At this time of night, traffic on the divided highway could only be described as nonexistent. So, when he noticed a pair of headlights rapidly approaching from behind, he paid attention.

He lifted the lid for the center console of the F-150 and extracted his Sig Sauer. "Heads-up, Apollo."

The dog, having fallen asleep on the back seat, jumped into the front passenger side, his attention on the back window.

Storm mumbled, "This could be nothing, but let's not take chances." The headlights approached rapidly and appeared to almost collide with the rear of the pickup. Just as fast, the vehicle swung to their left to pass.

The deputy slammed his foot on the brake pedal and the F-150 went into a skid. As the larger vehicle sped past, a loud crack sounded and a starburst pattern formed on the far-right side of the windshield.

The other truck accelerated and disappeared into the night. Looking over at Apollo, the dog appeared unharmed. He said, "You okay, boy?"

The dog just panted, but did not respond.

"Good." He pulled the truck over to the shoulder and parked. Consulting his cell phone, he checked for an alternate route north. "We need to find a less obvious way home."

Chapter Six

St. Louis, MO

Five hours after leaving the hotel in Memphis, Storm pulled up to his now burned-out house. The deputy who called him earlier stood next to a squad car talking to a fireman. One fire engine remained on the scene, and yellow crime scene tape roped off the perimeter of what remained of his home.

Storm walked up to the two men, Apollo close to his right heel. As he and Carter shook hands, Storm said, "Not much left, is there?"

"No, sorry, man." Carter nodded at the fireman. "Dakota, this is Jake Riley, he's the fire marshal."

As the two men shook hands, Storm asked, "Where'd it start?"

"We think we've identified three accelerant locations. All on the rear of the house. By the time the first engine got here, the back half of the house was fully engulfed. The house was lost before we even started fighting it."

"So, it was arson."

"Rather aggressive arson if you ask me. No effort whatsoever to make it appear to be an accident."

Taking a deep breath, Storm blew it out as he gazed over the charred remains of the house he and his wife purchased right after their wedding.

Placing his hand on his friend's shoulder, Carter said, "The captain's aware of what's happened. He asked me to tell you, anything you need, just let him know."

"I appreciate that." After a short pause, he turned to the fireman. "How long before I can access the site?"

"My team will have to search it first, but I'd say we can give you access sometime late today."

Storm returned to his pickup. Allowing the dog to jump into the Ford before he got behind the wheel, he said, "Now I'm pissed, Apollo. Except for the ones on my cell phone, all of my pictures of Judy and Todd are gone." He took a deep breath. "Let's find these assholes and shut them down."

Four Days Later

Negotiating with the insurance company about his house and replacing his old pickup with a different vehicle took most of the week. Storm found a used Ford Police Interceptor Utility vehicle available at a local dealership. Being the police version of a Ford Explorer, he traded the F-150 for the SUV. With a more powerful engine than a civilian Explorer, he would be able to outrun another highway incident. The vehicle also gave him another advantage; he knew how to maneuver it, having driven one as a deputy.

On day four, he met with Captain Guy McBride.

"Are you going to rebuild the house?"

Storm shook his head. "No, a real estate company has the lot for sale and I'll use the insurance money to buy somewhere else."

"I'm sorry this happened, Dakota."

"Sir, I have reason to believe the individuals who burned my house are also the ones who murdered Judy and Todd."

"Hmmm."

"It's personal now."

"Not a good combination, Dakota. As a friend, I'd advise against pursuing this vendetta."

"What would you do?"

McBride remained silent for a long time. Finally, he gave the deputy a grim smile. "Probably the same thing. What can I do to help?"

"Authorize me to be on loan to the Memphis police department."

"Do you plan to come back?"

"I plan to, but…"

"You're a good officer, Storm. I'd hate to lose you."

"If I don't help stop these guys, they'll eventually succeed in shutting me up. So, you'd be assisting my return to St. Louis."

Southwest of Memphis

Utilizing information provided by Judy's journal, Storm staked out an old run-down motel just outside of Tunica, Mississippi. According to the missive, the location served as a way station for transporting sex workers who worked the Tunica casinos.

Sitting in his Explorer with Apollo in the seat next to him, he watched the comings and goings of the area surrounding the inn. Hidden in the parking lot of a strip mall across from the building, he concentrated on a van parked at the northern end of the structure.

The van possessed a Louisiana license plate. Plus, the windows were heavily tinted, preventing observation of the passengers. At exactly 9:40 p.m., four young females entered the van and a burly man got behind the wheel. It pulled out and headed west toward the casinos.

Storm picked up his radio and said, "Target is traveling west on 713 toward Casino Strip Resort Blvd."

"10-4. We see it."

"Copy that."

Storm noticed another car pull out of the motel parking lot and follow the van. From his advantage point, he could see two men sitting in the front of the vehicle.

"White Toyota Camry with two white males following van."

"10-4." There was a pause. "Got it. Keep an eye on your location. Notify if needed."

"Roger that."

Putting the Explorer in gear, he eased the vehicle out of the parking slot and headed toward the motel to see if he could detect any additional activity. Just before he exited the mall parking lot, his radio went active.

"Shots fired, shots fired, officer down."

Without hesitation, Storm accelerated the vehicle in the direction the van and Camry traveled.

Coming up on the scene, Storm saw two men on the ground next to the Camry and another by the van with two officers administering first aid. The four females from the van faced it, their hands above their heads and palms against the vehicle. A female police officer and Stevens stood behind them. The SUV's tires screeched to a halt, and the deputy jumped out. Apollo followed.

Sergeant Stevens pointed toward a vacant field. "The van driver took off on foot, see if you and Apollo can find him."

With a nod, Storm took the dog to the driver's seat of the van. "Identify and seek." Apollo jumped up, sniffed the seat, hopped down, and sprinted toward the open field.

Yanking his badge attached to a lanyard out from under his sweatshirt, he gripped his Sig Sauer and followed at a sprint. The dog stopped and sniffed the ground for a few seconds. He then took off at a hard run heading toward Storm's left.

With a waxing gibbous moon in the eastern sky, Storm was able to follow Apollo fairly easily. As the canine neared a grove of trees, he slowed and glanced back at Storm. Catching up with the dog, the deputy kneeled beside him. "Where is he, Apollo?"

The canine took off again and Storm trailed close behind. After the dog rushed into the grove, the deputy heard a man curse. The burly man from the van exited the cover of trees at a run. Apollo, doing what the breed had been bred to do for hundreds of years in Scotland, basically herded the driver out of the brush by constantly nipping at the fugitive's heels and then backing off. Suppressing a chuckle, Storm took a Weaver Stance and yelled, "Halt, let me see your hands."

The man looked at Storm and then the dog. He stopped running, shook his head, and raised his arms.

As he approached the fugitive, the deputy said, "On your knees, hands behind your head."

After kneeling, he watched the deputy approach him. "You're Dakota Storm."

Ignoring the statement, the deputy placed handcuffs on the man's wrists and swung his arms behind him. The prisoner continued, "Hate to tell you this dude, but you're a dead man walking."

Memphis

George Stevens approached the desk currently occupied by Dakota Storm, with two cups of coffee in his hands. He set one in front of Storm and then settled into a chair at the desk next to his new friend. "Tomorrow's Christmas, Dakota."

Taking his attention away from the computer screen, he turned to Stevens. "Thanks for the coffee. Yeah, I know."

"Any plans?"

After taking a sip from the paper cup, Storm shook his head. "Not really. If the weather holds, I thought I'd take Apollo somewhere and let him run. Why?"

Stevens sipped coffee. "The wife and I are having a few friends over for Christmas dinner, would you like to join us?"

"I wouldn't want to intrude."

"Nonsense. Swing on by around one. I'm deep-frying a turkey."

Storm nodded. "Thanks, sounds good."

"Have you spoken to Jacob Gordon yet?"

"Not today, why?"

"He's been asking questions about you. Seems he's some kind of a big shot within the U.S. Marshals Service."

"No, he hasn't talked to me other than when I turned the van driver over to him."

With a chuckle, Stevens stood. "I meant to tell you, nice work bringing him in so fast."

"Apollo deserves the credit."

"Yeah, well, nice work anyway."

Chapter Seven

Memphis

Five minutes later Storm's coffee needed a warm-up. As he stood, Jacob Gordon made a beeline toward his desk.

After the two men shook hands Gordon said, "I understand you recently lost your house in a fire."

"Yes, I did."

"Do you have plans on where you'll live?"

"It's been a little hectic since the fire. I really haven't had time to think about it yet."

Gordon nodded. "Nice work bringing the van driver in so quickly."

"Thanks. Apollo did all the heavy lifting."

Standing two inches taller than Storm, the man folded his arms. "Ever thought about applying to the U.S. Marshals Service?"

"When I got out of the military, I did. But my late wife was pregnant at the time and didn't want me away from home. So, I took a job with the St. Louis County Sheriff's department."

"Sorry about your loss, Storm." He paused. "You were a dog handler in the military, right?"

"Yes, sir. Actually, I was a trainer at Lakeland Air Force Base in Texas."

Gordon nodded. "I read that. I've been authorized to offer you an opportunity to become a deputy U.S. Marshal. Are you interested?"

"Doing what, sir?"

"What you did the other day. Tracking down fugitives and bringing them in."

"What about Apollo?"

Gordon smiled. "I wouldn't want to break up a winning team."

"Can I think about it?"

"Sure. Let me know after Christmas."

Germantown, TN

Christmas Day

Arriving an hour late at George Stevens' house more than likely saved Dakota Storm's life. Approaching the residence located in a nice neighborhood of Germantown, the presence of police and EMT vehicles caused his stomach to clench. After parking on the street, he clipped his badge on his belt and opened the door. Turning to Apollo, he said, "Stay."

The dog relaxed and remained in the passenger seat.

Rushing across the street, he ducked under yellow tape and immediately went to an officer keeping attendance of who entered the scene. Showing his badge, Storm told the man his name.

The policeman wrote it down and said, "Deputy U.S. Marshal Gordon wants to see you. He's in the back."

Storm sprinted around the house. When he rounded the corner, he saw Gordon talking to several uniformed officers. As he approached their location, Gordon broke away from the group and met Storm. "Glad you're here."

"What happened?"

"Stevens was out here tending to a turkey in a fryer when five men in ski masks confronted him. They forced him inside."

"Is he dead?"

"No, but his wife and three of his guests are. He's critically wounded but was able to tell first responders what happened."

"I was supposed to be here at one."

"Best you weren't. Where's Apollo?"

"In my SUV."

"Get him."

Storm let Apollo sniff around where the turkey fryer had been. When the dog stopped and looked at his partner, he sat, his signal he had a scent.

When the deputy made a circling motion with his hand, Apollo took off toward the northwest, his nose close to the ground.

Following his partner, Storm could tell the canine had a strong trail. He did not deviate from his tracking, nor did he stop and sniff the air. He kept his nose to the ground and forged ahead. Located in a relatively new neighborhood, George Stevens' home was surrounded by numerous vacant lots. Apollo stopped at the curb of a cul-de-sac, raised his nose, sniffed the air, and sat. The trail ended there.

Catching up to the dog, Storm surveyed the few homes in the area. On one across from where he stood, he saw what he needed.

Christmas Evening

Jacob Gordon stood in front of the members of the task force in the briefing room. He said, "The hospital reports George Stevens is in critical condition. Prognosis is not good." Surveying the room, he continued, "Deputy Storm located a ring camera image of the attackers." He touched a button on an open laptop, and an image appeared on the screen behind him. "This is a still shot of the vehicle the men arrived in. Note there is a clear image of the license plate. Deputy Storm was able to trace it to the Avis rental kiosk at the Memphis airport." He touched the mouse again.

Another image appeared. "This is a photograph from the Louisiana Office of Motor Vehicles. Meet the individual who rented the SUV identified in the picture. His name is Frank Jackson, aka Gimpy. The vehicle was returned to the airport and, at this moment, is being processed by an FBI forensic team." The picture showed a dark-haired male in his mid-thirties.

A hand shot up in the back of the room. Gordon pointed at the man. "Yeah, Bob."

"His name was registered at the motel where the girls were found."

Turning to the image on the wall, Gordon took a breath. "Ladies and gentlemen, this might be our first break." He turned back to the group. "Let's find out everything we can about our Mr. Frank Jackson."

Storm parked his car outside the door to his hotel room. He turned to Apollo and held up the sack from a local Chinese carryout. "I know it's not a fancy Christmas meal, boy, but there's not much open tonight."

Apollo sat and panted. Suddenly, the dog's ears perked up, and he stared out the rear driver's side window. Dropping the sack, Storm grabbed the SIG Sauer he now kept within easy reach and ducked below the window.

Just as he pushed the door open, the driver's side window shattered. A shadow in his peripheral vision drew his attention. He rolled when he hit the parking lot and turned. A silhouette could be seen running from the scene. He raised his 9mm SIG and squeezed off a shot. Apollo dove out and chased after the figure.

The deputy gained his feet and took off in pursuit of Apollo and the assailant. A shot sounded and the bullet whizzed by his ear. Adrenaline pushed him forward with the need to protect Apollo at all costs.

The sound of the dog catching the running man came to his ears as he closed the distance. Apollo growled, and the man cursed. A streetlight illuminated the scene before him. The suspect stood with his pistol aimed at the canine.

When he saw the deputy running toward him, he raised his weapon. Storm fired just as the assailant's gun went off.

Midnight

Jacob Gordon leaned against the doorframe of the hospital treatment room, a smile on his face. "Well, Dakota, glad you're gonna live."

A sad smile came to Storm's face. "How's Apollo doing?"

"Fit as a fiddle."

"Good. Where is he?"

"He had a gash on his rib cage which the vet said probably came from Frank Jackson's pistol. He's resting comfortably at the vet's office."

"How'd you find a vet this late?"

"I'm with the U.S. Marshals Service. We take care of our team." He hesitated for a second. "How's the arm feeling?"

"Other than a bullet grazing it, fine." He paused. "Where's Jackson?"

"After he was patched up by EMTs, they transferred him to the FBI office here in Memphis. He's singing like a choir member. Apparently, once they explained to him how he was being charged with the murder of a police officer and three others, he found religion."

"Good."

"He told me he thought you were going to pull the trigger any second while you waited for backup."

"The thought crossed my mind." The deputy studied his new friend. "I heard you say Jackson goes by the name Gimpy."

"Yeah."

"An informant told me he was the man who ordered my wife and son's murder."

A frown crossed the marshal's face. "You have any evidence?"

"No. Just the word of a dying man." Storm took a breath and let it out slowly. "Any news about Stevens?"

"Yeah. He didn't make it. Sorry, Dakota."

"He was a good man."

"Yes, he was." The deputy marshal folded his arms and tilted his head. "The other day when I offered you the job as a deputy U.S. Marshal, I didn't tell you I've been named the U.S. Marshal for the Western District of Missouri. You'd be working for me."

Storm nodded. "Congratulations, sir."

"Have you had a chance to think it over?"

"I have."

"And?"

"As long as the deal includes Apollo."

"It does."

"Then my answer is yes."

Gordon offered his hand. "Welcome to the U.S. Marshals Service."

Part II

U.S. MARSHAL

Eighteen Weeks Later

Chapter Eight

Chesterfield, MO

An unusually cold wind for early spring swirled fallen leaves from the previous fall around the headstones of the cemetery. Storm sat in his Ford Explorer, chin resting on arms folded over the steering wheel. Apollo sat in the passenger seat and kept his gaze on the driver.

"Do you want to come with me, Apollo?"

The dog whimpered.

"I'm not looking forward to it, either."

Steeling himself to the cold, he pulled a black watch cap over his ears and zipped his windbreaker together. Cold invaded the warm interior of the SUV as he opened the door. Apollo did not move. "Don't blame you, old friend."

He shut the door and strode toward a specific headstone in the graveyard. When he reached it, he stood silently for several minutes studying the names etched into the granite:

Judy Marie Storm, Wife and Mother, Todd Jeffery Storm, Son.

There was room for his name, but including it would

come later. With his hands in his jacket pockets, he shivered. Partly from the cold wind but mainly from being near his family's final resting place.

"Sorry I haven't visited sooner. I don't have an excuse other than coming here still hurts too much." He paused and wiped his cheek with a sleeve of his coat. "It reminds me you and Todd are gone forever, and there's nothing I can do to bring you back."

He stood silent, lost in his own thoughts for another five minutes. Finally, he said, "I'm moving to Kansas City, my love. The house is gone, the lot was sold to a developer, and after eighteen weeks of basic training, I'm a newly sworn-in deputy U.S. Marshal. Apollo and I are a team. We'll be working out of the Western District office in Kansas City."

Bending over, he brushed several leaves from the base of the headstone. "The guy who paid someone to murder you and Todd is in prison." After several moments of silence, he continued, "I don't think he's the one who ordered it. That individual's still out there, and I won't rest until I find him."

Closing his eyes, he whispered, "I wish there was a way you could tell me what happened before we met. It might help me understand."

The wind picked up, and Storm shivered again. He placed his hand on top of the tombstone. "Gawd, I miss you and Todd." Taking a deep breath, he let it out slowly. "I miss your touch and your laugh. I miss Todd jumping into bed with us and burrowing under the covers to get warm." He closed his eyes. "I love you, Judy Storm. I will always love you."

The wind suddenly died, and the sun broke through the clouds. He looked up and smiled. "And I know you love me. I'll visit as often as I can."

With those words, he returned to the SUV.

Kansas City

Two Days Later

Storm double-checked the address. The small bungalow sat on the east side of State Line Road, which meant it was in Missouri. Across the street would be Kansas. He turned to Apollo. "Well, this must be the place, buddy." Storm exited the SUV with Apollo following.

An elderly man stepped out of the house. "You Storm?"

"Yes, sir."

"You didn't say anything on the phone about having a dog."

"You didn't ask."

"Don't rent to people with dogs, or cats, for that matter."

Storm stopped in the middle of the poorly maintained driveway. "His name is Apollo and he's a certified K9 police dog."

"Police dogs are German shepherds, that ain't no German shepherd."

Storm crossed his arms as he stood; Apollo sat next to his right leg. "Nevertheless, he is a police canine."

"You a cop?"

"Deputy U.S. Marshal."

"Same damn thing. I don't rent to cops."

"Who do you rent to?"

"Anyone who isn't a cop with a dog."

"Sorry I wasted your time."

"Don't be filing no discrimination lawsuit against me. I'll claim the mutt attacked me."

He walked toward to his SUV without a reply. But he did raise his right arm and extend his middle finger.

Back in the SUV, Storm pulled away from the curb and turned to Apollo. "I didn't like the neighborhood anyway. Did you?"

Apollo yawned and stared out the front windshield.

Storm smiled. "And people think dogs can't communicate."

That afternoon, Storm located an affordable ranch-style home with a fenced backyard north of 99th street on Riggs. The owner, a retired Kansas City police lieutenant, welcomed them as new tenants and even gave them a discount on the rent.

"How long you expect to be in Kansas City, Dakota?"

After signing the lease agreement, Storm looked up at his new landlord. "I hope for a while."

"You've not mentioned a wife."

With a shake of his head, Storm said, "Widower."

"I'm sorry for your loss."

"Thanks."

"As soon as the background check comes back, you can move in."

With a chuckle, Storm pointed at Apollo. "With the exception of a few clothes, this is the extent of what I'll be moving in."

Sam Pearce raised an eyebrow.

"My house in St. Louis burned. Apollo and I are making a clean start with a new job."

"So, what're your plans?"

"There's an IKEA somewhere in town, right?"

"Yes, in Merriam, Kansas. Not too far from here."

"My wife loved their furniture. Guess I'll start there."

"They deliver." He handed Storm a business card. "Check out this company for a mattress. They won't screw you like some of the large furniture stores."

Accepting the card, Storm studied it for a few moments. "Thanks, Sam. I appreciate your kindness."

Sam placed his hand on Dakota's shoulder. "Don't mention it. Glad to help."

———————

Monday

The door to Jacob Gordon's office stood open when Storm approached. He knocked on the frame.

Gordon raised his head and smiled. "Did you get settled in, Dakota?"

"Yes, sir." He paused for a moment. "You wanted to see me?"

"How familiar are you with the Mark Twain Forest area in central Missouri?"

"I've hiked there a couple of times. Why?"

Gordon held up a file. "I need you to take this one."

Storm accepted the folder and opened it. The mug shot of a man in his forties with long disheveled salt-and-pepper hair stared back at him. He checked the fugitive's name. "Reid Hicks?"

With a nod, Gordon said, "He was being held in the Pulaski County jail awaiting extradition to New Orleans for murder. He escaped two nights ago and was last seen driving off in a stolen pickup."

Raising an eyebrow, Storm said, "Where was the pickup stolen?"

"Waynesville. It belonged to a soldier stationed at Ft. Leonard Wood."

"How's the soldier?"

"Hospital with a cracked skull."

Looking up from the folder, Storm kept a neutral expression. "Who's going with me?"

"You're the only one I can spare right now. You'll be supplying manpower to the local sheriff's department there. They requested a good dog handler."

"Lucky me."

With a chuckle, Gordon said, "One of the reasons I recruited you, Storm, is because you do better by yourself. You're a loner by instinct."

"Two days is a long time for a fugitive. He could be anywhere by now."

"The locals don't think so. He was caught on a security camera breaking into a convenience store last night. Stole food and water."

"Does he have any relatives in the area?"

"Pulaski County sheriff doesn't seem to think so. However, he does have an ex-girlfriend they're talking to."

"Well, I've got my go bag in the Ford. Apollo and I can be there in about two-and-a-half hours."

Gordon smiled. "Contact info and warrants are in the folder."

Storm flipped through the pages in the file. "I don't see anything unusual at first glance."

"Keep reading."

Storm scanned the rest of the file then looked at Gordon. He raised his eyebrows. "Really?"

The senior U.S. Marshal nodded.

Chapter Nine

Somewhere In Pulaski County Missouri

Located in central Missouri, Pulaski County is a loosely populated area offering two features. I-44, a major interstate highway, dissects the southern part of the state from east to west and is a major economic engine for the county. Plus, Ft. Leonard Wood, a U.S. army training base, provides a huge tax base. More than half of the county's population live near this major interstate highway and the fort.

Northern Pulaski County is mostly rural, sparsely populated, and densely forested terrain. Having spent time in this part of the country as a youth, Reid Hicks took refuge there.

Near the Gasconade River, Hicks came upon an isolated house occupied by an elderly couple. Using the cover of the heavily wooded land surrounding the structure, he spent most of his third day of freedom sizing up the possible place of refuge.

Cold, hungry, and exhausted, Hicks invaded the home

at two minutes past four a.m. on his fourth night as a fugitive.

Ellis and Edith Wallace, both in their early eighties, could offer little resistance to his invasion.

As the sun peaked over the eastern horizon, Hicks studied the two individuals sitting at a small kitchen table, hands folded as they stared at their captor.

"What do you want?"

Hicks smiled. "Money, guns, and a car."

"I'm a retired army sergeant living off my pension, and Edith here is a retired school teacher. Not a lot of money in either profession. Guns I have. There's an old Ford F-150 in the garage out back."

"Where're the weapons?"

"A gun safe in the basement."

Hicks studied the couple. "As long as you two cooperate, you won't get hurt."

Having stayed quiet since their abduction, Edith said, "I remember you. You're that Hicks boy from Crocker. You were in my English class in high school. If I remember correctly, you dropped out mid-year."

Tilting his head, the fugitive pursed his lips. "Don't remember you. But then, I didn't pay much attention in school back then."

Ellis said, "Take what you need; just leave us alone."

"What I need is a place to hide out for a while. You two are in the way."

"You can stick us in the basement. We won't bother you down there."

"What's the safe combination?"

"That's the only bargaining chip I have. Not gonna tell you."

Hicks walked to a drawer next to the kitchen sink and

extracted a large butcher knife. He walked over behind Edith and held the blade against her throat. "What's the damn combination?"

The elderly man told him.

With the couple locked in the basement and the contents of the gun safe arranged on the kitchen table, Hicks made a sandwich and a pot of coffee. He studied an old paper map of the state of Missouri he had found in the gun safe.

Various spots were circled on the map with handwritten notes and a date. Each indicated where the retired army sergeant hunted. "You've been busy since your retirement, Ellis."

After several cups of coffee, he decided on an escape route. However, he thought it best to wait a few more days. If the authorities were looking for him, which he knew they were, staying out of sight a day or two longer might lead them to assume he had fled the county.

With his plan in place, he picked up the retired army sergeant's Sig Sauer M17 from the table and headed to the basement.

On the third attempt to call her parents without an answer, Brenda Wallace felt a bit of apprehension. Her parents always answered their phone. Looking at the clock on the wall, she gathered her keys and purse. She stepped into her assistant's office and said, "Something's wrong at my folks' house. They aren't answering."

"Hope everything's okay."

"I'm sure it is, but with Mom's health on the decline, I don't want to take a chance."

"I'll hold down the fort."

"Thanks, Sally. I'll call when I get there."

Thirty minutes later, as Brenda parked her car in the gravel drive next to the house, she knew something was amiss. Without getting out of the car, she dialed 911.

Dakota Storm watched as two body bags were loaded into an ambulance. Apollo sat on his left as the vehicle drove away from the isolated farmhouse. Pulaski County Sheriff Caleb Bradley walked up to the new deputy U.S. Marshal.

"What do you think, Deputy Storm?"

"Call me Dakota."

"All right. Any thoughts?"

"How did the daughter know something was wrong?"

"Her father always sits on the front porch at that time of day, regardless of the weather. The mother watches soap operas, and he can't stand them."

Storm took a deep breath, his arms folded, as the ambulance drove away. "How long do the EMTs think they've been dead?"

"Couple of days. The father's pickup is missing. We think they were in the basement for a while. There's a bedroom down there where they were found."

Storm continued to stare at the house as a deputy ran up to the sheriff. He whispered in his ear and then rushed back toward the house.

"Highway patrol helicopter spotted an abandoned pickup that matches the description of Wallace's truck."

"Where?"

"Couple of miles from here. You can follow me."

When Storm and Apollo arrived at the scene, they saw an older pickup parked in the middle of a narrow two-lane asphalt road. Police and sheriff's department vehicles surrounded the truck. Overhead, the deputy U.S. Marshal could hear a helicopter circling the area. Leading the canine to the abandoned truck, he signaled for him to start tracking. After several minutes of sniffing, Apollo jumped down from the truck cabin and sat, signaling he had a scent.

Kneeling beside his partner, Storm said, "Time to go to work, buddy," and made a circling motion with his right index finger. Apollo took off toward the east into the wooded area.

In this part of the state, the Mark Twain National Forest held shortleaf pines, oaks, and hickory with the occasional redbud and dogwood tree scattered about. Sparse underbrush characterized the area. Storm kept pace with his partner, his Sig Sauer P226 in his right hand, pointed toward the ground.

Apollo's pace remained steady until he stopped and raised his head. The dog turned his head toward the right, ears pointed up and tail ramrod straight. Storm froze where he stood, focusing his attention on his partner.

A growl deep within the border collie caused Storm to dive to the ground just before he heard the telltale double click of an automatic pistol slide being pulled back and released.

The shot passed over his head just as Apollo sprinted toward the sound. The pop of another shot broke the silence of the forest and then the cursing of a man. Storm rose and sprinted toward the noise. He kept track of the direction by the dog's growl and then the yelp of the fugitive being nipped by the canine. Within seconds, Storm came upon a small clearing. A man lay on the ground attempting to fend off the attacks of the black-and-white dog.

Storm blew a one-note whistle, and Apollo broke off his attack and ran to the deputy's side. The flustered man on the ground frantically searched for his weapon. Storm yelled, "Hands over your head."

The man, now on his knees, stopped his search and stared at Storm. "Who the fuck are you?"

"U.S. Marshal. Hands over your head, Hicks. I'll not repeat myself again."

Reid Hicks' eyes focused on Storm and then the ground. His hands were parallel to his shoulders as he once again trained his attention back to the man with the gun. He tried to rise to one knee, but a short whistle from Storm sent the canine back to the now-captured fugitive. Hicks screamed as the dog sank his teeth into the calf of the fugitive's leg.

Another whistle stopped the dog, who retreated to stand by the deputy.

"Keep that fucking dog off me."

"Do as I say, and I will. Now, hands on your head, Hicks."

When the man complied, Storm hurried to the rear of the prisoner and secured his hands behind his back with handcuffs. "Get to your feet; the dog will be right behind you."

After Apollo herded him back to the asphalt road, Pulaski County deputies took over and put the captive into the back of a squad car. Before leaving the clearing, Storm searched for Hick's weapon, found it, and used a stick through the trigger guard to carry it back for evidence.

As Bradley placed the gun in a plastic evidence bag, he said, "That looks like the gun Ellis Wallace used in the military."

"Probably the same one that killed the couple."

As the car with Hicks in the back seat drove off, the sheriff turned to Storm. "You made that appear easy."

With a shrug, the newly minted deputy U.S. Marshal said, "It helps when you have a good partner like Apollo."

Offering his hand, Bradley said, "Pleasure doing business with you, Dakota."

"Thanks, Sheriff. I think I'm going to like being a U.S. Marshal."

"How long you been a cop?"

"Since I got out of the military. I was a deputy for the St. Louis County sheriff's department for a little over eight years. Apollo and I just finished basic training to be deputy marshals a few weeks ago."

With a chuckle, Bradley patted Storm on the shoulder. "I think they made a good decision to bring you on."

"Let's hope so."

Chapter Ten

Kansas City

Late in April, weather in Kansas City can vary from cold and wet to pleasant and sunny. On this particular Friday evening, temperatures stood in the low fifties with a clear sky. Storm answered the doorbell, curious as to who would be visiting, considering his list of local friends lacked any names.

Jacob Gordon stood on his front porch with a six-pack of locally brewed beer in his hand. "Have you had dinner, Dakota?"

He opened the door. "No."

"Got any plans for the evening?"

"No."

"Good, I'll order pizza. Where's the fridge?"

Pointing to the right, he led his new boss toward the kitchen. Before the man placed the carton in the refrigerator, he handed a bottle to Storm. "Got a call from the Pulaski County sheriff today."

Opening the beer, Storm took a sip. "Hope it was a good call."

"He thanked me again for sending you. Once in jail, Reid Hicks became fairly talkative. Their discussions have cleared up a few cold cases there in the central part of the state. Louisiana wants a piece of him, too."

Storm leaned against the island separating the kitchen from a dining area. "That's good news. Who gets first crack at him?"

"State of Missouri."

With a contemplative nod, Storm took another swig of his beer.

Gordon opened his and took a gulp. "I had a lengthy discussion with my boss today."

Raising an eyebrow, Storm said, "About?"

"You."

"Jacob, is this a *sorry it's not working out* conversation?"

"If it was, I wouldn't be here with beer and a pizza. On the contrary, it's a *how about a promotion* conversation."

"I just started, Jacob."

"I know, but we don't have a regional fugitive task force here in the central part of the country. After what I've told him about you and your performance in Pulaski County, plus what I witnessed in Memphis, he and I think you're the perfect person to start one."

"Sorry, I'm not familiar with the term."

"U.S. Marshals have been providing assistance to local law enforcement agencies pursuing fugitives for years. Under the Presidential Threat Protection Act of 2000, the service has been setting up and overseeing regional fugitive task forces throughout the country. The purpose of these groups is to combine and coordinate the efforts of federal, state, and local law enforcement agencies. Their task is to locate and apprehend the most dangerous fugitives and assist in high-profile investigations."

"You sound like a recruiting video."

"I hope so. That little speech came right off our website."

"So, what does this have to do with me?"

"My boss and I agree, you're the perfect candidate to start up a Central Midwest Regional Task Force. You'd be responsible for covering Missouri, Kansas, Oklahoma, and Arkansas."

"Is this an as-needed position?"

"Nope. Full-time."

"What about Apollo?"

"Did I indicate he wasn't included?"

"No."

"Then he's involved. You two are too good a team to split up."

Storm looked at his dog relaxing on the floor next to him. "What do you think, Apollo?"

The canine simply stared at his master and panted.

"I like the idea, too." He turned to Gordon and offered his hand. "When do we start?"

Two Months Later

The first weekend after the Fourth of July found Storm adding a workbench and shelves to the garage. Since moving to the area with nothing except the few clothes he had purchased since the fire, he had accumulated a few tools. Weekdays, since his promotion, were filled with training and trips to surrounding Regional Fugitive Task

Forces to get ideas on how to succeed with the one he now managed.

Apollo stood and directed his attention at something in front of his house. An attractive woman in her late twenties or early thirties approached the open garage.

She waved. "Hi, I'm Melissa from across the street."

Wiping his hands on a shop towel, he said, "I'm Dakota and that's"—he pointed to his partner—"Apollo."

"She's a beautiful dog."

"She's a he, and thank you. I think so, too."

Staying outside the garage, she looked at the concrete floor and then back to Storm. "I've been meaning to introduce myself, but this is the first time I've seen you outside."

"I'm gone a lot."

She wrapped her arms around herself. "Uh, I know the feeling. I have to travel for my job, also."

Storm asked, "What do you do?"

"I'm a regional manager for Marriot hotels. I have Kansas and Missouri. What about you?"

"Deputy U.S. Marshal."

Her eyes grew round. "Really?"

He nodded.

"Well, that adds some security to the neighborhood. What about your wife? What does she do?"

"I'm a widower."

"Oh, I'm sorry. I didn't mean to…"

"It's okay. Are you married?"

"Divorced."

"Sorry."

"Like you said, it's okay. We grew apart and went our separate ways."

They talked for another thirty minutes and then she said, "You're busy, I'll stop bothering you."

"You're not bothering me. I've enjoyed the visit."

"Maybe we can do this again sometime."

"I'd like that."

"Well, nice meeting you, Dakota. You, too, Apollo."

Storm did not immediately resume his work. She crossed the street while he admired the graceful sway of her hips. He turned to Apollo. "It's not time yet, old friend. I'm not ready to even think about dating someone."

The dog raised his head and yawned.

———

The conference room in the Charles Evans Whittaker United States Courthouse in downtown Kansas City held only one individual when Dakota Storm walked through the door.

"I thought we had a meeting scheduled."

Jacob Gordon pointed to a chair. "Sit, Storm, we do. It's just you and me."

Taking a seat across from his boss, Storm sat straight with his hands clasped in front of him.

"The director is extremely pleased with reports he's getting about your efforts on getting the task force up and running."

Relaxing just a bit, Storm said, "Thank you, sir."

"Why are you always nervous when I call you into a meeting, Dakota?"

"Don't know, sir. Habit, I guess."

"Anyway, time for you to get a team selected. Who do you want?"

Taking a piece of paper from his utility pants pocket, he handed it to Gordon.

He scanned the list and said, "Good choices. Now, if

budgetary issues were involved, and I had to tell you only one person could be added to your team, who would it be?"

"James Russel."

Looking over his glasses at Storm, his boss chuckled. "That was fast."

"Yes, sir. But if I can only have one, Jimmie's the guy."

"I see. Consider him on your team. Hopefully, when our budget allows, we can add more members."

"Thank you, sir."

Taking his glasses off and placing them on the table, Gordon folded his hands. "Dakota, when was the last time you took a day off?"

"Last Saturday."

"Before that?"

"Uh…"

"You don't remember, do you?"

Storm shook his head.

With a fatherly smile, Gordon said, "You're doing exceptional work, son. But you also need to have a personal life. I don't want you burned out before you get started."

Storm did not respond.

"I know it's none of my business, but you still need downtime."

"I know, sir."

"I'll make sure HR notifies James. Anything else, Dakota?"

"No, sir." Storm stood to walk out of the conference room. Just before he exited, he turned. "Thank you for your concern, sir."

Gordon smiled.

Chapter Eleven

Somewhere on the Missouri-Arkansas State Line

On the Missouri-Arkansas border, a few miles west of where the Bootheel of Missouri dips south is a small town called Galesville. Both time and progress skipped this small community which happened to be in the wrong location when the state built a major north-south highway in the latter half of the twentieth century.

With a dwindling population, the area no longer held a strong enough tax base to stay incorporated. Without a city government or police department, it became the perfect place for a specific group of individuals to lie low.

Denzel Cruz stood in the doorway of his motel room watching the sunrise. With a cigarette in one hand and a cup of coffee in the other, his thoughts centered around his group's streak of bad luck. Since December, five members of his team were either dead or had been incarcerated. Replacing them would be more of an inconvenience than a problem. There were plenty of out-of-work twenty-some-things in the area. Finding ones with a semblance of intelligence seemed to be the largest stumbling block.

Denzel Cruz's second-in-command approached his room. "I've got bad news."

"Of course, you do. There's never good news anymore." He paused. "What is it, Lucas?"

"Reid Hicks was arrested. He's been charged with murdering an elderly couple north of Waynesville."

"Shit." Cruz threw the cigarette into the parking lot. "Wonderful. I always knew he was a fuckin' moron."

"Plus, Louisiana wants him extradited for murder."

"Of course they do. In other words, he's no use to us anymore."

"Nope. What do you want to do about him?"

"Can he be gotten to?"

"He's in a county jail. What do you think?"

"How far is it from here?"

"Two hundred miles, mostly back roads. About three-and-a-half hours."

Cruz kept his gaze on the eastern horizon as dawn turned to morning. "Eric Robles is from that area, right?"

"He's from Kansas City. Which is a long way from Waynesville."

"Better than where you or I come from."

"True."

"Send him. You and I have a meeting in Adams County, Oklahoma."

"Got it."

Waynesville, MO

Eric Robles sat in a pub sipping beer. Across from the establishment stood the county courthouse. Positioned on the main drag running through the northern section of the small city, the sheriff's department occupied the eastern side of the building.

A search on the Pulaski County sheriff's website confirmed Reid Hicks as an inmate. The downloaded document indicated he was being held on murder charges both locally and in the Louisiana Parish of Orleans.

The secondary reason Robles occupied a barstool in this particular pub stemmed from the fact there were more than a half dozen attorneys' offices within walking distance. He assumed there would be lawyers in the pub after a long day of chasing clients and performing their profession. He presumed correctly.

Two men sat at a table next to him, discussing the day's events. Both spoke freely, not concerned about who might be eavesdropping.

"Ever wish you practiced in a larger town than Waynesville, Brad?"

After a chuckle, the attorney said, "Every single day. How about you?"

"At first, I liked the slower pace. But that has also meant less earnings. So, yeah, I regret it, too."

"So, what do we do?"

Robles took a quick glance at the next table in time to see one of the lawyers lift his beer to his lips and shrug. Silence fell between the two as each sipped on their beer. After several moments passed, one said, "I talked to a prisoner today, his name's Hicks."

"Yeah, I spoke to him as well."

"What do you think?"

"I decided he's too toxic to touch. Besides, he doesn't have any money."

"Huh…"

"What'd he tell you?"

"I agree he's toxic, but he told me someone would pay his fees. When I asked him who that person was, he didn't answer."

"Well, there you go."

"My guess is he'll probably have to rely on a public defender."

"Yup."

Robles finished his beer, stood, and left the pub.

Oscar's Place, a smoke-filled gathering spot just outside the city limits of Waynesville, drew a different clientele than the pub across from the county courthouse. Dim lighting hid the cigarette burns and knife cuts on the rickety tables. Cheap well drinks and super-cold beer completed its appeal to locals and off-duty soldiers from nearby Fort Leonard Wood.

Into this environment strode Eric Robles at five minutes to eleven in the evening. He walked up to the bar and ordered a draft. When the bartender placed it in front of him, he turned, sipped the beer, and surveyed the crowd.

Spotting a table occupied by four gentlemen who appeared well on the way to inebriation, he studied them for a few moments. The more the four drank, the more agitated one of the fellows became.

Even from his position at the bar, Robles heard, "Fuck this shit. Send me back to prison. At least there I'd get three squares and a bed." The man slammed his beer down on the table.

One of his companions said, "Geez, Cash. You're never happy. You just got out six months ago."

"Yeah, and I haven't had a decent meal since. There weren't any damn bugs in my cell, either."

Robles walked over to a pay phone, slipped a quarter in, and dialed a number. He was on the phone for a few minutes and then returned to his spot at the bar.

Cash stood. "Thanks for the beer, boys. I'm outta here." He walked quickly out of the bar.

Robles followed.

In the parking lot, the man known as Cash stopped to light a cigarette. He inhaled deeply and stood looking up at the sky as he blew the smoke out.

Robles walked up behind him. "Got a solution for you."

The man whirled around and snarled, "Who the fuck are you?"

"I overheard your comment in there."

"None of your fucking business."

"You have a problem, and I have a problem. I'll give you a hundred bucks just to listen to mine."

Taking another long drag on his cigarette, the man tilted his head. "Hundred bucks?"

A nod from Robles.

"Pay up, then I'll listen."

Handing the man a bill with Ben Franklin's picture on it, he said, "What's your name?"

"You can call me Frank."

"Well, Frank, I need someone to take care of a problem inside the jail."

"What kind of problem?"

"Someone with a big mouth."

Raising an eyebrow, Frank folded his arms. "Sounds like something I can do."

"Good."

Robles proceeded to tell Frank what he needed and how much he'd be paid.

At nine a.m. the next morning, an ambulance arrived and hurriedly transported a prisoner to the local urgent care facility, where he was pronounced deceased. Frank, whose real name, Robles learned, was Brett Cash, was charged with first-degree murder. His victim, Reid Hicks, would not have the opportunity to make any deals with federal prosecutors.

Eric Robles checked out of his hotel and drove southeast. His destination, the area of the state known as the Bootheel.

Chapter Twelve

Kansas City

On a rare day off, Dakota Storm and Apollo spent a good portion of the morning at a park several blocks from his house. The dog chased a Frisbee, jumping and catching it before it landed. Storm enjoyed watching the dog's acrobatic exhibition as he chased, leaped, caught, and then returned the saucer-shaped object.

After one such chase, Storm's cell phone informed him of an incoming call.

"Storm."

"Dakota, I hate to bother you on your day off, but thought you would like to know Reid Hicks was attacked early this morning in his jail cell."

"Let me guess. He didn't survive the attack."

"No, he didn't."

Apollo offered the Frisbee to the deputy. After throwing it again, Storm asked, "Do they know who did it?"

"Guy by the name of Brett Cash."

"Never heard of him."

"The local sheriff says he's a not-too-bright local who's been in and out of the county jail so many times he has his name on one of the bunks. Most recently, he was paroled from the JCCC and had stayed out of trouble for about six months. He was in the state prison for running a stolen car ring. He's never committed a violent crime before."

Storm remained silent as he let the information sink in. Finally, he said, "Has Cash made any statements about why he attacked Hicks?"

"None whatsoever. Claims he didn't even know the guy."

"Does the sheriff think he was paid to kill him?"

"That's the prevailing theory."

"Want me to see what I can find out?"

"Not yet. The sheriff has a call in to Jeff City. Cash was on parole and will more than likely be on his way back to JCCC. You might be assigned to transport him."

"That would be convenient."

"My thoughts, exactly."

Storm paused for a moment. "Jacob, you and I both know there's more to the death of Reid Hicks."

"Yes, Dakota, I know that."

"So…"

"When you get here tomorrow, I want you to start making phone calls. We need more facts concerning this Hicks' character. Also, be prepared to head to Waynesville at some point."

"Got it."

The Next Day

By noon, Storm knew more about Reid Hicks than he cared to. To break up the inactivity, he took Apollo to a park close to the offices. Being cooped up inside all morning sometimes made the border collie antsy. When they returned, he took his notes to Gordon's office.

"How bad is it, Dakota?"

"Hicks has been a busy boy. The FBI has an extensive file on him, as do the states of Louisiana, Arkansas, and Tennessee."

"Ok. Give me the executive summary."

"FBI wants him on violation of US Code Title 18 section 2423 interstate transfer of a person under the age of 18 for purposes of prostitution."

Gordon raised an eyebrow. "You mentioned Louisiana, Tennessee, and Arkansas. Was this guy involved with the group you found in Memphis?"

Taking a deep breath, Storm blew it out slowly. "I hate to assume anything, but it sure appears that way."

Standing, the U.S. Marshal headed over to a coffeepot he kept on a credenza. "Want a cup?"

"No, thank you."

"Sorry I interrupted you. Go on."

"The murders he's wanted for in Louisiana also center around human trafficking. I spoke to a New Orleans detective this morning who said Hicks was known to travel to Central America on numerous occasions. He recruited young girls on the promise of education or good-paying jobs. Once they were inside the States, those girls were forced into prostitution up and down the Mississippi River.

"Apparently, a couple of coyotes double-crossed him and he made an example of them."

"What was he doing in Missouri?"

"Hunting down a couple of girls who escaped."

"Any evidence he found them?"

Storm shook his head.

"Why was he originally in the Pulaski County jail?"

"Traffic stop on I-44."

"That's one for the good guys. Did you hear back from the Pulaski County sheriff about Cash?"

Gordon nodded. "Yeah, his parole has been revoked, and the JCCC has requested his return. I volunteered you."

"When?"

"First thing tomorrow morning."

"Can I take one of the transfer vans?"

Holding up a set of keys, Gordon offered them. "All gassed up and ready for you."

Storm checked out of the hotel at five a.m. and arrived at the Pulaski County jail just as the sun peeked over the horizon. He was escorted to the sheriff's office where he shook hands with Caleb Bradley.

"Good to see you again, Deputy Storm."

"Glad to see you, too, Sheriff."

"So, you're gonna take Cash off my hands?"

The deputy handed the sheriff a set of documents. "Yes."

"Good riddance to him. He's been griping about the baloney sandwiches ever since he got here. Demanding to be sent back to JCCC so he can get a proper meal."

"Looks like he's getting his wish. When can he be ready?"

Glancing at his watch, the sheriff grinned. "I'll have the guards roust him out of bed."

"Perfect."

Thirty minutes later, Brett Cash sat in the back of the prisoner transfer van. When Storm let Apollo into the front, the man started cursing.

"Get that damn mutt out of here. I don't like stinking dogs. They're dirty."

Storm got behind the wheel and started the engine then turned. "Let's get some rules established, Cash. You're the prisoner. I'm a Deputy U.S. Marshal. The dog is Apollo. He's a certified K9 Deputy U.S. Marshal. If you want a pleasant journey this morning, you will keep your trap shut about dogs." Pointing toward his partner, he continued, "Particularly that dog."

"If I don't?"

"I'll let Apollo ride back there. I might even let him pee on your leg."

Cash's eyes grew wide. "I'm good. Keep him up there."

"Good, glad you understand the rules. This little trip will take about two hours. The more you cooperate, the quicker it will go."

"Can't go fast enough for me."

Forty minutes into the drive, Storm asked, "What possessed you to kill Reid Hicks?"

"Not sure what you're talking about. Who's Reid Hicks?"

"The guy you stabbed to death in the Pulaski County jail."

"Was that his name?"

Looking in the rearview mirror, Storm nodded.

"Huh. I didn't know his name."

"Did someone pay you to kill him?"

"Why do you say that?"

"'Cause your history doesn't include violence."

"Maybe I changed."

"How much did they pay you?"

"A thou…" The prisoner closed his eyes. "Shit."

"So, it was a thousand bucks? Who paid you?"

"I didn't say anything."

"Yes, you did. Brett, I don't care why you did it. I want the guy who paid you."

With a frown, Cash tilted his head. "Why?"

"Because he may be connected to someone who likes to hurt little girls."

"I didn't hurt any girls."

"I know that. Tell me who paid you."

"Don't know his name. I met him at a bar just outside of Waynesville."

"Had you ever seen him there before?" Storm glanced at the rearview mirror as the man shook his head.

"No."

"What did he look like?"

"I don't know. Regular guy: dark hair, beard, taller than me." The man paused. "He had a New Orleans Saints ball cap on. I do remember that."

"What color were his eyes?"

"How the hell should I know? I don't notice that kind of shit."

Keeping his eyes on the road, Storm stopped his questioning for a while.

Within five minutes, Cash said, "You know, he did do something kind of weird."

"What's that, Brett."

"He made a phone call on the bar pay phone. I've never

seen anyone use it before. Everyone uses cell phones in that place."

Storm glanced in the mirror at the prisoner. "Didn't know bars still had pay phones."

"This one does. The owner keeps the phone there for soldiers from the fort. I always thought I was the only person in the world who didn't have a cell phone. But some of those kids in basic training don't have the money for one."

"What's the name of the bar, Brett?"

"It's called Oscar's Place. It's just outside of town on old Route 66."

"Huh. Didn't know Route 66 went through Waynesville."

"Yeah, main drag through downtown."

"Interesting. Thanks for the history lesson."

"How much longer, Deputy?"

"About twenty minutes."

"Thanks."

Storm returned his attention to the highway.

Chapter Thirteen

Waynesville

Dakota Storm showed his badge to the bartender at Oscar's Place.

The man glanced at it and shrugged. "I don't know anything."

"I haven't asked a question yet."

"I still don't know anything."

Pointing at the phone, Storm said, "Someone made a call on that the night Brett Cash was arrested."

"So?"

"I would like your permission to get the phone records."

"I don't allow anyone to use it for illegal purposes."

"Not what I'm looking for. I need the number of the person he called."

The bartender gave Storm a bored expression. "That's it?"

"Yes."

"Go for it."

Storm pulled out his cell phone and had the number within thirty minutes. With the number in hand, he called his boss.

Gordon answered on the third ring. "What've you got for me, Storm?"

"I need a phone number identified."

"Where'd you get the number?"

"Owner of the bar where Brett Cash was solicited to kill Reid Hicks."

"Give it to me."

Storm recited the number and remained silent.

"I'll call you back when I have it."

With this accomplished, Storm ended the call and turned his attention to Apollo. "Guess we need to get this van back to KC. You good?"

The border collie yawned.

"I'll take that as a yes."

At the intersection of I-70 off Highway 5, Storm headed west. At the same time, he accelerated onto the interstate, his cell phone vibrated with an incoming call. "Storm."

"It's Gordon."

"Did you learn anything?"

"Yes and no. The phone number belongs to a prepaid cell phone, which, at the time, was located near the Bootheel of Missouri."

"Where is it now?"

"Hasn't made a call since it received the one from the bar."

"Is it a burner?"

"Phone company says no, because whoever is using it continues to buy more minutes with cash."

Storm remained silent as he drove west. Finally, he said, "Jacob, there's a chance Reid Hicks crossed paths with our friends at the DEA. Do you have any contacts with them?"

"As a matter of fact, I do. What're you thinking?"

"I found several references of him making a few trips to Central America. Maybe the DEA has a file on him."

"I've got a buddy over there. Won't hurt to ask him."

"Okay. I'm about two hours away. It'll be dark before I get back."

"I'll probably still be here. Call me when you arrive."

At exactly seven thirty-two, Storm entered Gordon's office and watched his boss complete a phone call. When he hung up, he looked at the deputy. "Good idea about the DEA. They have an extensive file on Hicks."

Storm sat in a chair in front of Gordon's desk. His hand automatically reached down to scratch Apollo on the head.

Gordon continued, "It seems our Mr. Hicks had an associate, a guy by the name of Eric Robles. Both are well-known by ATF and the Border Patrol."

"Why?"

"They're suspected of smuggling guns, drugs, and humans into the country. DEA has a warrant out on both of them. They didn't know Hicks was dead until I told them."

Continuing to scratch Apollo's head, Storm grew quiet. "The Bootheel of Missouri is near Memphis."

"I'm aware of that."

"Where exactly was the phone located?"

Gordon slipped his glasses on and skimmed his notes. "A small town called Campbell, Missouri."

"I know where it is."

"What are you thinking, Dakota?"

"Can we get a mug shot of Robles?"

"I received it in an email. I'll forward it to you."

"Good." After a few moments of silence, Storm asked, "These two are considered fugitives, right?"

A nod became his answer.

"I think it's time for me to use my status as Regional Fugitive Task Force leader and start trying to locate these guys."

"Go home. Get some rest. Tomorrow you can start getting copies of any warrants on Robles together. Work with legal to get access to any phone records you can find. Once you have an idea of where you want to start looking for him, I'll approve your travel."

"Thanks, Jacob."

———

When Storm pulled his SUV into his driveway, his neighbor across the street was having what appeared to be a heated discussion with a man on her front porch. A Mercedes sedan sat in the driveway with the lights on.

Instead of minding his own business, he decided to walk over to see if he could assist Melissa.

With Apollo following on his right, Storm approached the scene. The pitch of her voice sounded an octave higher than normal, and she shook her finger in the man's face. As he approached, her wide eyes diverted from the man's face to his.

She said, "Dakota, could you please tell this man to leave me alone?"

Storm reached down and showed his palm to Apollo. The dog stopped following and kept his eyes locked on the unknown man. "What's the problem, Melissa?"

"This man claims to be an attorney for my ex-husband."

The unknown man turned to Storm and said, "I would advise you not to get involved."

"She's already asked for my assistance." He displayed his badge. "Dakota Storm, Deputy U.S. Marshal. Who might you be?"

The man raised an eyebrow. "This doesn't concern you."

"It does if you're threatening her. And from what I heard walking over here, you appear to be. Now, I will ask nicely one more time. Who are you, and what are you doing here?"

The man stared at Storm and then at Apollo. "I would advise you to keep the dog under control."

"Don't worry about my friend. He's a certified K9 officer. Last chance before I place you under arrest for harassment. Now, who the hell are you?"

"Attorney-at-Law William Becker. I have a legitimate reason for being here."

Storm turned to Melissa. "Is this man trespassing?"

"Yes. I did not invite him onto my property."

"Well, Mr. Attorney-at-Law William Becker, I would suggest getting into your vehicle and leaving."

With his legal bluff called, Becker turned to Melissa. "You'll receive a formal request for your testimony in the mail, Ms. Perry." He turned and hurried back toward his car, nervously looking over his shoulder at Apollo. The border collie kept his eyes on the man's back.

When the SUV drove away, Melissa broke down into tears. In between sobs, she said, "Thank you, Dakota."

"I don't mean to pry, but what was that all about?"

"Can we go in before I tell you?"

"Sure." He patted his right leg, and Apollo followed.

Storm sat on a stool at the breakfast bar as Melissa made coffee. "You have a nice home."

"Thank you." Her eyes remained puffy from her earlier experience with the lawyer. "I guess you're wondering what all the fuss was about."

"I figure you'll tell me when you're ready."

She pressed the start button on the coffee machine and then turned toward him. Folding her arms, she took a deep breath and sighed. "My ex-husband is trying to get out of paying alimony."

Storm remained quiet.

"I put the son of a bitch through medical school. Paid his tuition and spent more time alone than a spouse should. Then, when he started his practice, he dumped me for someone he met during his residency."

"I'm sorry."

"It happens. In our divorce settlement, my lawyer laid out how I helped him, and the judge sided with me. He was ordered to pay me retribution on both his school costs and loss of future sharing of his income. Now he's claiming I make more than he does, and he should not be required to continue paying me."

The coffee finished brewing, and she poured a cup for him and one for herself. "Do you take anything in it?"

"I'm a cop, Melissa. I like it black."

She chuckled. "Thanks, I needed a little humor."

"Does your ex-husband make less than you?"

"I highly doubt it. He's an orthopedic surgeon."

Storm let out a slight whistle. "I hear those guys make big bucks."

"Yeah, I've heard that, too. Not sure how good he is. But I do know he's already divorced from his second wife."

With a shrug, Storm said, "Well, there you go. He's a jerk."

She laughed again. "Yes, he is." She stared at the dark liquid in her cup. "Thank you, Dakota. I was about to lose my cool when you interrupted."

He raised his mug. "My pleasure. Helping a fair maiden in distress is what we U.S. Marshal's do."

"Do you enjoy your job?"

"Very much." He looked at Apollo. "My friend here and I make a good team." He paused and took a sip of coffee. "He also saved me from myself."

Chapter Fourteen

Overland Park, KS

Melissa Perry raised her eyebrows. "He saved you from yourself?"

Storm took a deep breath and nodded.

"Care to explain, or is that a secret?"

"Not a secret. I'd spent two years grieving the death of my wife and three-year-old son. On the night I found Apollo, I had decided to do something about the pain." He turned and viewed the collie lying on the floor with his eyes closed. "He had been abandoned and left to starve. I guess you can say I saved him from being trapped. But I've always thought of it as the reverse. He rescued me."

She was leaning on the breakfast bar, coffee cup in hand, and looked at Apollo on the floor next to where Storm sat. "Funny how life works sometimes. I'm glad he saved you." She took a sip of coffee and then returned her attention to the deputy. "You lost a son along with your wife?"

"Both were killed by a drunk driver." He chose not to go into any additional details.

"I'm sorry for your loss."

"Thank you." He paused for a moment. "Do you need to get your attorney involved, again?"

"I was hoping I wouldn't have to. But I think I'm going to need to."

"Melissa, do you have any security cameras on your house?"

"No."

"Okay. Tell you what. I may have to be out of town for a few days this week."

"I do, too."

"Well, this weekend, I can help you install a few Ring cameras around the perimeter of your house. They'll keep you informed about who might be nosing around."

"You'd do that?"

"Sure. I'd be happy to."

"Where would I get the cameras?"

"You can order them from Amazon or buy them at any Lowes."

She smiled.

An hour later, Apollo followed Storm back toward their house. The lateness of the hour left the neighborhood quiet and serene. Halfway across the street, Storm glanced down at his companion and said, "Don't worry. I'm just trying to be a good neighbor."

Looking up at the deputy, the dog's tongue hung out as he panted and seemed to smile.

"No, really. I'm just trying to be a good neighbor."

Apollo broke into a run to the back of the house, leaving Storm behind.

"Guess he didn't believe it, either."

Wednesday morning found Dakota at his desk, his ear smashed against the phone receiver, listening to a New Orleans detective.

"Eric Robles, huh. Well, Deputy, they don't come any meaner than the likes of him."

"How so?"

"Not sure where to start. We think he began his career as a coyote, smuggling folks into the U.S. using the Mississippi River Delta. First, it was migrant workers; then, he switched gears and started smuggling young girls."

"Do you have any proof about the latter?"

"Yes. There are several federal warrants out for his arrest for interstate transport of minors."

"Under what name?"

"Oh, let me see…" The silence on the phone allowed Storm hear the clicking of a computer keyboard. The detective said, "Eric Roberts, Edward Rollin, Enrique Romero, and, my favorite, Eddie Rosenblum."

"Does he have IDs for all of these?"

"Most of them. There are probably more names he uses, but those are the ones we know about."

"Can you send me any mug shots?"

"Sure. You going after him?"

"We're putting a task force together."

"Well, Deputy, if you need a detective from New Orleans, count me in. I've been chasing these guys for a long time."

"Guys?"

"Oh yeah. Robles isn't the only one we're looking for."

"How many of them are out there?"

"More than we can count."

"Huh." Storm was silent for a few moments. "Where was Robles' last known address?"

"Lower Ninth Ward."

"Oh boy."

"Yeah, the neighborhood Katrina blew away. Only 37 percent of the residents returned."

"Well, finding fugitives is what the U.S. Marshals Service does best."

Waynesville

Later That Afternoon

Sheriff Caleb Bradley stood next to Storm as the deputy U.S. Marshal showed the mug shot to the owner of Oscar's Place.

"Yeah, that's him."

Bradley asked, "You sure?"

"Yeah, I remember him. I'd never seen him in the bar before, so I kind of paid more attention to him. Most of my guests are regulars. He wasn't. He also acted way too curious about everyone in the place."

"Have you seen him since?"

"Nope."

"Do you remember how he paid for his drinks?"

"Yeah, he gave me a hundred-dollar bill. We rarely get those. I checked it with one of those testing pens and found it to be legit."

"You said he seemed too curious. What made you think that?" Storm asked.

"Most of the time, he stood around the bar. Occasionally, he'd walk by or stand close to a table and just listen for a moment. Then he would wander back to the bar and survey the crowd again."

"He didn't know Cash?"

"Not that I could tell. He never talked to him inside the bar. When Cash left, he followed him out the door."

Turning to the sheriff, Storm said, "Brett Cash was a random encounter. He was looking for someone he could entice into killing Reid Hicks."

Bradley said, "Yeah, that's how we figured it."

Holding the mug shot, Storm studied the image. "Our Mr. Robles came here with one purpose and one purpose only. To find someone to silence Reid Hicks."

Driving back to Kansas City allowed Storm time to think. Apollo, asleep on the seat beside him, did not, as usual, offer any advice on his search for the man who hired Brett Cash. Other cases were piling up on his desk and, with the current investigation going nowhere, he thought it best to move forward on the ones he could close fairly quickly.

Apollo opened his eyes, shifted position and watched Storm.

The deputy glanced at his partner. "About time you woke up."

The dog yawned.

"What do you think, Apollo? Is it time to stop chasing Eric Robles and move on to something else?"

No response came from the border collie. He just kept his eyes on Storm.

"Or, should I recruit a few other deputies, invite the

detective from New Orleans to join us, and we all meet in Tunica? What do you think?"

With his tongue hanging out one side of his mouth, the dog panted and crossed his paws in front.

After another quick glance at the canine, Storm grinned. "Yeah, that's what I think I should do, too." He paused. "I'll talk to Jacob in the morning."

Friday

"I think your idea has merit, Dakota. How many deputies do you think you need?" Gordon poured a cup of coffee and handed it to Storm.

"I spoke to Max Blanchard this morning. He's the detective from New Orleans who's assigned to investigate these guys down there. They have leads on the whereabouts of six members of the gang and would like to coordinate an early morning raid with the Marshals Service. One of those individuals might give us a lead to Eric Robles."

"And you want to be a part of the raid, don't you?"

"Yes, sir."

Gordon walked back to his desk and sat. "That's a long drive from here, Dakota. You sure that's what you want to do?"

"It makes the most sense."

"Yes, it makes sense, but what about the time?"

"It's only thirteen hours, and I go through Memphis, which means if we get any leads, that's the way I would drive back. I can head down Sunday and be there Monday morning. Max thinks we can have everything ready to go by early Wednesday morning."

"I'll talk to the Eastern Louisiana District Marshal. He was just appointed to the position. Plus, he and I have worked together in the past."

"Thank you, sir."

Storm stood to leave and just before exiting the marshal's office, Gordon said, "Dakota?"

Turning, he looked at his boss. "Yes?"

"Go home. You've got a long week ahead of you."

The deputy smiled and closed the door as he exited.

Chapter Fifteen

Kansas City

Saturday

By late afternoon, Storm finished placing three security cameras on Melissa's ranch-style home. One over the garage, a doorbell camera, and one covering the backyard. Satisfied with his efforts, he tested the effectiveness of each and by 5:25 p.m. declared the system operative.

"Thank you, Dakota. I'm not sure how to thank you."

"No need. I enjoyed doing it. Plus, having someone to talk to was a bonus."

With a shy grin, she said, "I agree, it was nice to have someone to talk to." Pausing for a few moments, she continued, "Could I fix you dinner as a thank-you?"

He started to decline but stopped himself. "Uh, sure, that would be nice. But don't do anything fancy."

She laughed. "I don't do fancy in the kitchen. We could grill some burgers."

"I believe that would be perfect. Let me go home, clean up, and change. When should I be back?"

"Let's say, an hour."

"See you then."

As he walked home, Apollo walked beside him on his right. Looking down at the dog, Storm said, "Do you know how long it's been since I've been on a date with a woman?"

Apollo barked once.

"It's probably been at least ten years. Probably longer."

The border collie looked up, his tongue out and once again seemed to smile.

"Thanks, buddy. I noticed you like her, too."

The dog did something very uncharacteristic. He moved in front of Storm, rose up, and put his paws on the deputy's chest. Without hesitation, he put his arms around the dog and gave him a hug. "Thanks, Apollo. We'll see where this goes."

Melissa Perry's back deck worked perfectly for the evening's events. She owned a large gas grill and a tall bistro table with four matching chairs. The evening temperatures were mild for this deep into summer, so they stayed outside on the deck. Before the light faded, Melissa threw a tennis ball, which Apollo relished chasing and retrieving. During this time, Storm built a fire in the deck's chimenea, which would provide a nice glow to the area after darkness fell.

Storm sipped on a beer and watched the two. It made him smile seeing them engaging with each other. Back on the deck, Apollo slurped water from a bowl, and Melissa sat next to Storm, a fresh beer in her hand. "I didn't realize how much fun throwing a ball around with a dog can be."

"You should see him with a Frisbee. He can jump higher than I am tall to catch it."

"I hope I get a chance to see that."

The statement caught Storm by surprise. "Why wouldn't you?"

She shrugged. "Not sure if this evening is the result of you feeling sorry for a damsel in distress or if you really want to be here."

Setting his beer down, Storm smiled. "First, I didn't think of you as a damsel in distress. I enjoyed helping with the cameras today. Second, if I didn't want to be here this evening, I would have turned down the invitation for dinner."

"I'm glad to know that." She paused and took a sip of beer. "I was hoping that was the case."

"Besides, the burgers were excellent."

"Thank you." She stared off into the growing darkness. "Can I tell you something personal, Dakota?"

"Sure."

"Since my divorce, I get a bit defensive around men."

"I can understand that."

"Unfortunately, I didn't realize it until about five minutes ago. I apologize for the rude comment about damsels in distress."

"I didn't take it as rude."

"Well, sometimes I can come off as a little snarky."

With a chuckle, he picked up his beer. "No need to apologize." They sat in silence as Apollo laid down on the deck and put his head on his paws. Storm continued, "Melissa, let's face it. We've both experienced a traumatic event in our lives. When I was a sheriff's deputy, I saw on more than one occasion what divorce can do to a person. It messes with your mind. It might be worse than having a spouse die."

"I don't see how that's possible."

"When a spouse dies, there's closure. You know you will never see them again. But the love you felt for them survives, and you will always love them. With divorce, closure takes a long time. Love has turned to either hate or loathing. You'd be surprised how many divorced men attempt to kill their ex-wife or the person she's with. The scene is always messy, and the outcome is never good."

She stared at Storm, her beer on the table and her hands clasped. "I've never thought of it that way. I always thought having a spouse die would be worse."

He chuckled. "I've never been divorced, so I might be full of shit."

With a shake of her head, she said, "No, I think you're right. Divorce is pretty traumatic." She paused and lifted the beer to her lips. "So, where does that leave you and me, Dakota?"

After a deep breath, he let it out slowly. "I hope friends." They remained quiet in the darkness. "And maybe more, at some point."

She reached out for his hand and squeezed it. "Do you have plans for tomorrow?"

He nodded. "I have to drive to New Orleans first thing in the morning."

She displayed a slight frown for a brief moment. "How long will you be gone?"

"Probably most of the week. Why?"

"I don't know, just curious when I might see you again."

"It will depend on how things go in Louisiana. I hope to be back by next Sunday."

She lowered her gaze, diverting her eyes from his. She recovered quickly and raised her head, displaying a smile. "Do you like baseball?"

"I do."

"Are you a Royals fan?"

"Uh, I'm from St. Louis. I bleed Cardinal red."

"Well, learn to be a Royals fan. I get season tickets through work every year. The reason I asked is next Sunday is our first home game in a long time. I was hoping you and I could go."

"I'll be home by Sunday. How's that for an answer."

"Perfect, I'll plan on it."

———

The time was after midnight, and Storm lay in bed, his hands behind his head, staring at the ceiling. Apollo lay next to his bed asleep. He found his enthusiasm for driving to New Orleans the next day, waning.

"You awake, Apollo?"

The dog raised his head and stared at his owner.

"Am I making a mistake getting interested in Melissa?"

Apollo followed his normal protocol and did not answer.

"She's a pretty woman, and I thoroughly enjoyed talking to her this evening."

The dog lowered his head to the floor but kept his eyes on Dakota.

"I guess I'll just think of her as a friend." He paused. "Or, maybe I'll forget about it. Nothing is going to happen. It doesn't work that way." He closed his eyes. After a few moments, they popped open. "Who am I trying to kid." He leaned up on one elbow and looked at Apollo.

The dog raised his head.

"You like her, don't you, Apollo?"

His tongue came out, and he panted.

"That's what I thought."

He lay back down and once again put his hands behind his head. "I like her, too. The question is, what am I going to do about it?"

Chapter Sixteen

New Orleans

Katydid and cricket sounds filled the early morning darkness as Storm and Apollo waited at the back of the house under surveillance. Dakota wore jeans and his U.S. Marshals tactical vest with Apollo in his U.S. Marshals K9 Unit tactical harness. Their job, to keep anyone from escaping out the back door. The deputy checked his watch. Five minutes before his five partners breached the front door of the house.

Apollo's attention remained fixed on the door as Storm adjusted his earpiece. He heard, "Stand by."

Another voice said, "I've got movement in the front window."

"Can you identify?"

"Negative. Just a shadow."

"Male or female?"

"Broad shoulders. Appears to be male."

"Roger."

The voice of the lead New Orleans police officer from their SWAT team came back on the air. "One minute."

Storm released the snap-hook on Apollo's harness then clenched his fist and pointed to the door. His signal to the canine to be ready. The dog dipped his head, preparing to charge.

The deputy withdrew his Sig Sauer from its holster and stood next to Apollo.

Commotion in the front of the house indicated the breach team had entered the residence. Not two seconds later, a figure shot out the back door, and Apollo leapt into action, Storm right behind him.

The dog barked and snarled at the man who froze at the top of the steps leading to the patio. Storm yelled, "Halt, police. Hands where I can see them."

The man grabbed the railing on the short staircase and hesitated. After glancing at the back door, he narrowed his eyes and continued down the concrete steps.

Storm planted his feet, took a Weaver stance, and yelled, "Halt. Hands where I can see them."

Apollo growled as he dashed in to nip at the man's heels. Just as fast, he backed off. The canine repeated the move several times.

After several attacks by Apollo, and Storm keeping his Sig Sauer pointed at him, the man finally said, "Aww, shit," and stopped. He raised his hands and remained still while Apollo barked and the deputy placed handcuffs on his wrists.

New Orleans Detective Max Blanchard studied a driver's license, it's owner facedown on the floor with his hands cuffed behind him. He glanced toward the rear of the house and saw Storm pushing another man into the living room, Apollo keeping a watchful eye on the prisoner.

"Who's that, Deputy?"

"A jackrabbit. He apparently didn't want to join the party."

"See if he's got an ID on him."

"You got it."

Storm patted the man down and extracted a billfold. Opening it, he grinned. "Well, well, well, guess who we have here. Seems we've found the elusive Eddie Rosenblum."

Blanchard walked over to the man captured by Storm. "Huh, you don't look like a Rosenblum." He turned to Storm. "Hey, Deputy, does this guy look like a Rosenblum?"

As the NOPD detective spoke, Storm studied a photo he had pulled from his tactical vest. "No, he doesn't, but he does resemble Eric Robles." He handed the picture to Blanchard.

"You know, you are correct, Deputy. He sure does." Blanchard returned his attention to the prisoner. "Well, Eric, you are wanted by the states of both Louisiana and Missouri. What do you have to say about that?"

"Don't know what you're talking about. The name's Rosenblum."

"Right."

At that moment, Apollo let out a series of sharp barks.

Storm turned to see the dog scratching at a door. The canine whimpered and barked again. He walked over to him and knelt down.

"What've you got, boy?"

Apollo sat.

Storm stood and immediately withdrew his weapon

from its holster. He said, "We've got something behind this door, gentlemen."

A Louisiana deputy U.S. Marshal fell in behind Storm. "I've got your back, Dakota."

"Thanks, Sam." Storm tried the knob. Locked. Turning to the man behind him, he said, "Get the breaching bar."

Sam bent down, studied the doorjamb, and raised a finger. "Just a second." He straightened, raised a foot, and slammed it against the wood near the knob. The flimsy entryway flew open and banged against the wall of an upward-inclining staircase. "There you go."

Apollo ascended the stairs with grace as Storm followed close behind him. At the top, the dog stopped and looked back at Storm. Another door created a barrier to what lay behind it. Using the same tactic as the other deputy, Storm slammed his foot against it, causing the jamb to shatter and crash against a wall. From the interior of the completely dark room came the sound of terrified girls sobbing and crying.

Once on the scene, New Orleans Social Services took charge of the six teenage girls. All were Hispanic, and none spoke English. With his rudimentary knowledge of Spanish, Storm learned all were under sixteen.

Eric Robles sat in a straight-back chair in the kitchen. His cuffed hands behind his back caused him to sit slightly forward as he glared at Storm with defiance.

"I ain't saying shit, man. I have no idea where those girls came from."

Apollo sat next to Storm. His attention trained on the

prisoner. An occasional growl emitted from the dog's throat caused the prisoner to snap at the deputy.

"Keep that mutt under control. I know my rights."

"What about the rights of the girls we found upstairs?"

"Like I said, I don't know anything about them."

"Whatever."

One of the deputy U.S. Marshals from New Orleans approached and whispered something into Storm's ear. A slight grin appeared on the Missouri deputy's face. "Really?"

"Yup. The other two's stories collaborate each other."

Storm folded his arms as the other deputy returned to the living area of the house. "Your buddies said you're the one who brought the girls here. They were scheduled to be moved to Memphis later today. Care to comment?"

"I want my lawyer."

"That's fine. You can call him after you're processed at the county courthouse."

"I'm done talking to you, asshole."

Turning, Storm started to leave the room. Before he did, he gave Apollo a hand signal to guard the prison.

"Don't leave me alone with that mutt, Storm."

At the mention of his name, the deputy turned. "What'd you say?"

"You heard me. You're Dakota Storm." He paused. "You're also a dead man walking, dude."

The deputy tilted his head. "Care to explain how you know my name?"

Robles grinned. "Everyone knows who you are, and everyone took their turn with that woman you married."

Taking a step toward the prisoner, Storm clenched his fists. He stopped himself just before raising an arm. He took a deep breath and kept his glare on the man sitting in the chair.

"Have I got your attention, Storm?"

The deputy remained quiet. His eyes fixed on the prisoner.

"Kind of thought that would wake you up. You haven't got a clue what the woman you married did before she got away from us." He paused. "Want me to tell you about it?"

Folding his arms, Storm listened as Robles told him.

The sun peeked over the horizon as the three men captured in the raid were driven off the property in a police van. Detective Blanchard stepped up behind Storm as the vehicle drove out of sight.

"You don't believe all that crap about your wife, do you, Dakota?"

The only response the deputy could give without revealing the turmoil he felt inside was a shake of his head.

"Good, because Robles was baiting you."

"I know."

"Thanks for the assistance this morning."

"Glad I was here."

"You heading back to KC?"

"Thought I would detour through Memphis. There's a hotel there I want to check out."

"Need any assistance?"

"Not yet. I'm just going to watch it for a few days."

"Well, let me know. My chief is gonna be thrilled with this bust. We're finally making some headway."

Turning to Blanchard, Storm asked, "Has your investigation discovered who runs this group?"

"One name keeps popping up. A guy by the name of Denzel Cruz. He's a mystery. We can't find any records on him, nor do we have a photo."

"Any aliases?"

"When we bring any of these guys in, they refer to him as Cruz. Nothing else."

"How many of them have you arrested?"

"Including the three we got this morning, ten."

"Over what kind of a timeline?"

"I've been on the case off and on for two years. This morning's raid was our most successful one yet, since we found three of them in the same house as their abductees. The district attorney will request no bail."

"Think you'll get it?"

"Yeah. There's a judge who isn't happy with the fact when they're released on bail, they disappear. We've been told he wants to make an example of the next ones we capture."

Storm offered his hand. "Good luck with that." As they shook, Storm continued, "I think Apollo and I will head out. If you need me, you've got my number."

"Thanks, Dakota."

Chapter Seventeen

Southwest of Memphis

The old hotel on the outskirts of Tunica, Mississippi appeared abandoned when Storm drove his Ford by the property. No cars graced its parking lot, plus, a sign on the front door apologized for the inconvenience of being closed for renovation.

He attached a leash to Apollo's collar, and the two walked the perimeter of the building. The room where the young girls had been held captive still displayed yellow crime scene tape stuck to the door.

Pulling out his phone, he called the U.S. Marshals travel agency. When the call was answered, he said, "This is Deputy Dakota Storm. Can you check availability at a motel in Tunica, Mississippi called Casino Row Inn?"

"Identification number?"

Storm provided it.

"Just a moment, please."

An instrumental version of a pop tune he did not recognize could be heard. Thirty seconds later, the female voice returned. "Deputy Storm, we're showing that particular property closed indefinitely."

"Does it say why?"

"No. But reservations are not being accepted, and any current ones will not be honored."

"Huh."

"Can I make you another reservation?"

"Yes, please. Find one close by."

"I'll text you the confirmation number."

"Thanks."

He checked his watch and determined the Tunica County Courthouse might still be open. He googled the location on his cell phone. With this in hand, he and Apollo returned to their vehicle and drove to the address.

With Apollo asleep in the back seat and with cloudy skies, a light drizzle, and temperatures in the mid-sixties, Storm left the window cracked on the SUV. Once inside the courthouse and in the collector's office, he showed his ID and asked to see the county official.

A young clerk escorted him to a room where a middle-aged woman occupied a typical government-issue desk. When she looked up, she sighed heavily and clasped her hands together. The name plate on her desk indicated her name was Ruth Bender. Storm offered his ID and stood in front of the desk. She glanced at it, handed it back, and offered a fake smile.

"What can I help you with, Deputy Storm?"

"I need to know who owns a property at"—he referred

to a small notebook he held—"2740 Casino Strip Blvd, Robinsonville, MS."

"That's public information. You could have found it on the internet."

"I could have." He paused for a second. "But, since I'm already here, I'll ask you."

She sighed heavily and turned to a computer monitor and typed on the keyboard below it. She lifted the glasses hanging by a strap around her neck, studied the data Storm could not see, and said, "Huh."

"What's wrong?"

"It is owned by a company out of Louisiana. The property taxes are delinquent."

"How delinquent?"

"Over three months."

"Is that unusual?"

She used a mouse with her right hand as she studied the screen. "Going back ten years, they've always been paid early." She took her glasses off, turned to Storm, and asked, "What brought this property to the attention of the U.S. Marshals Service, Deputy?"

"Several individuals were arrested there who are suspected of being involved with a human trafficking ring. They were supplying young girls to work at the casinos."

She shook her head. "Damn casinos. They just aren't worth the revenue they generate for the county or the state."

Storm continued, "I drove by the motel. It's closed for renovation, but when I called to make a future reservation, I was told it was permanently shut down."

She put her glasses back on and turned back to her computer screen. She typed, stopped, typed again, and then studied the screen for a few moments. "Well, Deputy Storm, it's for sale."

"Since when?"

"When did you say the arrests took place?"

"Just before New Year's."

"It went up for sale on the second of January."

"Can you tell me the name of the company?"

"I can do better. I'll print out the county assessment statement. That will give you all the public information and the name of the corporate entity that currently owns it."

"Thank you, Ms. Bender."

One of the benefits of having Apollo as his teammate was they could exercise together. An hour, either in the morning or evening, seven days a week kept both of them in shape for whatever the U.S. Marshals Service threw at them.

After one such session, back in their hotel room in Tunica, Storm made a call to a contact he knew in the Information Technology Division. She answered on the third ring.

"IT Division, this is Lisa."

"Hey, Lisa, it's Dakota Storm."

"Nice to hear from you, Dakota. How's Apollo?"

"Doing great. What about your border collie?"

"She placed first in a local working dog competition over the weekend."

"Fantastic."

"What can I do for you?"

"I know it's late, but I need some background on a company call Bayou Global." He spelled the name.

"How extensive?"

"As much as you can. I believe they might be a front for a sex trafficking and drug smuggling ring I'm investigating."

"Can I get back to you tomorrow? My shift's almost over."

"Yeah, no problem. You've got my number, right?"

"I sure do, I'll talk to you then."

The call ended. His next call went to New Orleans Detective Max Blanchard.

"Blanchard."

"Max, it's Dakota."

"What'd you find?"

"Ever hear of a company in New Orleans called Bayou Global?"

"Can't say I have. Why?"

"When I first got into this investigation, we discovered a motel near all Tunica casinos providing rooms for girls and their handlers. The motel is now closed and for sale. Plus, they haven't paid their property tax bill for the past year. Something the county tax collector said they'd never failed to do before."

Dakota heard the clicking of a computer keyboard.

Thirty seconds later, the detective said, "How about that."

"What?"

"Bayou Global is a property management company specializing in hospitality and entertainment. They own several casinos up and down the Mississippi, plus a number of hotels and motels in St. Louis, Biloxi, Memphis, and here in New Orleans."

"Those are the same locations where we've encountered the human trafficking gang. I'm not sure that's a coincidence, Max."

"Now that I'm looking at it, I'd have to agree with you, Dakota."

"I've got a friend in our IT division doing a deep dive into the company tomorrow. Think you could snoop around and see what you can learn?"

"Sure, I'll call you if I find anything we can use."

"Thanks, Max."

The call ended, and Storm placed the phone on the nightstand. Apollo curled up on a cushioned armchair.

He sat on the edge of the bed, placed his elbows on his knees, and buried his face in his hands. The conversation with Eric Robles replayed in his mind, word for word.

"She wasn't the innocent woman you thought she was, Storm." Robles narrowed his eyes. "The chick loved to party. Man, did she like to have a good time. I took advantage of that fact several times. Just like the others who knew her. I'm talking about knowing her in the biblical sense. Get my drift?"

When Storm did not respond, the prisoner chuckled. "We cut her some slack and kept her off the circuit because of this. We didn't want to use her up like some of the other sluts who worked for us. So, we kept her in one place during her stay. That way, we had her available when a party broke out."

Keeping his emotions buried deep inside, Storm asked, "Where was this?"

"In Memphis. A place down on Beale Street."

"What was the name of it?"

"You think I'm going to tell you? Fat chance."

Withdrawing his Sig Sauer, Storm pulled the slide back and chambered a round.

Robles stared at the weapon. "Put the gun away, man, or I'll start screaming."

"Go ahead." He placed the muzzle against the prisoner's forehead. "See if anyone gives a shit."

Squeezing his eyes shut, Robles said, "Blues on Beale."

Pressing the gun even harder against the man's skin, Storm growled, "Why there?"

"The company owns it. The girls we let work there can make extra cash."

"How?"

"You know, go home with the customers. They don't have to pay a percentage of what they make. It keeps them happy, and we don't have problems with them."

The room spun as Storm heard these last words. He began to put pressure on the trigger but stopped. He removed the gun from Robles' forehead, holstered it, and walked out of the kitchen.

A misty, overcast gray sky greeted Storm as he stepped out of the motel room. His already dark mood intensified as he opened the Ford's door for Apollo to scamper into the back seat.

He input an address in downtown Memphis into a GPS app on his cell phone and drove north. At noon, with his SUV parked in a lot, he walked a famous area in downtown Memphis: Beale Street. The area ran from the Mississippi River to East Street, a little less than two miles. The section of road of particular interest to Storm only occupied three blocks. This area was known as the Beale Street Entertainment District. He found the establishment mentioned by Robles in this area, Blues on Beale. What to believe of the man's tale remained a mystery.

After stepping out of his Ford, Storm slipped on his U.S. Marshals windbreaker and secured Apollo's harness, depicting his status as a police dog, around his chest. While unnecessary, Storm held the leash attached to the harness. Apollo knew to walk next to the deputy.

When they arrived at the establishment, a sign on the door indicated Blues on Beale opened at four in the afternoon. But he could see someone behind the bar working, so he knocked on the door.

The man eventually came to the door and pointed to the times printed on the frontS. "We're closed."

Holding his badge, Storm said, "U.S. Marshals Service, I need to ask you a few questions."

With a frown, the man unlocked the door and allowed Storm and Apollo to enter.

"Who are you looking for, Deputy?"

"The owner."

"The owner's a big company. I'm the manager."

"Can I have ten minutes of your time?"

With a shrug, he motioned for Storm to follow him. "Just make sure you keep that dog on its leash."

Chapter Eighteen

Beale Street Entertainment District - Memphis

The manager returned to the area behind the bar, basically trying to ignore the deputy. He continued restocking the bottles. "So, what's this about?"

Storm stood in front of the bar and kept Apollo's leash around his wrist. "What's your name?"

"Call me Bob."

Searching the back wall for a business license, Storm noticed the manager's name was Robert Trent. "Okay, Bob. Is this place owned by Bayou Global?"

As the manager placed several bottles of scotch on the liquor shelf, he nodded.

"I need you to look at a couple of pictures."

Turning, the man gave a sigh and placed his hands on the glass-rinsing sink. "So, show me."

Holding a picture of Eric Robles, he showed it to the manager. "Do you know this man?"

He pulled glasses out of his shirt pocket and put them

on. Trent took the picture, studied it for a while, and then handed it back. "Yeah, he's one of the owners. That looks like a mug shot. He in trouble?"

"You could say that. What name do you know him by?"

The man pursed his lips and regarded Storm for a few moments. "Edward Rollins. What's he done?"

"I'll get to that. What about this person?" The deputy handed him a picture of Judy taken during happier times.

"Not sure. She does looks familiar, but I can't place her." He returned the picture to Storm. "Want to tell me what this is about, Deputy?"

"The man you know as Edward Rollins' real name is Eric Robles. He is a person of interest in a human trafficking and drug smuggling ring based out of New Orleans. The trail of the scheme runs through Memphis up to St. Louis."

"Shit."

"Beg your pardon."

"I knew something wasn't kosher about him."

Storm put the pictures back into an inside pocket of his windbreaker. "Care to explain?"

"I'm not in trouble, am I?"

Shaking his head, the deputy said, "No. Edward Rollins is in custody, and I'm trying to track down where the woman might be."

"Let me see her picture again."

Extracting it again from his jacket, he handed the photo to Trent. The man studied it for a long time.

"Now I remember, it's been a while. Maybe nine or ten years ago. She was a waitress here. I don't remember her name."

"Was it Judy?"

"No, something different." He stared at the photo for a

few more moments. "Now I remember. Her name was Summer. Summer Cole."

Storm swallowed hard and blinked several times. Summer Cole was a name Judy had mentioned numerous times while they were together. "Did you know anything about her?"

"No. Back then, it was wise not to get too familiar with the staff. Particularly the women. They would be here for a few months and then disappear. I don't remember too many of them. Summer was different. She was reserved, did her job, and didn't get too chummy with the customers. She also seemed sad all the time."

Taking the picture back, Storm glanced at it and then returned it to the pocket of his jacket. "What do you mean sad all the time?"

"Like she really didn't want to be here but had nowhere else to go. During those years, the waitresses were supposed to wear low-cut T-shirts. You know, give the customers a show. Summer didn't possess a lot of cleavage, so she wore more conservative tops."

This truth about Judy felt like a punch to Storm's gut. Flashbacks of their lovemaking almost brought a tear to his eye. But, using his training as a cop, he kept his face neutral. "You said most of the girls didn't stick around long. Do you know why?"

"Yeah. Back in those days, they were on a circuit. They'd serve drinks here and then head up to St. Louis for a while. Some came back, others didn't. The reason I remember Summer…she was here for almost a year and then one day disappeared. I used to get a couple weeks' notice before they rotated the girls out. Not Summer."

"Did the girls ever get too familiar with customers?"

Trent frowned. "I don't run that kind of place, Deputy."

"But you said the girls were rotated out on a regular basis. That's the pattern for a strip club."

"I know, but…"

"So, what happened?"

"When?"

"When Summer disappeared."

"Rollins came for her one day and, when he found out she was gone, he blew a gasket." Trent seemed to be getting into the conversation. "Say, do you want a cup of coffee?"

"Sure."

"I'll get us both a cup."

After the manager returned with the steaming mugs, he leaned against the bar and sipped his. "I'm glad those days are gone."

"When did it change?"

"Not too long after Summer disappeared. I was allowed to start hiring my own staff. I also did away with the tight outfits, and now the girls stick around longer. I still have turnover, but it's not as bad as it used to be."

"Back to the girls getting too familiar."

"I knew some of them went home with customers. I tried to discourage it but was told to mind my own business. So, I did."

Storm asked, "How often?"

"Rollins only had to tell me once."

"No, how often did the girls go home with customers?"

Taking a breath, Trent let it out slowly. "More times than not." He took a sip of coffee. "You said Rollins was in jail for trafficking. Sex trafficking?"

Storm nodded.

"Shit."

"Were the girls of legal age?"

"Yeah, they were. I had to submit a copy of their ID to the liquor board so they could legally serve drinks."

Taking a sip of coffee, the deputy thought of a different question. "When they started letting you hire your own staff, did anything else change?"

The manager stared at the top of the bar for a few moments. "Yeah. Rollins stopped coming around. I've been left alone since."

"Who brought the girls to you back then?"

"Oh shit."

"Let me guess. Rollins?"

A nod from Trent. "Yup. It was always him."

"You didn't find that odd?"

"Like I said, they were on a circuit."

"How much do I owe you for the coffee?"

"On the house, Deputy."

"One last question."

"Sure."

"Do you still have employee records from those days?"

"Are you kidding? Once a girl leaves, I have to send her file to corporate. All I'm allowed to keep are current employees' records."

"Figures. Thanks, Bob." He looked down. "Let's go, Apollo."

Back in the parking area, Storm sat behind the wheel of the SUV and checked for missed calls. He had one: Lisa in Washington. He dialed her number. She answered right away.

"Boy can you pick them, Dakota."

"What'd you find, Lisa?"

"Bayou Global is a privately held company, incorporated in the Cayman Islands. They maintain a headquarters in New Orleans."

"Okay. What's its main business?"

"Hospitality. Lodging, entertainment, casinos, and men's clubs."

"Men's clubs?"

"Yes, they still exist and, from what I can see, are quite profitable."

"Really. Is there one in Memphis?"

"Yeah, but it's not owned by Bayou."

"Where's the closest one?"

"St. Louis."

"Give me the address."

She did.

"Okay, Lisa, what else did you find out?"

"CEO is a man named Denzel Cruz. They have a CFO named Lucas Toro."

Storm hesitated for a few moments. "Does it give an address for them?"

"No. Just the one in the Caymans."

"This gets weirder every time I learn something new about this company."

"Why do you say that, Dakota?"

"Because Denzel Cruz and Lucas Toro are suspected by the New Orleans police department of being involved with the trafficking ring I'm investigating."

"That's interesting. Is there anything else I can do for you?"

"I have another name I need you to do a search on."

"What is it?"

"Summer Cole."

"Who is she?"
"Good question. That's what I am trying to determine."

Chapter Nineteen

St. Louis

Two hours later, as Storm passed the city of Cape Girardeau, Missouri on Interstate 55, his cell phone buzzed.

"Storm."

"Dakota, it's Lisa."

"Did you find anything on Summer Cole?"

"Yeah, she disappeared off the face of the planet ten years ago."

"That corresponds with the information I obtained in Memphis. Anything else?"

"She was a ward of the state of Tennessee from the time she was ten until eighteen. She stayed with foster parents in and around Memphis. She was apparently a difficult child. I found records of eight different sets of caregivers."

This information gave Storm pause. "Any juvenile records?"

"Shoplifting when she was fourteen. But, other than that, none."

"What about her biological parents? Any info?"

"Her mother died right after her birth. The father apparently dumped her with a great aunt because she became the child's legal guardian until her death. I would say she never knew either of her parents. The aunt died when she was ten, and that's the reason for the foster care."

"Any other known relatives?"

"A paternal grandfather."

"Why didn't he take her?"

"From what I found out, he was with the state department at the time and overseas on assignment. He retired ten years ago about the same time Summer disappeared."

"Really?"

"Want the grandfather's address?"

Storm grinned. "Yeah, where is he?"

"Chesterfield, Missouri."

"You're kidding? Can you email it to me?"

"I can. I'll send his personnel file from the state department as well. There are several good pictures of him."

"Bless you, Lisa. I owe you big-time."

"Promises, promises. Just take good care of Apollo."

"No problem doing that. Thanks."

The call ended and Storm looked over at his partner who had transitioned to the front passenger seat so he could watch the road. "We just got lucky, buddy. I know where Judy's grandfather lives."

The dog glanced at the deputy, started panting, and returned to watching the highway.

Chesterfield, MO

The door to the well-maintained ranch-style home opened. A gentleman in his mid-seventies appraised Storm up and down. "Dakota Storm. It took you long enough to find me."

The deputy could only blink with this revelation.

"Beautiful dog. What's its name?"

"Thank you. His name is Apollo." He paused a few moments. "How do you know me, Mr. Cole?"

"You married my granddaughter. I'm sorry for your loss." He paused for a moment. "Please call me Frank."

"May, I come in, sir. I have a lot of questions."

"I'm sure you do." He stepped aside, and Storm and Apollo entered the home.

"Let's talk in the kitchen, I just made some iced tea. Would you like a glass?"

"Yes, please."

As the deputy followed the elderly man, he stopped in front of a shelf, with multiple pictures of the same young girl, and studied them.

Cole said, "Those are pictures of Summer. My sister used to send them to me while I was in Europe."

Turning to his host, Storm said, "I understand you were with the state department."

"That was my cover. I was a station chief for the CIA. One of the reasons I couldn't take Summer after my worthless son dumped her on my sister."

Holding one of the pictures, he said, "I've never seen a picture of her as a young child. She was beautiful."

"Yes, she was. Come. Let's sit down, I've got a lot to tell you."

After they sat and Frank Cole finished stirring his iced

tea, he said, "If you found me, you're obviously investigating those assholes who took over her life."

"I'm a deputy U.S. Marshal and yes, I am trying to find out more about them."

"Congratulations. I knew you were a sheriff's deputy but didn't know you went to work for the Marshals Service."

"How did Summer Cole become Judy Thorn?"

With a sly grin, Cole said, "Friends in low places."

"I'm sorry, but she never mentioned having a living grandfather."

Taking a deep breath, the older man let it out slowly. "That was the price I had to pay for leaving her to fend for herself all those years. Once I found her, I brought her to St. Louis, changed her name, and made her agree to my terms."

"Which were?"

"To protect her, I couldn't exist in her world."

"But you kept in touch with her?"

"In my own way. I attended your wedding and sat in the back of the church. However, I left just before you two walked down the aisle together."

"Did she know you were there?"

"No."

"Surely, you two kept in touch somehow."

Cole took a sip of iced tea and nodded. "We did. But not in St. Louis."

"Those frequent trips she took with friends to Silver Dollar City."

"Very good, Deputy."

Storm turned his iced tea glass clockwise and then counterclockwise. Finally, after a long pause, he asked, "How did the human trafficking group get a grip on her?"

"Another one of the many regrets I have. When she turned eighteen, she fell out of the foster care program. I was undercover in Turkey at the time. Some guy befriended her one night, and they took control of her."

"How long?"

"Couple of years."

"Did she…"

"She never told me, but I believe they made her—uh—date older men for money."

Taking a breath, Storm studied his iced tea glass. "Knowing what I know about them, I suspected they did." He paused and returned his attention to the older man. "How did you find her?"

"In Europe, I got to know a lot of military types over the years. When I retired and moved back to St. Louis, I started renewing those acquaintances. One of them lived in Memphis and called me one day. He'd seen her at a bar on Beale Street."

"Yeah, I talked to the bartender. He said she just disappeared one day."

"She did, because I was waiting for her one morning before she got to work and brought her here to my house."

"My sources with the Marshals Service told me that Summer Cole disappeared into a black hole and basically vanished."

"That's correct. She became Judy Thorn."

"How…"

"Don't ask."

"Okay." Storm studied the table top. "How did they find her?"

"I don't know."

"Did you ever get to meet your great-grandson?"

A tear formed in the older man's left eye. "Only once.

Todd was about one-year-old, and she brought him to see me. That's the only time she ever came back to this house after she married you."

"Then, you and I both lost something special."

"Yes, Dakota, we did." He kept his gaze on the younger man. "I was so happy when she told me you two were dating. I checked your military record. You were highly regarded as a dog trainer. Why didn't you stay in the service?"

"Looking back on it, if I had, no one would have found her, and she and Todd would still be alive."

"You can't know that."

"No, but we would have been somewhere besides St. Louis."

The two men fell into silence as each dealt with his private memories. Finally, after several minutes, Cole asked, "Did you two have a wedding picture put into the *St. Louis Dispatch*?"

"Yeah, her picture. How would that—" Vertigo swept over him as he realized the ramifications of doing so. "Oh my gawd. That's how they found her."

Cole nodded. "More than likely."

Storm stood and paced in the small kitchen. Apollo raised his head and watched the deputy.

After several minutes, he stopped pacing, his attention trained on his late-wife's grandfather. "Do you still have contact with other retired CIA operators?"

"Maybe."

"Do they like you?"

A chuckle was his answer.

"Good. Want payback?"

"What've you got in mind?"

Storm told him.

Kansas City

Jacob Gordon read the letter from Storm for the second time. He turned his attention back to the younger man and asked, "You sure you want to resign?"

"I don't want to, but I have an obligation I need to attend to, and I don't have any idea how long it will take."

"What about a leave of absence?"

"Didn't know if I'd been with the Marshals Service long enough to request one."

"You let me worry about that. I don't want you quitting. You've got too much potential."

"Thank you for your confidence, sir."

"This about your late wife?"

Storm nodded.

"You're not planning on doing anything illegal are you?"

"No, sir, I'm not. I located her grandfather and need to help him for a while. For her sake."

"Family matters. I can use that."

"Yes, sir."

"What will you do for money?"

"I still have some left from the house insurance settlement, and the grandfather is well-off. I'll be fine."

"Any idea how long it will take?"

"Couple of months. Maybe less."

He handed the letter back to the deputy. "Change that to a request for a leave of absence, and I'll approve it." He paused. "What's on your desk?"

"Nothing I can't clean up in a week."

"Good. I can get all the paperwork submitted by Friday."

"Thank you, sir." He turned and walked toward the door of Gordon's office.

"Storm?"

He turned. "Yes?"

"Don't get caught."

Chapter Twenty

Kansas City

The Following Weekend

"How long do you think you will be gone, Dakota?"

Storm stood on the front porch of Melissa Perry's house. His purpose for being there was to give her a key to check his house on occasion. "Month, maybe six weeks."

"Glad we got to see the Royals play last weekend."

"I had fun. Thanks for getting the tickets."

"You're welcome. Would you like to come in and have a cup of coffee?"

He checked his watch. "Sure, I've got time. I don't have to be in St. Louis until this afternoon."

They sat in silence for a few moments after she poured the coffee. Melissa grasped her mug with both hands and studied the steam rising from the dark liquid. "Dakota, can I tell you something?"

"Sure."

"It's a little personal."

He gave her an encouraging smile.

"I've really enjoyed the time we've spent together this week."

"Me, too. Glad I got to show you I know my way around an outdoor grill."

"Yes, you did." She paused. "I'm going to miss you."

Reaching over the small table, he placed his hand on hers. "I enjoy being with you, too, Melissa. But if I'm ever going to be able to move on with my life, this trip is something I have to do. My hope is it will bring some closure concerning my wife and son's deaths."

She gave him a sad smile and leaned forward. "I hope you're able to find peace. You'll be careful, won't you?"

"Of course. I won't be doing anything dangerous. I found Judy's grandfather. He has—uh—some law enforcement in his background and has offered to help me find out more about the accident."

She stood. "Give me your hand, Dakota."

He offered it.

Pulling him up, he stood facing her. She kissed him on the lips and then led him back to her bedroom.

Storm arrived at Frank Cole's house by midafternoon. When he and Apollo were inside, the older man asked, "Where are you staying?"

"There's a Hampton Inn not too far from here. I've got a reservation there."

"Nonsense, you'll stay here. I have a guest room with its

own bathroom. That way Apollo has access to the backyard whenever he needs to run."

"I wouldn't want to impose on you."

"It will be nice having someone here for a change. Besides, it will be easier for us to plan our next moves."

"That's very kind of you, Frank."

"Good, then it's settled. Make yourself at home. A few of my old friends and I have been busy this week."

Storm raised an eyebrow.

Cole displayed a sly smile. "I know where to find Lucas Toro."

"Where?"

"It seems our Mr. Toro had a slight falling out with his associates. He's currently in an assisted living facility in Tulsa. He's Native American and is living under his real name, Lucas Wohali. My source tells me he grew up on the Cherokee Nation."

"Why's he in an assisted living facility?"

"Same question I asked. Apparently, someone shattered his kneecaps with a hammer."

"Ouch." Storm grimaced. "I'll go down there and have a talk with him."

The older man said, "Probably not a good idea at the moment. My source also told me Mr. Wohali has a serious problem with authority. Going in as a U.S. Marshal won't get us anywhere."

"I've taken a leave of absence. I'd be talking to him as Dakota Storm."

"I was wondering how you were going to handle being gone for a while."

Folding his arms, Storm said, "How did your source locate this man so fast?"

134

Cole used a napkin to wipe the sweat off the outside of his iced tea glass. "Dakota, men like Lucas Toro are easy to find if you know how to look for them. I can help you become a more effective U.S. Marshal if you'll allow me the opportunity."

Storm remained quiet as he let the older man speak.

"Part of my job for the CIA revolved around locating and silencing international terrorists."

"Did you personally silence them?"

Cole raised the tea glass to his lips and took a drink. He then slowly shook his head. "No. We had others better trained and suited for that task. My job was to trace the sources of money allowing those types of men to operate. If you compare the men who took control of Summer and others like her to the organizers of various terrorist groups around the world, you'll see similarities."

"Such as?"

"Ego, greed, and narcissistic tendencies."

"Okay, I'll buy that. But they fight for a cause."

"Bullshit. They fight for power and its sister, money."

"So, how did you locate Lucas Toro?"

"Just like I did in Europe and Asia, social media and bank records."

"Show me."

"My pleasure."

"How familiar are you with computers, Dakota?"

The younger man contemplated the question from his late-wife's grandfather. "I know how to use them, but I can't explain how they work."

"That's a good answer. I don't know how they work,

either. But I can show you how to get the most out of one. Have you ever heard of the Dark Web?"

"Yes, I've heard of it, but not much more."

"Very few individuals have. Let me explain. The internet is made up of three types of sites. The open internet is accessible by any search engine, such as Google. The deep web is composed of websites that require sign-in credentials, like a bank, PayPal, or a credit card. The Dark Web is a subset of the deep web and can only be accessed with special software. The Dark Web is where I hunted terrorists during the years before I retired. It's how I found Lucas Toro."

"I'm listening."

"When I got back from Europe and learned what had happened to Summer, I used the skills I'd acquired to find her. The thugs that kidnapped her called themselves The Collectors. Sounds innocent enough, but they marketed themselves on the Dark Web as procurers of pleasure for all tastes."

Unease swept over Storm and he shuddered.

"I know, it made my skin crawl as well. There were several of these groups, but The Collectors seemed to be the most sophisticated. They also import girls from South and Central America."

"How did you find Judy—I mean Summer?"

"I knew her as Summer; you knew her as Judy. The names are interchangeable for me." He paused and took a deep breath and let it out slowly. "I found her picture on the Dark Web. From there, I discovered where she was and where she worked."

"Did she recognize you?"

"Oh yes. I've never forgotten her reaction when I pulled up next to her on the curb. She was walking to work."

"Let me guess, a gleeful giggle and she probably said, 'I was wondering when you'd show up.'"

"No, she didn't giggle. All she said was, 'Please take me home, Papa.'"

Storm wiped his eye with the back of his hand and turned away from the older man.

"It's okay, Dakota. I've done my fair share of shedding tears since that day."

Both men remained quiet, lost in their private thoughts of a granddaughter and a wife.

"Okay, Frank. How'd you find Lucas Toro?"

After a chuckle, the retired CIA field agent said, "Those morons discussed the attack in a chat room they have for members."

"You're kidding?"

"Nope. A buddy of mine found it and told me how to access the chat room. Apparently, Toro was some kind of big shot within Bayou Global."

"He was. In the corporate papers I was given, he's identified as their CFO."

"Well, he was accused of misappropriating a rather large sum of money into a secret bank account he held in the Cayman Islands."

"How much?"

"Ten million."

"And they only broke his kneecaps?"

"They got the money back, so it became more important to make an example of him."

"Huh."

"Want to learn more about the Dark Web?"

"Absolutely."

Chapter Twenty-One

Tulsa, Oklahoma

The odor became Storm's second impression of the assisted living facility. While the exterior did not communicate a homey, or even an agreeable, place to live, the smell inside sealed the deal. A place for the least affluent members of society to spend their last remaining days in a depressing atmosphere reminiscent of Dante's nine circles of Hell.

With this image in mind, Storm approached the reception desk and waited for the middle-aged woman to acknowledge his presence. It took a full minute for her to glance up with bored eyes.

"Whatta ya need?"

"Lucas Wohali."

"Yeah, what about him?"

"I'm here to visit him."

She checked the clock on a wall and continued in a monotone. "Well, you're in luck; visiting hours are noon to four, it's just three." She thumbed through a small plastic box on her desk and extracted a 3x5 index card. "This place is so cheap we don't even have computers yet." After studying the card, she returned her attention to Storm. "Huh, what do you know. You'll be his first visitor. He's not the most likable man we've had here."

"Nevertheless, I would like to visit with him."

"Name?"

"Dakota Storm."

"What the hell kind of name is that?"

"Mine."

"Who the hell would name their kid something like that?"

"My parents."

She looked at him like he had a third eye. "Wait in the room next door. Someone will bring Wohali to you."

"Thank you."

Fearing the ancient furniture might have been in some of the residents' rooms at one time, Storm chose to stand. Five minutes later, a thin, young woman wheeled a man into the room. As soon as she set the parking brake on the wheelchair, she made a hasty retreat, leaving the two men alone.

The resident looked at Storm and growled, "I don't know you."

"You have no reason to. Are you Lucas Wohali?"

"It depends on who you are."

Storm pointed to the casts on the man's legs. "I'm the guy trying to find the individuals who did that to you."

"You a cop?"

The deputy shook his head. "Used to be. Not now."

"Then why you looking for them?"

"They stole someone from me, and I want payback."

Wohali tilted his head. "These are not guys you want to fuck with."

"They haven't met me yet."

The man in the wheelchair laughed. "Pretty sure of yourself, aren't you?"

Storm shrugged.

"What's your name?"

"Dakota Storm."

With narrowed eyes, the injured man tilted his head. "I've heard that name before. Is it supposed to scare me?"

"Just stating a fact. Now, where can I find the assholes who busted your kneecaps?"

Wohali studied the man in front of him for a few moments. "I fell down a staircase."

The deputy slowly shook his head. "No, you stole ten million dollars from them, and they used a ball-peen hammer on your legs. You were then dumped in the parking lot of the Tulsa County sheriff's department. Someone used a Sharpie to write the word traitor and thief on your forehead."

"I'm impressed. But I'm still not going to tell you where to find them."

With another shrug, Storm moved toward the door of the room. Just before he exited, he called over his shoulder, "It was worth a shot."

"Storm."

He returned. "Yes."

"It wasn't my idea to have your wife killed."

"Whose was it?"

"Denzel Cruz."

"You're the second person to mention his name. Where can I find him?"

"They'll kill me if I tell you."

Looking around, Storm chuckled. "It appears you're already in hell, Lucas." He turned and walked out of the depressing facility.

With visiting hours from noon until four in the afternoon, Storm spent those hours over the next few days observing the comings and goings of the assisted living facility. Apollo, sitting on the passenger seat, watched the activities with him. With a laptop mounted on a bracket between the front seats, pictures of the known characters of Bayou Global were displayed for his reference.

On the third afternoon, right at three thirty, a man matching one of the pictures on his laptop parked in the visitor area and walked in. Storm clicked on the picture and read about the individual.

Storm said, "This is Victor Landry, Apollo."

The canine glanced at the deputy and then returned its attention to the man walking into the facility.

Storm lifted binoculars to his eyes. "According to the information we have on this guy, he's a gofer for the organization."

Apollo increased his panting.

When the man disappeared inside, the deputy lowered the binoculars. "We'll see where he goes after he completes his business."

They did not have long to wait. At exactly ten minutes of four, Landry returned to his vehicle. Storm punched a number into his cell phone. "Light-gray Chevy Silverado. Single white male. Leaving parking lot." He recited the license plate. "Name is Victor Landry, and he just visited Lucas Wohali."

"I'll take the first five minutes and then you slip in."

"Got it." Storm started the Explorer and left the parking lot.

Storm kept his distance behind Frank Cole's Lexus RX350, his cell phone still connected to the call.

Cole said, "He's merging onto north I-44, I'm going straight, you pick him up, and I'll be behind you for a switch-off if needed."

Settling in two cars behind Judy's grandfather, he said, "I'm on him." Storm set his cruise control, ended the call, and followed the pickup. Sixty minutes later, his cell phone rang. "Yeah."

"I'm two cars behind you. What's our boy doing?"

"Steady seventy-five miles an hour."

"Good. When you need a break, let me know?"

"At this pace, we'll be in Joplin soon. If the cars ahead of me don't exit, we can switch then."

"Sounds good." The call ended.

An hour later, Storm exited the interstate for gas and to let Apollo do his business. Ten minutes later, he was back on the road and called Cole. "Where's Landry now?"

"He took an exit and is headed north on I-49."

"Shit."

"What's that mean?"

"Kansas City is two hours north."

"Oh dear."

"Well, Frank, it will be dark soon, and we can follow a little closer."

"Got it."

Ending the call, Storm looked at Apollo. "Let's hope this is just a coincidence."

Apollo whimpered.

"Yeah, I don't believe it, either."

By eight thirty, Storm suspected where Landry was headed. His house in Overland Park. He called Frank Cole on the phone.

Cole answered. "He's headed to your house, isn't he?"

"It appears that way. If he exits onto Metcalf, we'll know for sure."

"If he doesn't?"

The deputy paused before he answered. "We follow him until we know where he's going."

"Got it. How far behind me are you?"

"Three cars."

"Okay. We're coming up on Metcalf Avenue."

Storm held his breath.

"Nope, he stayed on I-435 heading west."

"Huh." The deputy remained silent for a few moments. "What now, Frank?"

"Let's see where he goes."

"Okay, I'll take the lead and follow him."

Storm accelerated around the Lexus and fell in behind the Silverado as they passed the I-69 intersection. They continued to head west.

The time approached nine when Landry pulled into a driveway on the outskirts of Topeka, KS. Storm drove by just as Landry turned his pickup into a driveway attached to a ranch-style dwelling. No lights could be seen inside the house.

He dialed Cole's phone. "He just parked inside a garage." He recited the address. "Doesn't look like anyone else is at home. When you go by, see if you notice any lights. I'm going to a restaurant a few blocks from here and get on their Wi-Fi. I'll check the property tax records for the address."

"Want me to keep the house under surveillance?"

"Yeah. Just in case he decides to bolt."

"Got it."

———

Storm parked his SUV behind Cole's Lexus. He entered the car on the passenger side and closed the door. "House is owned by Bayou Global."

"Imagine that."

"There's more. The Silverado is registered to Victor Landry at this address."

"Then he's lived here awhile."

"It would appear so."

"Dakota?"

"Yeah?"

"Does it strike you as strange these guys appear to be leading normal lives?"

"Hadn't thought about it until you mentioned it. Maybe they're just hiding in plain sight."

Cole shook his head. "There's something else going on. Any other names listed on the personal property tax file?"

"Only one person, Victor."

"Then we only have to contend with one person inside."

The deputy did not comment immediately. Finally, he said, "I'd hate to assume anything, but there's a good chance of it."

"If he was sent to deliver a message to Lucas Wohali, knowing what that message was might be helpful. Think we should have a chat with him?"

"Not a bad idea. You take first shift. I've got to get

something for Apollo to eat and give him some exercise. Then I'm going to a Walmart not far from here. What size pants and sweatshirt do you wear?

Cole stared at the house containing Victor Landry. "Thirty-six, thirty-two, XL."

"See you in a bit."

Chapter Twenty-Two

Topeka, KS

At 1:35 a.m., two men, dressed in black, their faces covered by ski masks, and a dog invaded the home of Victor Landry.

They entered his bedroom and caught him asleep in his bed. One man zip-tied his hands while the other did the same to his feet. Before the resident could react, duct tape covered his eyes and mouth. Landry lay in his bed, blind and helpless.

With the home's resident secured, Storm removed his ski mask and started looking through a desk containing several drawers with files. At the same time, Frank Cole attacked a laptop found on a table in the kitchen.

By 3:15 a.m., both Storm and Cole were ready to confront the man. They carried him into the kitchen. With his arms and feet still bound, they placed him into a straight-back chair. Cole spoke in a gravelly voice. "If you want to live, speak only when asked a question. Is that understood?"

Landry nodded his head.

They removed the duct tape from his mouth, leaving his eyes covered by the gray material.

Storm pressed his Sig Sauer against Landry's head just above the ear, while Cole asked the questions.

"You visited Lucas Wohali yesterday. Maybe you know him as Lucas Toro. What did you discuss?"

"Who the fuck are you?"

Cole slapped him, bent down, and growled, "I'll ask the questions. Again, what did you talk to Lucas Toro about?"

"Haven't got a clue what you're talking about."

Storm charged the automatic pistol and placed it, once again, against the man's temple.

The ex-CIA station chief slapped Landry again. "Wrong answer."

"Like I said, I don't know anybody by the name Lucas Toro."

Another slap. "You don't listen too well, do you, Victor? Now answer the question. What did you discuss with Lucas Toro?"

The mention of his name caused Landry to stiffen.

"Yes, we know who you are, and we know who you work for. Now, last time before things get ugly. What did you discuss with Lucas Toro?"

"Uh…ah man, you're gonna get me killed."

"Who's to say we won't kill you? Now start talking."

"Shit."

"Yes, Victor, something you are extremely deep in right now."

"Ahhh, geez."

Cole looked at Storm, who nodded. The deputy slapped

Landry hard with the pistol on the back of his head. He bent forward and growled, "Answer the question, asshole."

"All right, all right." He took several breaths. "I told him not to talk to anyone, or someone would come and check him out of that dump."

"And?"

"He'd end up in a landfill somewhere."

Cole folded his arms and studied the bound man for a few moments. "Who sent you to talk to Landry?"

"The boss."

"What's his name?"

"I don't know. He's just the boss."

Storm struck the bound man again with the Sig Sauer, only harder.

"Shit, man. You're gonna crack my skull with that thing."

"Good."

Cole gave Storm a smile. "Victor, my colleague and I are getting impatient with you. What is the name of your boss?"

A long silence ensued. Finally, Landry said, "Denzel Cruz."

"Good for you, Victor. Now, where is he?"

"How the hell should I know? He contacts me; I don't contact him."

Storm gave Apollo a hand signal. The canine moved closer to the man in the chair and made a deep, menacing growl.

Landry's body grew stiff. "Ah, shit, there's a dog in here. Keep it away from me, man."

"Tell us where we can find Denzel Cruz, Victor."

"Get the dog away, and I will."

With another hand signal, Apollo retreated, sat, and kept his eyes on the prisoner. Storm then said, "Now, where is he?"

"He's got a house in New Orleans, but he's never there. When he's out of town, he stays in hotels the company owns."

Leaning over, the deputy spoke into Landry's ear, "Where's the fucking house?"

"How the hell should I know, I've never been there. I'm a nobody."

"Somehow, I doubt that. What's your role in the company?"

"Like I just told you, I'm a nobody. I do odd jobs like drive ten hours to Tulsa and back, just to tell some poor schmuck to keep his trap shut."

Cole picked up a file Storm found in a desk and looked through it. "Not according to what we found in your desk, Victor."

"You guys were in my desk? Ah, geez."

"You're lying to us, Victor. And my friend with the gun doesn't like that. Now, according to your last year's tax filing, you claim your occupation to be a consultant. Plus, you made over two hundred thousand dollars. Pretty good money for a nobody."

"I can explain that."

"I hope so."

The eastern horizon showed the first signs of dawn as Cole and Storm drove toward the Missouri state line. Landry, still bound to a chair by duct tape, would soon have visitors

149

from the FBI field office in Kansas City. Information concerning his many illegal transgressions was neatly stacked on the kitchen table and labeled for the convenience of the investigating agents.

With Apollo asleep in the Explorer, the two men sat in a coffee shop just as the sun popped over the horizon.

Storm asked, "Who did you call?"

"A retired FBI agent I've known for a while. He took care of alerting the local field office about Victor Landry's whereabouts and what information waited for them. I told him the guy was involved in the death of my granddaughter. He agreed to keep yours and my name out of it."

After a yawn and a sip of coffee, Storm nodded. "I'm not sure how deep the information we found will penetrate the trafficking ring, but Landry is going to have a lot of explaining to do."

Cole chuckled. "They'll chalk it up to an anonymous tip and run with it. You'd be surprised how many felons they take into custody because of phone calls like the one I made."

The deputy yawned again. "I'm aware of those types of tips. What now, Frank?"

"It would probably be a wise idea for you and me to lie low for a few days. Why don't you go home and get some sleep. We can meet up later in the week."

After a third yawn, Storm nodded. "Yeah, that's a good idea. With what you've taught me about social media and how to utilize it, I'll spend a few days seeing what I can find."

Cole picked up the check and stood. "Thanks for helping with this, Dakota. Maybe, when this is all over, we can both have a little closure."

"You don't have to pay for breakfast."

"No, I realize that. But I feel responsible for the loss of Summer and Todd. I'll take that to my grave." He turned and headed toward the cash register to pay for their breakfast.

Storm, weary from the lack of sleep over the previous thirty-six hours, could only watch him walk out. Five minutes later, having finished his coffee, he pushed himself up, left the café, and drove the half mile to his house in Overland Park.

———

The following day, he took Apollo to a park for an hour of chasing Frisbees. The two arrived home at the same time Melissa pulled into her driveway. The man and dog walked over and greeted her as she stepped out of her car.

"Dakota, what a surprise. I thought you were going to be gone for a while?"

"We're back for a few days. I'm working out of the house until I have to leave again."

She gave him a quick hug. "Do you have time for dinner?"

"Yeah. Can I take you out?"

"I was thinking about making something at home."

"Tell you what. Why don't you come over around six? I'll make a pizza."

"I'll bring the wine."

"See you then."

As he walked back toward his house, he looked down at Apollo. The dog appeared to be smiling.

"Take it easy, boy. It's just dinner."

The dog jumped up toward his outstretched hand and barked once. Looking back at Storm, he ran toward their back door.

"I swear, that dog is smarter than a lot of people I know." He jogged after his canine friend.

"Can you tell me what you're doing?" Melissa lifted the wineglass to her lips.

Dakota said, "I'm helping Judy's grandfather research. He's been showing me how to do inquiries on social media. We're both of the opinion there is someone out there who knows more about Judy and Todd's accident. We might find them on social media."

"How?"

"Sometimes people like to brag. If they brag, we can find it."

"Then what?"

"We turn them over to the police."

She tilted her head. "You're not involved, then?"

He shook his head. "At this point, no. If they turn out to be fugitives, then I'll get involved."

"What have you found so far?"

His recent exploits did not need to be discussed. "Not much. But I'm just getting used to the techniques he taught me."

"What did he do before he retired?"

"State Department. He worked in a number of embassies in Europe and the Middle East. Apparently, he learned a lot about finding information on social media."

"Sounds interesting."

"He's an interesting guy."

"So, what's next for us, Dakota?"

"What do you want for us, Melissa?"

"I'm hoping you can find closure and move on with your life. When you do, maybe we can become more than just friends."

He reached for her hand. "I'd like that."

Chapter Twenty-Three

St. Louis

One Week Later

Storm and Apollo returned to the home of Frank Cole after an early morning run. The owner of the house grasped a cup of coffee in both hands as they entered the kitchen from the back porch.

Checking his watch, Storm said, "You're up early."

"Couldn't sleep."

"Hope Apollo and I didn't wake you."

The older man shook his head. "No, I heard you two leave. Grab a cup and sit. I want to get your opinion on something."

Storm filled Apollo's food bowl and then poured a cup of coffee for himself. Once he sat across from Cole, the older man said, "I think we're going about this backward."

"Okay. How so?"

"You're a deputy U.S. Marshal, right?"

"Yeah."

"You're the leader of a fugitive task force, aren't you?"

"Yes."

"For all intents and purposes, Denzel Cruz could be considered a fugitive."

"If he isn't, he should be."

"Your position within the Marshals Service should give you access to any available information regarding his whereabouts, correct?"

"I see your point. Time for me to get back to work."

Cole nodded and sipped his coffee. "While you're doing your job, I can use my resources to keep searching for the man." He paused. "My methods might not be deemed acceptable by your employer and the FBI." With a smile, he continued, "If it is determined you assisted, some of my actions might cause you to lose your job. I don't need any more regrets on my conscience."

Storm tasted his coffee.

"You and Apollo need to get back to your regular routine," Cole went on. "Consider it an alibi. I'll call you when I have more information. For now, you need to search for Cruz within the boundaries of the law."

"And if we don't find him that way?"

"We'll cross that bridge when we get to it."

"How long do you think it will take us?"

"I thought we would have learned more by now. But we haven't come up with anything concrete since we started. I'll work in the background while you search for him within the bounds of federal law enforcement. Since I have access to different sources, maybe between the two of us we can discover where the son of a bitch is."

After another sip of coffee, Storm nodded. "I don't want to leave this all on your shoulders."

"You're not." He paused. "I didn't spend all those years with the CIA and not learn a few tricks. Best if I do them myself."

The Next Day

Jacob Gordon looked up from his desk after the knock and waved Storm in. "Didn't expect to see you back so soon."

"It didn't take as long as I thought it would."

"Everything okay?"

"Yes. I learned a few things while I was gone."

Gordon tilted his head. "I won't pry."

"It's okay. Judy's grandfather showed me how to search for individuals on social media. I'm anxious to see if it helps me find fugitives."

"In that case"—the U.S. Marshal for the Western District of Missouri handed Storm several file folders from his desk—"glad you're back. You can test your newfound knowledge with these." He paused for a moment. "Learn anything about Judy's accident?"

Storm shook his head. "Unfortunately, whoever may be responsible is keeping quiet about it."

"After the amount of time it's been, that's probably the case. Or they're dead."

"That thought also occurred to me."

Gordon smiled. "Welcome back, Dakota. You're officially on the clock again."

"Thank you, sir."

Later in the afternoon, after getting all the paperwork

required by the Marshals Service HR department completed, Storm sat in his cubicle and did a few preliminary searches. With Apollo taking a nap next to his desk, he started with the top file given to him in the morning.

A fellow deputy stopped by his cubicle. "Welcome back, Dakota."

Turning, Storm smiled at his occasional partner, James Russel. "Hey, Jimmie. What've you got going on this week?"

"Court tomorrow."

"Okay, make yourself available this Wednesday. I just got a hit on someone we need to bring in."

Bending over, Russel studied the computer screen. "Want to explain what I'm looking at?"

"Facebook post by the guy's girlfriend."

"Huh."

"Our fugitive has been hiding in plain site near Warsaw. He doesn't post as himself but uses a series of letters and numbers. According to the information in the file Gordon gave me, the girlfriend's name is Brenda Samuels. I found a profile by that name with references to a boyfriend." Storm pointed to a particular post. "Note the selfie she posted. In the background you can see the city limit sign. Her comments indicate she was visiting a friend. The shadow in the picture appears to be male."

Russel moved closer to the monitor. "That's kind of thin, Dakota."

"Yes, but what about this?" Storm scrolled down a little farther and clicked on a picture of the fugitive posted over two years ago. "That, my dear Jimmie, is our man."

"Son of a bitch. It sure is."

"While you're in court tomorrow, I'll see if I can narrow his location down a little more."

Standing straight, Russel chuckled. "Glad to have you back, Dakota."

"Good to be back."

Warsaw, MO

Wednesday

By dawn, Russel and Storm, accompanied by Apollo, were positioned near an old motel situated northwest of the small community. Known for its proximity to the Harry Truman Dam and on a major tributary of the reservoir, the motel served as a place for fishermen to rest after a long day on the lake. And, occasionally, it provided a place for individuals to avoid scrutiny by law enforcement authorities. The motel, several miles west of US 65 highway, provided an easy access point for anglers to launch their boats from their trailers.

The Lake Vista Motel owners maintained a relatively clean place but believed property updates only meant an occasional fresh coat of paint for the rooms.

The team from the U.S. Marshals Service kept cover in a stand of birch trees and viburnum shrubs. Their hiding spot lay perpendicular to the southern wing of the hotel. This allowed them to keep tabs on both a room occupied by the fugitive they sought and the parking lot.

As the sun peeked over the eastern horizon, Daryl Thorton stepped out of his room and lit a cigarette. Dressed in jeans, minus shoes, socks, and shirt, he stood watching the brightening day, his back to the deputies.

Storm made a hand signal, and Apollo took off toward the man. The dog remained silent as it rapidly approached him. When it reached the suspect, it nipped at his heels and started barking.

Thorton turned toward the fast-approaching animal and started cursing. Russel appeared from the side of the motel and pushed the fugitive against the building. "U.S. Marshals, Daryl. You're under arrest."

While Russel held him against the wall, Storm yanked the man's hands behind him and cuffed his wrists. The door to the hotel room flew open, revealing a woman holding a sheet around herself. Her eyes widened and she slammed the door shut. Storm heard the security chain scraping into place. With Thorton now in custody and guarded by both Storm and Apollo. Russel displayed a grin and knocked on the door. "Ms. Blanch, open the door. U.S. Marshals."

Thorton chuckled. "That ain't Vivian, dude." He paused and shook his head slowly. "So that's how you found me, that stupid bitch Vivian. I knew that Facebook crap of hers would come back and bite me."

Turning to their prisoner, Russel asked, "Who's in there?"

With a shrug, Thorton just smiled.

Before Russel resumed pounding on the closed motel room door, Storm said, "Hey, partner, step to the side of the door."

Russel nodded and moved to his right. He then pounded on it. "You're trapped, lady. Come out with your hands where we can see them."

Two bullets tore through the door, missing everyone on the outside. Storm pushed Thorton farther down the row of rooms and tripped him. With the prisoner now facedown on the parking lot, the deputy applied a zip tie to secure his feet. Returning his attention to his partner, he saw Russel talking on a handheld radio asking the local sheriff for backup. Storm made a hand signal to Apollo. The canine placed himself beside the prone prisoner. At the slightest movement, the canine barked and nipped at the man's heels.

Looking down at the prisoner, Storm asked, "What's her name?"

"Don't have a clue. I picked her up in a bar last night."

"Daryl, do you really expect me to believe that?"

"Believe what ya want."

"Don't move, Thorton. The dog looks harmless, but he isn't."

With Thorton secured, Storm moved cautiously back toward the door where the barricaded woman remained. From the side of the entrance, he said, "Hey, Vivian, there's no way out. You need to put the gun down and come out with your hands where we can see them."

A muffled voice could be heard behind the door. "Name's not Vivian."

"That's what Daryl told me."

"He's a lying sack of shit."

"What's your name?"

"You can call me, Kate."

"Okay, Kate. Time to come out." Storm paused and remembered a name from the file he had on Thorton. "You're Kathleen Bossing, aren't you?"

"Damn that Thorton. He told you, didn't he?"

"Nope, we know about you." He paused. "I might want to warn you, if the sheriff gets here and you're still behind that door, they'll use gas to get you out."

Russel smiled at Storm, knowing what his partner was trying to do.

The woman behind the door said, "Gas? What kind of gas?"

"The kind that makes your eyes water. Then you gag and puke."

"Shit."

Storm stifled a laugh.

"Okay, I'm coming out. Don't shoot."

"Come out with your hands empty and in front of you."

The sound of a security chain being released could be heard and then the door opened. The disheveled woman held her arms straight out and used one hip to open the door. She wore jeans and a baggy sweatshirt.

Russel grabbed one of her outstretched arms, twisted it behind her, and pushed the woman against the wall next to the door. He quickly handcuffed her and patted her down around the waist. With a quick glance at Storm, he lifted the back of the garment and pulled a Colt 1911 out of her waist band. He handed it to Storm and continued his search.

Storm examined the gun and then said, "Awful big gun for such a little lady."

The woman turned her head so she could see Storm. "Fuck you."

Chapter Twenty-Four

Kansas City

Friday

Jacob Gordon stopped at the entrance to Storm's cubicle and said, "How'd you and Russel manage to bag two fugitives so fast? I just gave you the list on Monday."

Turning from his desk, Storm looked up at his boss. "One was planned, the other just happened to be in the same motel room."

"No, seriously, Dakota, how did you find Thorton so fast? He's been on the Marshals Services' watch list for over twelve months."

"Really?"

"Yes."

"Huh." The deputy paused. "Didn't know that."

"Okay, so how'd you two do it?"

"Remember I told you about Judy's grandfather?"

"Yes."

"He showed me a few tricks he used during his time with the State Department."

Gordon closed his eyes and shook his head. "State Department?"

Storm nodded.

He folded his arms and glared at the deputy. "Let me guess—he was the cultural attaché?"

"Nope. CIA station chief."

"Oh dear. You'd better tell me how you did it."

"Facebook."

A small grin appeared on Gordon's face. "That's it?"

"Yup. He showed me how to dig into the posts a little deeper. In the file you gave me on Thornton, several of his girlfriends were identified. I found him through one of their posts. He was hiding in plain sight north of Warsaw in one of those old no-tell motels."

"Was the Bossing woman his girlfriend?"

"One of many. We think they hooked up at some bar the night before. Guess we got lucky."

Patting the deputy on the shoulder, Gordon chuckled. "Sometimes luck is more than half the battle, Dakota. Glad you're back."

Tuesday the Following Week

Storm entered Gordon's office at ten minutes after eight in the morning. "You wanted to see me, Jacob?"

The U.S. Marshal handed his deputy a picture. "The FBI have that man in custody here in Kansas City. His name is Victor Landry."

The muscles in Storm's stomach tightened. "If he's in custody, how does that affect us?"

Gordon pointed at the photo. "He's part of the human trafficking group you and I investigated in Memphis."

Keeping his eyes on the picture, Storm's mouth felt like a dust bowl. He chose to remain quiet.

"Apparently, the bureau found extensive files in his house linking him directly to the group as both a money launderer and a mid-level lieutenant."

Returning his attention to his boss, the deputy said, "A mid-level lieutenant? What does that mean?"

"He knows a lot."

"Huh." He paused for a moment. "Why did the FBI contact you about this guy?"

"Professional courtesy." After a chuckle, Gordon continued, "They won't admit it, but they're a little embarrassed they didn't know about him. All of a sudden, their interest in this group has increased tenfold. They're requesting someone to brief them on the details."

Realizing his boss was not aware of his involvement with Landry, he exhaled quietly. "I hope you aren't asking me to do it."

"You're the perfect individual. You know the case better than anyone. Besides, you need to get to know the agents who work in this area."

"Why?"

Gordon took the picture back from Storm. "The agent in charge is a good guy. Some of his agents have their nose stuck in the air, but that's standard procedure."

"That doesn't answer my question, sir. Why?"

Gordon's tone hardened. "Because, like it or not, Deputy, we have to work with our FBI cousins. We are all on the same team, regardless if they believe it or not."

Taking the hint, Storm stood at attention. "Yes, sir. When?"

"They are expecting you this afternoon."

"I'm taking Apollo."

"Wouldn't have it any other way. Good luck."

Dakota Storm viewed the recording of Victor Landry's interrogation on a monitor in a conference room. Next to him stood the FBI Special Agent in Charge of the Kansas City Field Office who had watched the entire interview at the same time.

Adam Lowe stood with his arms crossed as the video ended. "Well, Deputy Storm, what do you think?"

"Agent Lowe, from my experience with these guys, everything he said was more than likely a lie."

"That was our assessment as well." He paused and tilted his head. "Jacob Gordon speaks very highly of you."

"That's good to hear."

"Relax. Jacob's an old friend of mine. We go back more than a few years."

Storm maintained his neutral gaze and kept quiet.

"The briefing you gave us earlier was eye-opening. We had no idea how widespread this problem is." He paused. "May I call you Dakota? Using our titles feels a little silly when it's just the two of us."

Storm gave the FBI agent a slight smile. "It is my first name. Please do."

"I'm Adam, okay?"

The deputy nodded.

Lowe continued, "Jacob told me your late wife and son were killed by this group. Is that correct?"

"Yes."

"Is that going to cause a problem?"

Folding his arms, Storm studied the FBI supervisor for a few moments. "Let me explain something, Adam. Before I started investigating these guys, no one even knew they existed. Plus, no one seemed to give a shit about them until I discovered those girls in the Memphis warehouse. These clowns burned my house down and tried to kill me in a hotel. Still, no one paid a whole lot of attention to them. Now, the FBI has a suspect in custody, and, all of a sudden, your hairs on fire to learn as much as you can about them. I've already assisted in the arrest of Eric Robles, aka Edward Rollins. Plus, a guy named Lucas Toro, aka Lucas Wohali, can be found in an assisted living complex in Tulsa. He was their accountant until he diverted a couple of million dollars into his own account in the Caymans. Because of that, they broke his knees, to set an example. So, is it a problem for me? No."

With a wide grin, Lowe nodded. "Good, I like your attitude. What else can you tell me about them?"

"Denzel Cruz."

"Who's he?"

"Their boss. He's also a mystery. No one will talk about him. Those who do, disappear."

"Guess we need to ask Landry about him."

"It would be interesting to see his reaction."

"Want to be there?"

"Sure. When?"

"How about now."

Fifteen minutes later, the interrogation room once again held Landry and a single FBI agent. Lowe and Storm watched from a video monitor outside the room.

The agent started the conversation. "Some additional

information has presented itself, Victor. We wanted to get your take on it."

Landry sat across from the agent and shrugged. "Whatever."

"Does the name Denzel Cruz mean anything to you?"

The prisoner stiffened. "I didn't give you that name."

"But you know who he is, right?"

"I didn't say that."

"Then, how do you know his name, Victor?"

"I want a lawyer."

"Now, Victor, we had a nice conversation this morning without involving attorneys."

"Well, I ain't saying shit until I have one present."

Lowe turned the volume down on the monitor and looked at Storm. "You're right. This Denzel Cruz person scares the shit out of these people."

Still staring at the monitor, Storm said, "Ask him about Cruz's house in New Orleans."

Raising an eyebrow, Lowe walked to the interrogation door and knocked. The agent opened it and stepped out.

Storm watched on the monitor as Landry pounded on the table and said, "Shit. If Cruz knows I told them anything, I'm fucked." He stared at the ceiling. "Not fucked. Dead."

The door opened, and the agent sat across from the prisoner again. Lowe took his place next to Storm in front of the monitor.

"Okay, Victor. One more question."

A shrug from Landry.

"We understand Denzel Cruz owns a house in New Orleans. Care to comment?"

Landry did something that even surprised Storm. He let out a low cry. "Ahhh, geez, I'm dead."

Lowe smiled and turned to Storm. "Well, it appears he just confirmed the information about the house. Any idea where it might be?"

Still watching Landry, Storm said, "If you remember, I mentioned Bayou Global in my briefing this morning. Check on houses owned by the company. It seems to own a lot of property all over the country."

"How so?"

Storm turned his attention away from the video monitor. "Check the lease on the warehouse in Memphis. I guarantee Bayou is paying the rent. There's also a bar on Beale Street owned by Bayou." He paused and turned back to watch Landry bury his head in his hands as the FBI agent asked one more question. "How did you learn about Landry, Adam?"

"Anonymous tip."

"Then you know where he lives?"

"We do."

"Check the ownership." He turned to face the FBI agent. "Want to bet it's owned by Bayou Global?"

"Dakota, at this stage, I'm not betting on anything."

Chapter Twenty-Five

St. Louis

The process to shut down Frank Cole's cell phone only required him to remove the SIM card and the battery. With this accomplished, he placed the phone and battery inside the refrigerator toward the back, covered by an egg carton. He locked the front door and set the alarm system before he exited the house through the garage. Lambert International Airport would be his destination after a stop at a local cemetery.

A light mist fell from water-laden gray clouds as he walked to a familiar headstone. Protected from the dampness by a fedora and trench coat, he stood and read the engraved names: Judy and Todd Storm.

Touching the top of the granite, he said, "You married a fine man, Summer. His devotion is total. He still mourns you and Todd after all these years." A notable catch in his voice occurred and he paused for a moment. Taking a calming breath, he continued, "I'm sorry I wasn't there to help protect you and your son."

The mist eased while he stared at the marker, lost in his own thoughts. After ten minutes, he returned to his vehicle and continued the drive toward the airport.

His passage through the TSA security area went without issues, and he arrived at the gate for his flight to Phoenix. After checking his watch, he settled in to wait. Ten minutes later, an elderly tall male sat next to him. Neither man acknowledged the presence of the other.

Cole casually removed his boarding pass from his coat pocket and laid it on the seat between him and the newcomer. Reaching into his pants pocket, he retrieved the SIM card from his phone and laid it on the boarding document. The other man casually placed a paperback book on top of them. Thirty seconds later, the retired CIA operator stood and walked out of the boarding area.

The other man moved the book to his lap and placed the boarding pass with Cole's name and the SIM card between the pages. He then pretended to read until his flight was called.

When the gate personnel announced the boarding, the man stood and passed through the door after presenting Frank Cole's documentation. For all intents and purposes, documentation of the arrival of Frank Cole in Phoenix, Arizona would be available for inspection later in the day.

The car, rented using one of the many aliases Frank Cole obtained while undercover in Europe, sped south on I-55 heading toward the Missouri Bootheel. Approximately twelve miles past Sikeston, Missouri at the junction of I-55 and MO-80, Cole stopped at a Flying J Travel Center. Once he filled the gas tank on the rental, he walked into the store and purchased two prepaid cell phones with two hundred minutes calling time on each. Returning to his car, he drove back to south I-55 and set the cruise control to seventy. His next destination: New Orleans. A little over seven hundred miles away.

Kansas City

At the same moment Frank Cole purchased his new prepaid cell phones, Dakota Storm and Apollo entered the office of the Western District of Missouri U.S. Marshal.

"You wanted to see me, Jacob?"

"Yeah, Dakota. Shut the door and sit down."

Storm complied with shutting the door but remained standing. "Is something wrong?"

With a chuckle, Gordon shook his head. "On the contrary. I have good news for you. Have a seat."

Raising an eyebrow, Storm sat in the wood captain's chair in front of his boss's desk. Apollo sat next to him, tongue out and panting. The deputy's right hand immediately rested on Apollo's shoulders. "Glad to hear it's good news."

"You trained Apollo yourself, correct?"

"Yes, sir, we trained each other."

Gordon raised an eyebrow. "Explain, please."

"Sir, a handler has to be trained by the dog, just as the handler trains his K9 companion. It's a two-way exercise."

"Got it." Referring to a letter in his hand, Gordon said, "I received this memo this morning. It concerns you." He read, "By virtue of Deputy U.S. Marshal Dakota Storm's devotion to details and innovative techniques in the field of U.S. Marshals K9 training, he is hereby transferred for temporary assignment to the U.S. Marshals K9 training center in Lawrence, Kansas. In addition to this temporary assignment, Deputy Storm and K9 Deputy Apollo are elevated one pay grade and title. New title: Supervisory Deputy Storm. At the conclusion of this temporary assignment, he will return to his position as team lead on the Central States Fugitive Task Force." Laying the paper down, Gordon returned his attention to the man sitting in front of his desk. "The order is signed by the director himself." Gordon paused and smiled. "So, Dakota, what do you think?"

The deputy kept his gaze on his boss but did not respond immediately. Finally, he said, "I think it's fantastic. When do I report?"

"Next Monday. I want to add, the facility is not owned by the Marshals Service. We contract with the owner. You'll be there a couple of weeks, maybe more."

"Thank you for your recommendation, Jacob."

"I just filed the paperwork. Your accomplishments are why it happened."

"Well, thank you anyway."

"One more thing."

"What's that, sir?"

"You know the proposal you submitted for additional electronic equipment?"

Storm now sat on the edge of the chair as he leaned forward, elbows on his knees. "Yeah?"

"Funds were approved because of your and Apollo's success."

After a fist pump and an excited, "Yes," he paused. "Full funding?"

A nod was his answer. "One of the reasons you're being assigned to the facility in Lawrence. The Marshals Service is starting a pilot program. You're going to train four additional teams."

"So, a total of five teams?"

"Yes, they will be assigned to your Fugitive Task Force and be available to Missouri, Arkansas, Oklahoma, and Kansas."

Taking a deep breath, Storm leaned back in the chair and scratched Apollo behind his ears. "Jacob, this is huge."

"I have to agree."

"Will these be new teams?"

"Unfortunately, no." Gordon handed Storm a sheet of paper.

"What's this?"

"Resumes of the teams you're going to train."

"They're all German shepherds or Belgian Malinois."

"Is that a problem?"

"Not for me. Apollo will get to show off his skills and how smart he is."

Gordon chuckled.

The deputy grew quiet as he stared down at Apollo.

Gordon frowned. "What's the matter, son?"

"I was just thinking how excited Judy would have been at this news."

The office grew quiet.

Frank Cole drove past the address given by the Orleans Parish property tax records as the location of a house owned by Bayou Global. With the time approaching ten p.m., he noticed few lights in the neighboring houses.

The condition of the house did not match his experience with the company. It appeared old and neglected. The landscaping, visible in the glow from streetlights, gave the impression of an abandoned house. After driving a few more blocks, he stopped the car behind another car parked at the curb.

Keeping to the shadows, he made his way back to the structure and slipped into the backyard. Here, there were no lights to expose his presence. The only illumination visible within the house came from the reflection of lights shining through uncurtained windows. No furniture occupied any of the rooms visible from his position.

He turned to examine the out building. Thirty yards from the back door, Cole opened the entrance to the small shed. Cobwebs and a dirt floor greeted him but nothing else.

A slight smile graced his lips as he left the property.

Back in his rental, he drove out of the neighborhood.

An hour and a half later, a few minutes before midnight, he checked into a Marriot Courtyard in Biloxi, Mississippi. His appointment with an old associate would take place at an oyster bar on the Gulf Coast at noon the next day.

Cole sat across from his friend and offered his hand. "How are you, Pete?"

Peter Khan shook his old boss's hand. "Better, now that I'm retired." He remained lean, tall, and could fade into any crowd with his every-man appearance. He had been one of Cole's best operators in France and Spain. His once coal black hair now possessed more silver strands than dark.

"Yeah, I don't miss a lot of it, but I do miss the people."

Khan laughed. "You got to spend way too much time in

the embassies. I had to be on the street. I don't miss those experiences at all."

"No, I don't miss the streets, either." He looked up as a waiter approached.

"Can I get you two anything to drink?"

Pointing at his friend, Cole said, "He'll have a Stella Artois in a bottle with a cold glass and I'll have a Coors Light draft if you have it."

"Very good, I'll be right back."

Khan appraised his old boss. "You remembered."

"It was part of my job to remember." He paused and tilted his head. "How was your trip to Phoenix?"

"Uneventful."

"Good. What else are you doing these days, Pete?"

"Little bit of this and a little bit of that."

"In other words, you're still active."

A shrug was his answer.

The waiter deposited the beer on the table. "I'll be back for your order in a few minutes."

Once he was gone, the old CIA Chief of Station took a sip of his beer and watched his friend pour his brew into the cold glass. "I need a favor, Pete."

A smile appeared just before Khan took a sip. When he put the glass down, he said, "Who do I need to find for you, Frank?"

"The man who ordered the death of my grand-daughter."

Chapter Twenty-Six

Monday

Dakota Storm studied the operating manual for the K9-XR Camera system. He and Apollo would have three days to test and acclimate themselves with the new equipment before other handlers and their partners arrived. The more he studied the system, the more his excitement intensified.

Assessing Apollo, who now wore a new U.S. Marshals K9 Unit harness, he said, "This stuff is better than I anticipated, buddy. I can monitor you up to a little over a quarter mile away."

Apollo kept his eyes on his handler, tongue out and panting.

"It's got two-way audio. I can hear what's going on around you, plus, I can talk to you."

As was Apollo's habit, he made no comment.

"Heck, this thing has a thermal camera so we can detect heat signatures of hidden bad guys." He closed the book and returned his attention to his dog. "We've got a lot of work to do, buddy. Let's get started."

Kristin Duffy, the owner of the training facility, approached Storm. "Mornin', Dakota."

"Good morning, Kristin."

"Did you find everything without any trouble this morning?"

"Yes, thank you for giving me the tour last night. Hope I didn't get here too late."

"Nonsense. It's normally just me and the dogs here. I enjoyed having human company for a little while."

The owner of the facility stood as tall as Storm. Slender, she wore her long blonde hair tied back in a ponytail. Blue eyes studied him as he noticed a hint of mischief in her slight smile. He guessed her age to be close to his. He said, "Have you ever worked with the K9-XR?"

"Once when a team of Navy SEALS came through here."

"Navy SEALS?"

She nodded and flashed the smile he found charming. "Since this place is in the center of the country, I get everybody, FBI, U.S. Marshals, sheriff's departments, large police departments, Rangers, SEALS, and military police. Which means, I don't have to cater to rich people who want their poodles trained. I've been fortunate. I do a good job, keep my fees reasonable, and the good guys keep coming back."

Storm chuckled.

"So, to answer your question, yes, I'm familiar with the K9-XR. Good system."

"We just got five units for the Western District. I'm anxious to learn more about it."

Kristin bent down to rub Apollo's head. "I've worked with border collies before. Amazing creatures. How many words does he know?"

"Right now, he has a 300-plus word vocabulary and recognizes over a hundred hand signals."

"And you trained him?"

"Yes, ma'am."

"Call me Kristin or Duffy, or Hey You, just don't call me ma'am, Dakota."

"Deal."

"How old is he?"

"I found him when he was about one. We've been together for three years now."

"Found him?"

"Long story."

She patted him on the chest. "Make sure you take time to tell me the story before you leave." She started to walk away but stopped and turned back. "Where did you say you live?"

"I didn't. But I live in Overland Park."

"Huh. We're practically neighbors."

She turned and Storm caught himself admiring the view as she walked away. Folding his arms, he said, "Pretty lady."

The dog barked once.

———

Friday

The time neared six p.m. as Storm packed his Ford for the trip back to Kansas City. He noticed Kristin approaching. She wore jeans and a white blouse instead of her normal navy utility pants tucked into tan hiking boots and tight T-shirt.

"Are you back next week, Dakota?"

He nodded. "I am. I'll be here for a few more weeks. We have more teams coming through. I appreciate you opening up your academy for us."

"No problem. Hell, I learned so much this week, I should be the one paying you. Need a job?"

He shook his head. "Already got one. But I'm enjoying working with dog handlers again. Plus, I really like your facilities here. Well thought out and efficient."

She folded her arms. A faraway look passed over her face. Just as quickly, it was gone. She asked, "Why'd you leave the military?"

He grew quiet. "Uh, I had a family at the time and my wife didn't like Texas."

"I'm sorry. Divorce?"

He shook his head. "No, drunk driver."

Raising her hand to her mouth, she took a deep breath. "Oh, Dakota. I'm sorry. I didn't know."

"No way you could."

"How long ago."

"Two years before I found Apollo."

"So, five years?"

"Yes. It sounds like a long time, but it sure doesn't feel like it."

"You've never told me how you found him."

He glanced at his watch. "You have plans for dinner?"

She smiled. "No, but it sounds like I do now."

Storm lifted the wineglass and chuckled. "I've never used Grubhub. Kind of cool."

"Cool? Did you just say cool, Dakota?"

"I did."

"How old are you?"

"Old enough to realize I probably shouldn't say cool anymore."

She chuckled. "Grubhub is the only way to get decent food this far out in the sticks."

"You don't cook?"

"I do, but I'd rather clean out a dog kennel."

"I enjoy cooking. It's relaxing."

She tilted her head and appraised him. "You're a unique man, Dakota Storm. Good with dogs and enjoys cooking. Where have you been all my life?" She paused. "Sorry, that was rude of me to say."

"No problem. I've never met a woman who has the same passion for dogs as I do. It's refreshing."

Her cheeks turned slightly pink and she changed the subject. "You never found the person who abandoned Apollo?"

"No. I really didn't try too hard. Within a day or two, he and I developed a rather strong bond. I really didn't want him going back to someone who would tie up a dog and leave him to starve."

"Trust me, there are a ton of them out there. They shouldn't be allowed to have a dog, let alone be parents."

He sipped his wine and said, "I've met them." He stared out the darkened window in the dining area. Returning his gaze back to her, he asked, "You ever think about having children, Kristin?"

She stared at her wineglass. A sad smile graced her lips. "I did at one time."

"Sorry, I didn't mean to pry."

"It's okay. I started this academy with someone I thought I was in love with. He changed his mind after he found out how much hard work is involved. He signed his share over to me and now it's all mine. So, to answer your question, I'd need to find the right guy to consider it again."

"Yeah." He took another sip of wine. "Finding the right individual is important."

"Why'd you ask?"

"Just curious."

She narrowed her eyes and grinned. "You making plans without consulting me?"

"It's the wine talking."

"Speaking of wine, you're not planning to drive home, are you?"

Glancing at his watch, he shook his head. "I've enjoyed getting to know you better. Guess I'll sleep in the Ford and take off in the morning."

She reached for his hand. "You'll do no such thing. I've got a spare bedroom you can use." She pointed at Apollo asleep on the floor. "No need to wake him. He's tired from a long week."

After they cleaned the kitchen, she showed him the room. "It even has its own bathroom with a shower."

"Good, I'll take one and then get to bed."

With a devilish smile, she asked, "Alone?"

He began to unbutton her blouse. "I hope not."

The drive back to Overland Park never occurred on Saturday or even Sunday. Storm helped Kristin around the academy getting a few neglected projects completed. He cooked dinner on Saturday evening and again on Sunday.

"So, what do I have to do to hire you away from the U.S. Marshals Service?"

Storm glanced up from the grill. She was sitting at a bistro table on a deck attached to the back of her house. She watched as he tended to a couple of steaks. "It's tempting, Kristin. Very tempting."

"But…"

"I enjoy the work. Plus, I have unfinished business to attend to."

"I understand." She took a sip of wine. "Can I be honest with you, Dakota?"

"I hope so."

She smiled. "I don't throw myself at men. Never have. Most have a tendency to disappoint me. You're different."

"I'll take that as a compliment."

"It was meant that way. What happens when you find the man who ordered your wife and son killed?"

"I don't know." He paused for a moment. "As a deputy U.S. Marshal, I'd have to arrest him. But putting a bullet through his head sure would feel good."

"You've got two more weeks assigned to the academy, correct?"

"Maybe three. Depends on what I tell my boss."

"Okay, make it three. You stay here, we get better acquainted, and then we find a female border collie and breed her with Apollo."

Storm contemplated the suggestion. "Never thought of doing that."

"Trust me, I've trained both German and Belgian shepherds. Apollo is something special."

Storm returned his attention to the grill.

Kristin frowned. "What's the matter?"

"Nothing."

"Yes, there is. You got quiet too quick."

He shook his head.

"Dakota, I'm sorry if I offended you."

He looked up. "It would be a betrayal to Apollo to use him for profit."

She tilted her head. "You're serious, aren't you?"

He pressed his lips together as he felt a sinking sensation in his stomach.

"Oh, my goodness. I've never met anyone like you."

He shrugged. "Sorry."

"No. That's a good thing."

He folded his arms as the smoke from the grill surrounded him. "What do you mean, it's a good thing?"

"I've always wanted to train service dogs and donate them to small police departments. Some of the ones around big cities need them but can't afford them. With yours and Apollo's help, I can make that dream come true."

"You don't want to sell them?"

She shook her head. "Hell no. The dream has always been to donate them."

"You'd need help?"

"Duh."

He smiled. "The steaks are done."

"Good. You'll need your strength later."

A slow grin appeared on his lips. "I can't believe I'm saying this, but it's been a long time since I've enjoyed being with a woman that I understand and understands me."

"Scary, isn't it."

"No, not really."

Chapter Twenty-Seven

New Orleans

The majority of neighbors surrounding the house owned by Bayou Global were blue-collar workers who labored through the daylight hours and buried themselves inside at night. Peter Khan's frustration at finding no one home in the neighborhood increased with each unanswered inquiry.

Until he knocked on the door of an elderly woman. She answered the door cautiously, the security chain still attached. "Yes?"

Khan, dressed in khaki slacks and a shirt with the parish emblem on the left breast offered ID claiming him to be an assessor from the parish. "I'm sorry to bother you, ma'am. Do you have a few moments?"

"What's this about..." She scrutinized the offered ID. "Mr. North?"

"I've been trying to contact the owners of the house across the street, but I can never find anyone at home. Do you have any information about them?"

"Oh yes." She unhooked the security chain and stepped out onto the front porch. "Indeed I do."

"Is anyone ever home?"

"A blight on our neighborhood if ever I saw one. No one's lived there since Ms. Thibodeau sold it two years ago. Poor thing. Her husband died working on the oil rigs in the Gulf and left her with those two boys. She sold the house, packed up, and, last I knew, had moved back to Houston. She has kinfolk there."

Finally, Khan sensed he had found the neighborhood watchdog. "I see. Do you have an address for her?"

"Sorry. I didn't speak to her very often. Those boys were a handful. Always in trouble, they were."

"Do you know who bought the place?"

She shook her head. "One day the For Sale sign disappeared, but no one moved in. Whoever bought it must be using it for a tax dodge or something. Not helping our property values at all, if you ask me. Never seen anyone over there fixing up anything."

Khan held his clipboard and made a few notes. "You say that was two years ago?"

"That's what I said. Try to listen closer, sonny."

"Sorry. The parish records show a company called Bayou Global bought it. Have you ever heard of that company?"

A shake of her head became her first silent answer.

"Thank you, Ms…"

"Mrs. Violette Gaudet, I hate the term Ms. A lady is either a Miss or a Mrs. By the way, there's only one T in the last name. Husband's been dead now close to ten years."

"I'm sorry for your loss."

"Don't be. He was a scoundrel."

Khan had a hard time keeping a straight face. He asked

his final question. "Mrs. Gaudet, have you ever seen anyone visit the property at night?"

"Hmmm." She trained her attention to the house and put her hands on her hips. "Only once. Just the other night. They drove by slowly, parked down the street, and then snooped around back. Whoever it was only stayed a few minutes then left."

"Do you know what time that was?"

"Yeah, around ten. The local news was on."

"How did you know they were there?"

She touched her temple. "I'm Cajun. I know things."

He smiled. "Thank you for your time, Mrs. Gaudet." Leaving the porch, Khan walked over to the empty house and studied it for a while.

Baton Rouge, Louisiana

Khan, using another of his many aliases, finished filling out the form in the Louisiana Secretary of State's office. He handed the paper to the clerk, and she studied it for a moment. "Bayou Global. Is that correct, Mr. McCarthy?"

"Yes. I'd like to see the articles of incorporation."

She returned her gaze to the paper. "You could have found the information on the internet, you know."

"I was in the neighborhood."

Her mouth twisted into a smirk. With a huff, she left her position behind the counter and walked briskly to a desk with two computer monitors angled together. After several moments of clicking on the keyboard, Khan heard a laser printer spool up and spit out numerous sheets of paper.

The clerk stood, retrieved the stack, and returned to the counter. "That will be ten dollars."

He smiled and handed her a twenty. "Smallest I have. Keep the change."

Her smirk turned to a grin as she accepted the money and handed over the paperwork. Khan left the office and hurried to his rental car in the parking lot.

When he sat behind the steering wheel, he handed the stack to Frank Cole who occupied the passenger seat. "Check out the CEO's name."

"Alexi Yankovic."

At the same time, he started the vehicle, Khan said, "Wanna bet Yankovic and Denzel Cruz are one and the same man?"

Flipping through the pages of the document, Cole said, "No thanks. I'd lose. Why is that name so familiar?"

"You mean, Alexi Yankovic?"

"Yeah."

Khan put the car in gear and backed out of the parking space. "Think back to the summer of 2005 when you were assigned to the embassy in Moscow for a few months."

Cole raised an eyebrow. "Damn."

"Remember now?"

"Yankovic was the leader of a prison riot in Saint Petersburg. If I remember correctly, he was deported after the incident. Is this the same guy?"

"Don't know, but if he is, you've got Russian Mafia involved with Bayou Global."

Cole stared out the window as Khan drove out of the parking lot. "Pete, do you know how we could get a picture of Yankovic?"

"Some of your old buddies at Langley probably could."

"Not my first choice." He turned to look at his friend. "Would the FBI have a picture?"

"Might."

"I know they don't have one of Denzel Cruz, but under the name Alexi Yankovic, they might. And I know someone who can check without raising suspicions."

———

Dakota Storm's cell phone vibrated, and he checked the caller ID. *Unknown.* He hesitated about answering the call, but something Frank Cole once told him made him accept it. "Hello."

"Good afternoon, my friend. No names. Is this a good time to talk?"

Cole's familiar voice allowed him to breathe easier.

"Yes."

"I need you to check with your friends at the bureau about a name. If they have files, we need a picture and a profile."

"What's the name?"

"Alexi Yankovic."

"Spell it."

Cole did.

"Okay, is this a priority?"

"More than a priority. He might be the answer for a big question we have."

"Got it. How do I get in touch?"

"I'll send you a text message. When you know something, reply to it, and I'll call. Don't call me." The connection ended.

Storm rested his hand on Apollo's new harness. "Frank

has a lead. I need to make a call and then we can start testing the range of that thing on your back."

At eight that evening, Storm studied a picture on his laptop. The photo appeared to be from a passport of a man in his late forties. The name Alexi Yankovic appeared in English under Cyrillic script. Recognizing the writing as Russian, he studied the photo for a few moments.

He sent the text message.

The phone call came thirty seconds later. Storm answered. "Hello."

"Did you get it?"

"Yes."

"It needs to be shown to our friend in Tulsa."

Storm looked closer at the photo and rested his chin on the palm of his hand. "Who do you think this guy is?"

"The one who, so far, has eluded us."

"I take it you are not in your normal location."

"No, I am farther south."

"I can meet you at the assisted living facility on Saturday."

The caller said, "I'll be there."

The call ended, and Storm stood. Time to tell Kristin he would be taking a trip this coming weekend.

Chapter Twenty-Eight

Friday Evening

Apollo sat quietly as Storm packed his SUV for a possible two-day trip to Tulsa. Part of his plans included testing the range of the K9-XR camera system in a real-world environment. During the past week, they had discovered the range exceeded a quarter of a mile, but they were testing in the flat plains of Eastern Kansas. How the system would work in an urban jungle of concrete and steel buildings remained unknown.

Kristin came out of the house as Storm finished stowing his equipment in the vehicle. She said, "Why don't I go with you?"

After shutting the hatch, Storm looked at her. "I might not get back until midday Monday."

"So?"

"Don't you have to get the academy ready for next week?"

"The teams don't get here until late Monday."

"I don't know what may happen in Tulsa, Kristin."

"When are we ever certain what's going to occur?"

He gave her a slight grin but remained quiet.

"Dakota, Bruno and I can provide backup for you and Frank. If the guy in Tulsa is as connected as you think he is, someone might be watching the place."

"Hmmm. Bruno and Apollo do get along."

"Yes, they do. Plus, having a Belgian Malinois along might make anyone thinking of ambushing us reconsider."

Storm did not comment right away. After several moments, he said, "Makes sense. But this is my fight, Kristin. I don't want you to get hurt because of it."

"Dakota, I have a funny feeling my involvement with you already makes it my fight."

He reached for her hand. "You don't know how much this means to me."

"I think I do. Because I believe you and I feel the same way about each other."

He placed his arms around her and they embraced. The hug lasted a long time, neither saying a word. Finally, he broke free. "If we have time, we can test the K9-XR system in downtown Tulsa."

"Another good reason for me to go."

After taking a deep breath, Storm said, "I have no idea what to expect. It could be dangerous, and I'd worry about you getting hurt."

"And you don't think I wouldn't worry about you? If I go, we can at least worry together."

After a chuckle, his grin turned to a smile. "It's a long drive. I would enjoy the company."

"Good decision, Deputy."

Tulsa, OK

Frank Cole and Peter Khan entered the diner at 11:26 a.m. Cole pointed toward the table where Storm sat. He noticed a woman sitting next to the deputy. When they arrived at the table, Cole offered his hand to her. "Frank Cole."

"Kristin Duffy."

Nodding toward his companion, Cole said, "This is Peter Khan, an old associate of mine."

Both Storm and Kristin shook the man's hand. After Cole and Khan sat, Frank directed his attention to Storm. "I thought you'd be alone."

"Kristin owns the K9 training academy where I'm working for the next month or so. She offered to help out." Storm looked at Khan. "I don't believe we've ever met, Mr. Khan. How do you know Frank?"

"I was his nursemaid during the time he spent in Europe. I kept him from making social faux pas at embassy gatherings."

With a knowing grin, Storm nodded. "Nice to meet you."

Cole turned to Storm. "Can you show us the picture?"

The deputy handed his cell phone to the retired CIA field officer. "That's the picture of Alexi Yankovic, Russian Mafia. He was quietly escorted out of Russia in 2010 with the threat of being pushed out of a tall building if he ever returned."

"How old is the picture?"

"It's a booking photo from New York City, January

2015. He was arrested on extortion and sex trafficking. He's still on the FBI's most wanted fugitives list and the U.S. Marshals Service has him on their list as well."

Cole raised an eyebrow. "That makes him fair game for you to pursue, doesn't it?"

"It does."

Studying the picture again, Cole asked, "Does Alexi Yankovic use any aliases?"

"Not according to the FBI database. What are you thinking, Frank?"

"There's a good chance our Mr. Yankovic and Denzel Cruz are one and the same person."

"I checked and there aren't any records of a Denzel Cruz being arrested. Not even a parking ticket. So, if that's the case, we can identify him now."

"Well, to make sure, we need to show the photo to Lucas Toro. It will be interesting to see what his reaction is."

Nodding, Storm said, "As soon as we have lunch. Kristin and I got an early start and haven't eaten."

The odor in the assisted living facility seemed worse than during Storm's first visit. He and Frank Cole waited at the reception desk for the middle-aged receptionist to respond to their presence. After thirty seconds, Cole cleared his throat.

"I see ya. Be with ya in a moment."

Cole looked at Storm with a raised eyebrow.

The deputy just shrugged.

One minute later, she stood and walked to the reception window. "Whadda ya need?"

Storm offered his ID. "Deputy U.S. Marshal Dakota Storm. We need to talk to Lucas Wohali."

"Now I remember you. You were the one who asked to see him a few weeks ago."

"Yes." Storm glanced at the big clock on the wall of the woman's office. "It's just 1:30, so I assume visiting hours are in effect."

"They are. What's a U.S. Marshal want with that creep Wohali?"

"Official business, sorry."

She looked at Cole. "Who are you?"

"I'm with him." He pointed at Storm.

"That didn't answer my question."

"Sorry, need to know only."

She rolled her eyes. "Whatever." She went back to her desk. "Wait in the room next door, and I'll have the creep brought out to you."

Neither man sat after Cole observed the furniture. "It appears to be sticky."

"I didn't sit last time, either."

Twenty minutes passed. Cole turned to Storm. "You're my closest living relative. If I ever have to be put in a nursing home, please don't choose one like this."

"I promise. I won't."

The same ultra-thin woman wheeled Wohali into the room. The man appeared weaker than the last time Storm visited. When he saw Storm, he said, "Ah, shit, not you again." He turned his attention to Cole. "You look like a fed."

"Frank Cole."

"I don't give a fuck what your name is." He turned to his left. The woman who had wheeled him in no longer stood behind him. "Ah, shit. I'm trapped."

Storm held the cell phone with the picture of Alexi Yankovic displayed. "Recognize this man?"

Wohali's eyes grew wide for a brief moment. He shook his head rapidly. "Never seen him before."

Cole smiled. "Oh, come on, Lucas. We know you've used the name Lucas Toro, and you know the man in the picture. Might as well tell us."

"Haven't got a clue what you're talking about, Mr. Federal Agent."

"Oh, but you do. We know more than you think. Did you know you have it easy here? Where I could send you would make this place look like a luxury hotel."

Wohali looked at Storm and then Cole. He repeated the process two additional times. He then pressed his lips together and shut his eyes. "You guys are signing my death warrant. Go away."

Cole leaned over to be eye level with the man in the wheelchair. "Open your eyes, Lucas."

"No."

"It's your choice, Lucas. We can become your worst nightmare or your best friends. Now, open your eyes and answer the damn question. Who is the man in the photo?"

He opened his eyes and stared at the floor. He then slumped in the chair. "Denzel Cruz."

Storm put the cell phone in his back pocket. "Know where he is?"

The man shook his head. "No one ever knows where he is. Most times he just shows up. When he does, it's never a good thing. He pays good, but you don't want to fuck with him."

"Is there anybody in the organization who knows where he is at any given time?"

A nod from the depressed man. "I only know him as

Ivan. I've heard his last name a few times. It sounds like a brand of vodka. Don't have a clue how to spell it."

Cole smiled. "Smirnov?"

"Yeah, that's it."

"The guy's name is Ivan Smirnov?"

"Yeah, now that I've told you his name, please leave me alone. If anyone ever finds out, I'll be dead."

Storm started toward the door. "Don't worry, Lucas. This is the last time I plan to visit."

"Good. Take the fed with you."

The two visitors left Lucas Wohali alone to contemplate his future.

When they got back to the parking lot, Peter Khan asked, "Well, Frank, what did he tell you?"

"Another Russian name. One we've not heard before."

Chapter Twenty-Nine

Tulsa, OK

Dakota Storm studied the K9-XR monitor while Apollo sat patiently by his side. A video feed from a transmitter connected to Bruno's harness displayed on the screen. From his position at the corner of 3rd and South Boulder Avenue, the signal remained strong even though he knew two large skyscrapers were between the other camera and his monitor.

Kristin's voice came over the monitor's two-way communication feature. "We're almost to the Hyatt Regency on 2nd Street. That puts a lot of steel and concrete between the two of us. How do you copy?"

"So far, five by five."

"Is Apollo getting antsy?"

The deputy held a leash attached to the border collie's U.S. Marshals harness with another K9-XR camera unit attached. "Not yet, but he keeps looking up at me with pleading eyes."

The pleasant sound of Kristin's chuckle came over the radio. "We're going to cross..." Her voice dissolved into a barely audible hissing. The video image went to static at the same time.

"You're out of range, Kristin."

No reply.

Storm turned and walked toward 2nd Street, but the reception did not return. He picked up his pace toward the next corner. When they got to the corner of 2nd and South Boulder, the monitor came alive. "Can't hear you, Dakota." The image from Bruno's harness camera once again appeared on the monitor's screen.

"You got out of range, Kristin. Where are you?"

"We're at 2nd and Cincinnati."

Storm turned to his right but did not see her and the dog. "Head back this way, the range is good, but I believe these buildings are causing some interference."

"Copy, heading your way."

When they arrived back at Storm's SUV, he removed the harness and camera from Apollo and secured it in a storage case supplied by the manufacturer. Kristin did the same for Bruno's equipment.

With the two dogs sitting in the back, Storm drove the SUV toward the hotel where they planned to stay. Kristin turned to him and asked, "How are you going to determine who this Ivan Smirnov person is?"

"I haven't figured it out yet. My guess is he'll be operating under an alias. After Lucas confirmed Alexi Yankovic and Denzel Cruz were the same person, he implied Smirnov always knew where Yankovic was, or knew how to get hold of him."

"Did you believe him?"

"Not particularly. So, I'm going to see what the

Marshals Service might have on Smirnov. If nothing, then I'll let Frank have a shot at it. My bet is Cruz and this Smirnov character fly under the radar."

Storm's cell phone vibrated. He checked the ID and saw *Unknown* on the screen. "Hello."

"When are you going to be at the hotel?" A hint of urgency in Frank's voice concerned Storm.

"Soon. What's wrong?"

"Make it as soon as possible. Got something for you."

The call ended.

He looked at Kristin. "Tell me again where we're staying?"

———

Storm answered the knock on the hotel room door. Cole and Khan stood outside and entered as the deputy stood aside.

Cole said, "Pete called a buddy of his and asked about Smirnov."

"And?"

"You want to tell him, Pete?"

"Ivan Smirnov and Alexi Yankovic were both requested to leave the Russian Federation on the same day. They both received the same ultimatum if they returned."

Folding his arms, Storm kept his gaze on the tall man. "So, Smirnov is Russian Mafia as well?"

"According to my source, he is."

"Did anyone have a current location for him?"

"The last anyone heard, he was in Poland. So, this tidbit of information generated quite a stir within Homeland Security."

"Did they have a picture of him?"

Khan showed his cell phone to Storm. "It's an old photo from the Polish Foreign Intelligence Agency."

The deputy studied it for a moment then reached for the phone. "He looks familiar. Did they give you the profile picture as well?"

"Yeah. Just slide the screen to the right."

Storm did and pursed his lips. "I've seen this guy before."

Cole took the phone and considered the picture. "Where?"

"At the moment, I can't place him. Let me see it again." He studied the picture for a few moments. "I have to be mistaken."

The former CIA station chief handed the phone back to Storm. "Take your time. It might be important."

Seconds became minutes, and finally Storm raised his head. "Now I remember, but it doesn't make sense. So, I'm probably wrong. It was when I was a deputy sheriff in St. Louis County. I remember seeing him at a four-state conference of county sheriffs. I was on security patrol with Apollo, and he asked me about border collies as K9 officers."

"Do you remember his name?"

"No."

Khan tilted his head. "Do you remember what county he was from?"

"No, the incident was so brief, I'm sure I'm mistaken." He handed the phone back to Khan.

Cole folded his arms and contemplated Storm for a few moments. "What was the conference about?"

"It was one of those annual meetings for sheriffs in the four-state area to come together so they know each other better." He paused. "What do the Polish authorities want him for?"

"Well, Dakota, it seems he was doing the same thing there as he is here, sex trafficking."

Kristin frowned. "Is there a possibility Yankovic and Smirnov are importing young girls?"

Neither Cole or Khan answered her question. Storm started pacing. After a few moments, he stopped. "I wondered why some of those young girls held captive in the Memphis warehouse didn't speak. At first, I thought it was because they were scared. It may have been because they didn't understand English." He stopped and stared at Cole. "Do we need to bring the big guns in on this, Frank? This needs to stop. I'm not sure a simple deputy U.S. Marshal has the wherewithal to make things happen."

Cole put his hand on the deputy's shoulder. "Dakota, unfortunately, I think we do. When Pete and I discovered who Smirnov was, we came to the same conclusion." He looked at his watch. "Lucas Wohali is probably already in the custody of the FBI as we speak. Apparently, Victor Landry is still being difficult."

"What about Bayou Global?"

"Don't know yet."

Storm turned to Kristin. "Should we head back tonight?"

"It's up to you. Do you think you'll be called back to Kansas City?"

"I have no idea." He offered his hand to Cole. As the two men shook, Storm said, "Thanks, Frank. I appreciate your help."

"It was fun while it lasted. Thanks for letting me help."

After a few more pleasantries, Cole and Khan left the hotel room.

Storm kept his gaze on the closed door for several moments. After a sigh, he glanced at his watch. "It's late.

Not sure I want to drive four hours. Let's get these dogs fed and then we can figure out something for us."

She put her arms around him. "The hotel has a restaurant. We can try it."

He nodded and put a leash on Apollo at the same time Kristin put one on Bruno.

"Let's get some fresh air, buddy."

I-169 Somewhere in Kansas

The Next Morning

The flatness of the Kansas landscape always caused Storm to wonder how the pioneers who crossed this part of the country in the middle 1800s kept their spirits up. Nothing changed as they sped north. There would not have been fences or highways back then and, after a while, the land would have seemed endless.

He glanced at Kristin. "Do you ever wonder how the settlers got across this part of the country without going crazy?"

She shrugged. "No. I've never really thought about it. But, you're right, I have no idea how they did it."

Keeping her face turned from him, he asked, "What's wrong?"

After giving him a weak smile, she said, "Nothing."

"You haven't said a word for at least twenty-five miles."

"Just feeling sorry for myself."

"Somehow, I doubt that."

"It's true. I'm worried about how I'm going to handle you going back to Kansas City."

He did not say anything for a few moments. "My house is in Overland Park."

"Might as well be New York City or Los Angeles. I won't see you every day like the last few weeks. I've gotten used to you being around." She took a deep breath and let it out in a sigh. "And I like it."

"I haven't been called back yet."

"No, but it's going to happen." She looked at him. "I haven't felt this way about someone in a long time, Dakota."

He glanced at her and then returned his attention to the road ahead. "I know, I've been dreading going back myself."

"I realize we haven't been together long, but sometimes it doesn't take a lot of time. I'm falling in love with you, Dakota, and I don't want to lose that feeling or you."

Wanting to say something, he hesitated. Finally, after a long silence he said, "Kristin, I've had to suppress my feelings for a long time. My grief for Judy and Todd overwhelmed me. I even decided to end it all one night. Apollo saved me. Over these last few weeks, I've started to understand how much I need to move on. There is nothing I can do to bring them back, and I've reconciled with the fact they are gone. Something I refused to do for a long time. I will always love them and will always keep them in my heart. But if I am ever going to be happy, I need to be with someone else." He stopped and looked at her. Tears trickled down her cheeks.

He continued, "It's amazing. When you stop searching, that's when you find the one special person you love and can't live without. I found that someone in a lady named Kristin who owns a dog-training academy."

Chapter Thirty

Kansas City

FBI Special Agent in Charge Adam Lowe read over the report placed on his desk earlier in the morning. The more he studied the information, the better prepared he felt about confronting a prisoner he would be interviewing in a few moments.

Another agent walked into the interview room and placed a stack of folders on his desk. "Here are the files you requested, Adam."

"Thanks, Leah."

She turned to leave.

"Why don't you stick around. I'd like to have a witness."

"Sure." She sat next to Lowe.

He handed her the report he held. "Look over this. Mr. Landry has not been forthcoming with us about his organization. I intend to ask him about this man."

She read silently for a few moments. "Ivan Smirnov?"

"Yes."

"Russian Mafia?"

"It appears Deputy U.S. Marshal Dakota Storm has uncovered a rather sophisticated organization. His report concerning the raid on a warehouse in Memphis stated several of the young women found there did not speak. Reading these notes on Smirnov's history tells us some of those individuals may have been smuggled into the country and didn't understand English."

Concentrating on the report, the female FBI agent said, "I'm not surprised. Who's the lead on this case?"

"As of right now, you."

She raised her eyebrows. "Really."

"Yes, you need to get up to speed ASAP. This new revelation about Smirnov and Yankovic has pushed the case to high-profile status. The assistant director wants to be kept up to date on a regular basis."

"What does that mean?"

"Daily updates."

"Great."

"Don't make them novels, Sutton. Just an email with the subject and your report. Copy me on it."

"Got it."

The door to the interrogation room opened, and a Jackson County sheriff escorted Victor Landry into the room.

Lowe said, "Thank you, Deputy."

Landry stood there and stared at the two FBI agents. "I want my lawyer."

"Sit down, Victor."

"Not without my attorney present."

Lowe stood, glared at the man, and growled, "Sit down."

He did.

"Have you contacted an attorney yet, Victor?"

"Nobody's offered to let me."

"There's a reason for that. It's for your own safety."

"Hah… That's rich, Mr. FBI."

Lowe picked up the top folder from the stack brought in by Leah. He opened it and withdrew a sheet of paper. "Is it, Victor? Let me inform you of the fate of a few of your fellow employees of Bayou Global."

The prisoner kept the scowl on his face.

"Do you know a Reid Hicks?"

"Never heard of him."

"I doubt that's true, so I will tell you what happened to him anyway. A man named Brett Cash was paid to get drunk and arrested. He killed Hicks inside the county jail the next morning with a sharpened toothbrush."

The scowl softened a little.

"Fred Noble, Memphis. He was killed execution style with a shot to the back of his head. He was kneeling in a Memphis warehouse at the time."

The scowl disappeared, and Landry sat straighter in his chair.

"Lucas Toro, or Lucas Wohali. You visited him in Tulsa and communicated a warning."

"Old friend."

"Your old friend was in the assisted living facility because someone broke his kneecaps. They took a hammer to them after he decided to help himself to company funds. He was arrested by IRS agents in New Orleans after an anonymous tip. No one knows who made it. Were you aware of that?"

Now staring at the table between them, Landry did not respond.

Lowe continued, "Apparently, the kneecap incident

occurred after Wohali spoke to a lawyer hired by Bayou Global. We don't know who the attorney was, but the powers that be at your company didn't like the report." He paused. When Landry did not say anything, Lowe clasped his hands together. "Now, do you want to call them for an attorney?"

"You're lying."

"I can assure you we are not. We can have a public defender here to represent you. The U.S. Attorney General here in the Western District of Missouri would like to visit with you about a deal he plans to offer you."

"You guys are going to get me killed."

"On the contrary, we are trying to keep you alive, Victor. With your help, we can put Alexi Yankovic and Ivan Smirnov away in some dark hole for the rest of their lives."

"If I was to make a deal, what would I have to do?"

Lowe proceeded to tell him.

———

Leah Sutton walked out of the interrogation room following Adam Lowe. When they were out of the sheriff's building and back in the parking lot, she said, "Do you believe anything he told you?"

"Some of it."

She nodded.

"Have you met Deputy U.S. Marshal Dakota Storm yet, Leah?"

"No."

"He's an interesting fellow. He's the one who brought Yankovic and Smirnov's organization to our attention."

"How?"

"It seems they killed his wife and young son. Like I said

207

before, he's the one who discovered the young women in the warehouse in Memphis. The majority were underage and, we believe, smuggled into the US. We have agents in Memphis following up. We should know more within a few days."

"How did he know about it?"

"Apparently, his late wife kept a journal of her ordeal with Bayou Global. His discovery of the journal sparked his investigation."

She nodded.

"This case should have been turned over to the FBI from the beginning. Instead, Storm went rogue and tried to solve it himself. Now he's mucked it up. So, here's what I need you to do if you are going to be the lead in this extremely high-profile case."

"What's that?"

"Get the journal from Storm."

"I doubt he will want to part with it, Adam."

"That's immaterial, Sutton. Your job is to get the journal. It's the key to cracking open this sex trafficking scheme. You might even say your future with the bureau depends on how well you do with this investigation."

Her pace slowed and glared at the back of Lowe's head.

Leah Sutton drove past the home of Dakota Storm several times. No one appeared to be home. After the fourth pass, she pulled into the driveway and parked her unmarked Ford Explorer. Staring at the house, she decided to knock and see if anyone answered.

As she got out of the vehicle, a woman from across the street walked up behind her.

"Are you looking for Dakota?"

"Yes. I'm FBI Agent Leah Sutton."

"Melissa Perry. I live across the street. I was hoping you were Dakota. He drives a vehicle similar to this one."

"Is he not home?"

"No, he's been out of town for a couple of weeks. He said he was on a special assignment." She paused and hugged herself. "Do you know how to get in touch with him?"

Sensing a possible clue to the whereabouts of the deputy, Leah said, "I'm sure I'll see him sometime this week."

"Well, I need to tell him something."

"Maybe I can help. What is it?"

"Could you tell him I've been transferred and would like to talk to him before I have to leave."

"Well, congratulations. Where to?"

"Cincinnati. It's kind of a long way from here, and I don't know if I will see him again."

"That's kind of sad."

"We were just friends, but he helped me around the house."

Sutton glanced over at the house across the street. A For Sale sign stood prominently in the middle of the yard next to the street. "I see you already have your house on the market?"

"Yes. I have to be in Cincinnati this coming Monday. I was hoping he'd be home before now."

"Well, I'll give him the message when I see him. Does he have your phone number?"

"I gave it to him." She stared at the house and then down at her feet. "He hasn't called and, when I call him, he doesn't respond." She took a breath and sighed. "This transfer happened so quickly."

"I'm sorry, Melissa."

"It's okay. We were just friends."

Sutton picked up on the woman's sadness. This was the second time she had mentioned they were just friends. "Maybe he lost your number. Why don't you give me your phone number, and I will ask him to call you."

"Would you? I certainly would appreciate it."

The FBI agent pulled out a small note pad and asked, "What's the number?"

After Melissa Perry left, Sutton got back into her Ford and drove away. She had not picked a lock since her academy days. Looked like she would get to do so tonight when she returned to Storm's house.

Chapter Thirty-One

Lawrence, KS

Two Nights Later

At the end of another week training other deputy U.S. Marshals and their K9 partners, Storm felt proud of the progress he and Kristin were making. After not being home for three weeks, he felt like he needed to go back to check on things.

As he packed the Ford, Kristin threw a duffle bag into the back next to his and announced, "I'm coming with you."

"I didn't think you wanted to."

"That was last night; this is today. I changed my mind. Besides, it's only a forty-minute drive." She stopped and folded her arms. "By the way, why haven't you been back before now?"

"Didn't see the need."

"Liar."

"Okay, I enjoy being with you. If I went to the house, you'd be here and I wouldn't. I'd miss you."

She chuckled. "That was the correct thing to say." After a pause, her smile disappeared. "What are we going to do when you have to go back, Dakota?"

He stopped arranging the cargo space and turned around. "I've been thinking about it. This place is only thirty-five miles from my current residence. That's within the guidelines for how far I can live from my primary office."

Her smile returned. "And?"

"If the proprietor would allow me, I'll cancel the lease on my place and move in here."

The smile turned into a sly grin. "And if the proprietor says no, what then?"

"I'll have to pitch a tent and live in it."

With a gleeful laugh, she threw her arms around his neck and gave him a kiss. "Oh, Dakota, I think this is a splendid idea."

"I was hoping you would think so. Apollo gets more exercise here, and he's learning a lot being around the other dogs. While I might be gone more than I am now, I'd be here when I'm not chasing bad guys."

She actually giggled like a teenager.

What few reservations the deputy possessed about making the decision to move in with her disappeared when he saw the joy in her eyes.

Pulling into his driveway in Overland Park, he knew something wasn't right the second he saw the house. Apollo sat in the back seat and a low growl emerged from his throat. "I sense it, too, Apollo." He stepped out of the vehicle and opened the back driver's side door. He made a circling motion with his index finger, and Apollo leapt out, making a mad dash toward the left side of the home.

Kristin stepped out. "What's wrong, Dakota?"

"I don't know. I left several lights on timers in various rooms, and they should be on by now. I don't see them."

The barking of Apollo brought both of them to attention, and they sprinted in the direction of the sound.

As Storm rounded the back corner of his house with Kristin right behind him, he saw Apollo on the deck staring at the back screen door, which was open and hung on one hinge. Storm withdrew his Sig Sauer and gripped it with both hands. "Stay here, Kristin. Apollo senses something."

He circled around to the deck stairs and cautiously ascended. Apollo had not taken his eyes off what caused him to give the alert.

"What is it, buddy?"

Other than one bark and a quick glance at Dakota, the border collie did not move.

Pointing the gun toward the open back door, he backed up against the wall next to it and took a quick glance in. A body lay on the floor just inside. He looked over at Kristin who still stood at the corner of the house. "Call 911. There's a body in the kitchen."

He backed away from the door and made a hand signal to Apollo. The dog immediately went to his side. He patted him on his ribs and said, "Good boy."

By 10 p.m., the quiet neighborhood was anything but quiet as paramedics, police officers, and detectives swarmed over the outside and inside of Dakota Storm's home. With his alibi firmly established, he and Kristin waited near his vehicle as he watched the activity.

Jacob Gordon arrived at 10:15 and stood beside Storm. "Do they know who the victim is?"

Storm shook his head. "Once they knew I had been out of town for three weeks, they left Kristin and me alone."

Gordon shot a glance at the woman standing next to Storm and raised an eyebrow. "Kristin Duffy?"

She turned and nodded.

"Owner of the K9 academy we assigned Deputy Storm to?"

"Yes."

"Huh." He paused. "Guess I'll inject myself into the investigation. Wait here."

The U.S. Western District Marshal spoke to a police officer at the front door and showed his badge. He was admitted inside immediately.

Fifteen minutes later, he returned to where Storm stood. "Do you know an FBI agent named Leah Sutton?"

"Nope."

"Didn't think you would. Well, she is lying on your kitchen floor with a lock pick in her hand and a 9mm hollow point in the back of her head."

Storm frowned. "Why would she have a lock pick in her hand?"

"Use your imagination, Dakota. Anyway, the house has been ransacked by what appears to be pros. Do you know what they might have been searching for?"

Storm started to shake his head but stopped. "Ah, shit. Judy's journal."

Gordon closed his eyes for a moment. "Damn. Where was it?"

"My office desk, bottom drawer on the left. I had it hidden under the hanging files."

"Stay here, I'll be right back."

Kristin turned to Storm. "You don't think?"

"No, I don't think. I know it's gone. I also know who did this and who killed the FBI agent."

When the U.S. Marshal returned, he shook his head as he approached his deputy. "Not there, and all the files in the drawer are gone."

"Figures. You know who's responsible for this, don't you, Jacob?"

"Yeah, I can guess. As you know, the FBI took over the investigation. Apparently, the dead agent inside was the lead agent on the case. I just spoke to Adam Lowe on the phone, he's on his way over."

"You might want to ask him why his agent had a lock pick in her hand."

"Oh, don't worry, Dakota. That's the first question I'm asking him." He looked back at the house. "It's obvious you can't stay here tonight."

"We'll be heading back to Lawrence as soon as we can leave." He turned to his boss. "You can find me there for the foreseeable future."

"What about this place?"

"I'm just renting. When they finish their investigation, I'll have my insurance company settle with the landlord."

Midnight

Kristin kept her eye on Storm as he drove the SUV west. The dash lights illuminated his profile, allowing her to study it closer. She had recognized from the beginning he was a handsome man, but as her feelings grew, so did her attraction to him. "Adam Lowe didn't have a lot to say, did he?"

"I don't know the man. When I first met him, I thought he was a good guy. But I didn't like the way he danced around the lock pick in his dead agent's hand."

"Maybe he didn't know."

Storm shrugged. "I find it hard to swallow he didn't."

"Dakota, are we in any danger?"

"Probably, but guess what?"

"What?"

"You and I have two of the best trained police dogs in the country. I'll take that type of protection over anything the police, FBI or even the military can provide."

"You know, you're right. We do." She closed her eyes for a moment. "Thanks, Dakota. That makes me feel better."

"You also have a deputy U.S. Marshal living with you now."

"Oh, that. He'll be too busy."

Storm chuckled and kept his eyes on the highway ahead.

Storm answered his cell phone a little after nine the next morning. The caller ID showed *Unknown*. "Hello."

"I heard your house had an incident." It was Frank Cole's voice.

"Yes, unfortunately."

"I fear I made a mistake handing the information we gathered over to the individual I chose."

"I was a little disappointed in that individual's response last night."

"That's what I heard."

Storm thought about it for a few moments and realized Cole had a source within the FBI he knew nothing about.

His wife's grandfather said, "What did they find?"

"Everything."

"Oh dear. Even the journal?"

"Yes, even the journal."

"Are you safe?"

"In my opinion, yes. Not too many individuals know where I am."

"Let's keep it that way. I'll be in touch in a few days. I believe we're going to have to figure this out ourselves. Unlike the individual I gave the information to, we don't seem to have any leaks."

"I've noticed that."

"I won't remind you to watch your back."

"Good, I won't tell you to do the same."

Storm heard a chuckle just before the call ended.

Chapter Thirty-Two

Lawrence, KS

The call came at 4:34 p.m. on Sunday afternoon. Storm answered while tending a smoker with a beef brisket on the verge of complete perfection. He would need to report to his office at the district courthouse in downtown Kansas City at 8:00 a.m. the following morning. Despite the depressing phone call, the brisket survived.

At 5:00 the next morning, he and Apollo ran their customary five miles and were on the road to KC by 6:30. A passionate kiss from Kristin almost made him late, but he arrived at the courthouse by 7:32 and in his office by 7:49.

At 8:05, Jacob Gordon breezed past Storm's cubicle and motioned for him to follow. He and Apollo complied. By 8:09 the two men and the dog were in Gordon's office with the door closed.

"Are you sleeping with Kristin Duffy?" The U.S. Marshal's tone did not convey mere curiosity. It verged on the *are-you-crazy* side.

Apollo gave a low growl. Dakota touched the dog on the neck, and the growl subsided. "That's a personal question, sir. One I do not believe I am required to answer."

Taking a deep breath, Gordon pursed his lips as he blew it out. "The point is, she is a contractor with the U.S. Marshals Service and off-limits to you, Storm. Do I make myself clear?"

"Very, sir." Storm stood, removed his badge from his belt, and placed it on Gordon's desk. "You will have my resignation letter on your desk within the hour." He turned and headed for the office exit.

"Storm."

Before opening the closed door, he turned. "Yes, sir."

Gordon tossed the badge back. The deputy caught it with one hand.

"How serious is it, Dakota?"

"I'm more at ease than I have been since Judy and Todd were killed. I can actually sleep all night without waking up in a sweat."

"That was fast."

Storm shrugged.

"Were you responsible for getting the information to the FBI?"

"Judy's grandfather arranged for that to happen. I provided a supporting role in the discovery."

Rubbing his face with his hands, Gordon pointed to the chair in front of his desk. "Please, sit."

Storm complied. Apollo returned to sitting next to him.

After a chuckle, Gordon gave the deputy a smile. "Are you going to threaten to resign every time something doesn't go your way?"

"No, sir. This is different. Kristin has helped me realize I have to move on."

"Very well. I won't pry into your personal life." He paused for a moment. "Adam Lowe is experiencing the full wrath of the FBI this morning. From what I've heard, he is on the verge of being transferred to the FBI field office in Nome, Alaska."

"They don't have a field office in Nome."

"My point."

The deputy kept his face neutral.

Gordon continued, "The only thing saving his ass right now is Agent Sutton breaking into your house right before she was executed. Lowe claims she did this on her own initiative."

"They were waiting for someone to enter the house. It would have been me if I had come home early."

Staring at his deputy, Gordon remained silent for a long pause. "I didn't put that together, Dakota."

"They discovered where I lived. One of the reasons I've stayed away. Kristin and I decided the time might be right, so I came back. How long had she been dead?"

"Three days."

"The neighbors didn't smell anything and no one missed her?"

"Apparently not. She was supposedly conducting an investigation."

Storm nodded.

"Why Kristin Duffy?"

"It's personal, sir."

"Okay, I can respect that. But you have a job to do."

"I'm aware of that as well, sir."

"Stop calling me, sir."

"Yes, sir."

Gordon's expression softened. "I'm happy for you, Dakota."

"Thank you, Jacob."

"Now, back to the business of catching fugitives." He handed Storm a pile of folders from his desk. "Since you've been on vacation the last four weeks, here are a few folks we need found."

Standing, the deputy said, "My pleasure."

That Evening

Storm met Sam Pearce at the rental house at 5:30 p.m. The deputy handed the keys to his landlord and said, "Sorry for the damage. I gave the insurance company your number."

"They've already contacted me. We're good, Dakota. Glad you're all right."

Pointing to the house with the For Sale sign, Storm asked, "Do you know what happened to Melissa across the street?"

"That reminds me." He pulled a folded envelope out of his back pocket. "She asked me to give you this."

Unfolding it, the deputy saw his name written on the front. "Thanks."

"What about all your stuff inside?"

"I didn't have that much. I'll be donating it to charity."

"Even your clothes?"

"Yes, everything."

"Uh, Dakota, there is the matter of the lease you signed."

Storm handed the man a check. "That covers my rent for the rest of the lease term."

Pearce studied it for a moment, smiled and placed the

check in his wallet. "Well, I wish all my tenants were as conscientious as you, Dakota."

"I appreciate the kindness you extended when I needed it. Thank you, Sam."

The two men shook hands, and Storm returned to his SUV. He did not look at the house as he backed out of the drive. He had never developed an attachment to the place nor the neighborhood; it was just a place to stay when not working. As he drove down the street, using one hand, he dug the envelope out and tore it open. The note from Melissa took up one line in the center of a legal pad page.

I've been transferred to Cincinnati. Short notice. Very disappointed you never called.

Storm read the note, wadded it into a ball, and placed it on the seat next to him. As he drove away, he mumbled, "There was a reason, Melissa. A very good reason."

The Following Weekend

Between his duties as a deputy U.S. Marshal, Apollo's continued training regimen, and keeping up with the maintenance on the academy grounds, Storm stopped revisiting his grief for the loss of his wife and son. The heartache remained, but staring into space and letting his emotions paralyze him both mentally and physically did not occur.

The sun hung low on the western horizon that Saturday evening when Kristin approached him with two beers in her hands. He finished nailing the final board on a new fence for the obstacle course when she offered the beer. "Looking good, Dakota. I didn't realize how handy you'd be around here."

After taking a sip, he said, "So that's the reason you let me move in."

She smiled. "One of them."

After a few moments, he said, "I have to be out of town a few days next week."

Raising her eyebrows, she looked at him. "Where?"

"Omaha. We have a lead someone I've been searching for will be there next week. Jimmie Russel and I are driving up there on Tuesday. If all goes well, I'll be back late Thursday."

She took a sip of her beer. "We have a light week around here next week. Anything you need me to do?"

He shrugged. "Nothing I can think of."

"Do you have enough clothes to be gone three days?"

He chuckled and then took a sip of beer. "I have three pairs of Levi's, three shirts, and the appropriate amount of underwear. I think I can get by."

"Why don't you let me buy you a few new outfits while you're gone. One of these days, you're going to need dress pants and something besides flannel shirts."

"Why?"

She shrugged. "One never knows when one might need something besides jeans."

"Do you know my size?"

"I've seen you without clothes more than a few times now. I'm pretty sure I do."

He nodded and stared off into the distance.

"What's the matter, Dakota?"

"Nothing."

She moved closer to him and put her arm around his waist. "I know. I'm finding it hard to believe we've grown this close so fast. Do you think we're making a mistake?"

"Oh, the contrary. I think we're making up for lost time." He leaned over and kissed her. "Wanna have Grubhub deliver something tonight?"

"You read my mind."

Chapter Thirty-Three

Omaha, NE

Lying on the ground hidden by the surrounding brush, Dakota Storm used binoculars to keep watch on the isolated farmhouse. The only occupants he and Jimmie Russel had observed, so far, were a young woman in her twenties and their target, fugitive Boss Haggard. He was a thirty-some-thing biker wanted on federal warrants for interstate trans-portation of stolen vehicles. Haggard also ran a chop shop in Omaha and pursued a side hustle dealing in meth, cocaine, and fentanyl.

The time neared 3:15 a.m., and they had not seen any movement in the cabin for at least three hours. Russel said, "Think they're asleep?"

"Hope so."

"How old you think the girl is, Dakota?"

"Don't know. Using meth can age you. She might be younger than we think." He stood. "Let's find out."

Storm made a hand signal for Apollo. The dog took off

and circled the house. When he appeared on the right side and stared at his handler, Storm said, "Coast is clear. Let's do this. Apollo and I will go in the front. You go in the back."

Watching Russel disappear around the corner of the house, Storm quietly stepped onto the concrete front steps. The porch, also concrete, extended one foot on either side of the front door. Trying the doorknob, the deputy found it unlocked. Turning it with care, he made no sound entering the house. Russel appeared from the kitchen and nodded.

Apollo kept his eyes on Storm, waiting for instructions. When the deputy made a fist and then pointed toward the back of the house, the border collie silently padded through the structure. The canine stopped in front of a door, sniffed the threshold, and sat. His eyes not deviating from the door. A signal someone or someones were behind it.

Storm held up three fingers. The countdown began as he lowered the first finger. When he made a fist, Russel kicked the door in. Storm and the K9 officer rushed into the room, backed up by Russel. He went left and Storm right. Apollo started barking.

The two individuals in the bed appeared confused by the noise, as they tried to sit up.

While Russel used zip ties to secure the woman's hands behind her, Storm told the man to get on the floor with his hands behind him. He complied with little protest.

With both the man and the woman handcuffed and sitting on the living room floor, Storm searched the house with Apollo's help. What he found in a back bedroom caused him to yell out, "Hey, Jimmie, I'm sending Apollo out to guard them, I need you to witness this."

Looking at his companion, Storm said, "Guard." The

dog ran out of the room and positioned himself near the two prisoners.

The deputy heard the woman start to protest the appearance of Apollo, then he heard Russel growl, "Hush."

Several moments later, Russel entered the room. "What've ya got, Dakota?"

Moving toward a computer on a desk, Storm touched the space bar. The screen came alive and displayed the images of young girls.

Closing his eyes, Storm said, "Ah, shit."

Omaha FBI Field Office

With the two prisoners transferred into the custody of the Douglas County sheriff's department, an FBI computer expert gained access to the computer confiscated from the rural farmhouse.

The woman introduced herself as Linda something. Storm immediately forgot her last name once she said it. But she dissected the computer with skill. Within minutes, she discovered images of child porn and web addresses for various dark web sites that promoted these types of activities.

Standing with his arms folded, Storm watched horrific images appear on the laptop screen that made his skin crawl. After one particular picture, he said, "Stop. Go back to the previous photo."

Linda looked at him strangely but did.

Bending over, he studied the face of the girl. "Damn, that's one of the girls from the warehouse in Memphis."

Linda reached for a phone on her desk.

By midmorning, Storm had identified three additional images of girls rescued in Memphis. Chaos reigned supreme as more FBI agents inserted themselves into the investigation.

With inflated egos crowding out lesser ones, Storm retreated to an unused corner of a conference room to call Jacob Gordon on his cell phone.

"What've you got, Dakota?"

"The arrest of the fugitive went without incident. He's in the Douglas County jail. What we found in the house is another matter."

"Give me the 50,000-foot view."

"We found a computer containing images of some of the girls rescued in the Memphis warehouse."

"Oh boy."

"Yeah. On top of that, it appears Bayou Global is also involved with more than just human trafficking."

"We kind of suspected that, Dakota. What is it?"

"They seem to be prolific on the Dark Web with sites that cater to certain tastes."

"Does the FBI know this?"

"They do now."

"Why don't you and Jimmie quietly get out of there and head back to KC? If you leave now and take I-29, you can be here by three. I'll have a conference call set up with the powers that be in Washington. I'm tired of taking a back seat to the FBI. They haven't accomplished a thing, except getting an agent killed."

"We're on our way, Jacob."

Kansas City District Courthouse

The conference room where Gordon scheduled the Zoom call to the director of the U.S. Marshals Service held only three individuals: Jacob Gordon, Dakota Storm, and an IT specialist. She would help show the director what Storm had uncovered. Apollo lay on the floor next to his handler.

Gordon looked at Storm. "You ready?"

"Hope he doesn't mind my jeans and windbreaker. My shirt's got grass stains all over it."

"You work for a living, Dakota. The director will appreciate it." He turned to the tech and nodded.

The screen brightened, and a middle-aged woman smiled. "Good morning, Jacob. I'll get the director."

She left the camera's view and, momentarily, the image of a heavyset male on the cusp of his sixtieth birthday smiled. "Good afternoon, Jacob."

"Good afternoon, sir."

"Is this the deputy causing all the ruckus these past few months?"

"Yes, sir, this is Deputy U.S. Marshal Dakota Storm."

Calvin Fox's demeanor reflected the severity of the conference call. He said, "I'm extremely pleased to finally meet you, Deputy. I keep reading extraordinary reports about your work."

"It is nice to meet you as well, sir."

"Also, congratulations on the training you have conducted for our K9 handlers in the Midwest. I've heard nothing but stellar reports about your accomplishments."

Storm felt his face flush. "Thank you, sir."

Fox continued, "Now, let's get down to the purpose of this call." The director clasped his hands in front of him. "Jacob, please start."

"The organization uncovered by Deputy Storm has flown under federal law enforcement agencies' radar for years. It is extensive and encompasses most of the central United States, from the Gulf to the Canadian border, probably farther. We just don't know. Two individuals, Alexi Yankovic and Ivan Smirnov, appear to be the driving force behind this group. Both are originally from Russia and both have ties to that country's Mafia."

The director sat stoic, his face an unreadable mask.

Gordon continued, "Unbeknownst to Deputy Storm, his late wife left a journal outlining her experience with this group. He found her writings hidden in a personal lockbox. The information within revealed details concerning one side of this group's activities. This led Deputy Storm to the discovery of a way station for the transportation of underage females in Memphis, Tennessee. There is a strong possibility the route extends into Canada. We have contacted the Royal Canadian Mounted Police and asked them to investigate on their side.

"Unfortunately, the journal, along with notes made by Deputy Storm, were stolen and the lead investigator for the FBI was killed."

"How was this FBI agent involved?"

"Evidences suggests she illegally entered Storm's home and was executed by unknown persons. Why she broke in is a question no one can answer. FBI SAC Adam Lowe has chosen not to discuss the incident with us."

"Let me handle getting an explanation, Jacob. I have a meeting with the FBI director following our discussion."

"Yes, sir." Gordon looked at his notes. "Also, this morning, Deputy Storm and a fellow marshal uncovered another aspect to this group's activities. We now have evidence the group is active in producing child pornography and distributing it on the internet utilizing Dark Web sites."

The director frowned. "How extensive are the sites?"

"Elaborate and numerous."

"Go on."

"While we don't have hard evidence, we believe they are also smuggling drugs." Gordon proceeded to recap the results of Storm's investigations. After he completed the report, he looked at the director. "Sir, ever since this investigation was turned over to the FBI, absolutely nothing has happened. Except the death of one of their agents, who we suspect was searching for Deputy Storm's journal."

Fox narrowed his eyes. "What are you suggesting, Jacob?"

"If, in fact, Agent Sutton broke into Dakota's home looking for the journal, we believe she may have done so at the request of Special Agent in Charge Lowe."

"That's a serious accusation, Jacob."

"I am very aware of the ramifications of my statement. I have known Adam Lowe a long time, sir. I find it hard to believe he would have given such a directive. But the fact is, the agent is dead."

Fox nodded. "If there is any chance he told her to do so, I would be obliged to report this to my boss, the attorney general."

Gordon clasped his hands in front of him.

The director tapped his lips with a finger. "Very well. I will address the situation with the AG. In the meantime, I will have warrants prepared for Yankovic and Smirnov. Capturing these two men as fugitives falls under our jurisdiction." He paused. "Deputy Storm."

"Yes, sir."

"Good work. Now let's finish the job."

Storm smiled. "Yes, sir, and thank you, sir."

Chapter Thirty-Four

Lawrence, KS

Storm parked his SUV in the detached garage. He exited the building, a duffle bag over his shoulder, as Apollo playfully nipped at his heels. The dog appeared happy to be out of the vehicle and free to run. The deputy bent down and picked up a stick. He tossed it toward the gravel approach road, and the dog tore after it.

Kristin stood on the back deck and folded her arms as he approached. "Glad your home."

"Good to be home." He climbed the four steps to where she stood and kissed her.

The border collie came running back, dropped the stick, and bounded up the steps. Kristin bent down and rubbed his head. "Good to have you back, Apollo." His tongue hung, and his eyes sparkled with excitement.

After they were in the house and the duffle bag deposited in the laundry room, Storm headed toward the bedroom. "I'll be in the shower. You won't believe what's happened over the last thirty-six hours."

Following him, Kristin pulled the academy T-shirt off over her head. "I'll join you, and you can tell me all about it."

He shot a quick glance at her, smiled, and said, "There are other things we can discuss in the shower besides my day."

Two Hours Later

The burning charcoal briquettes cast a warm glow on the back deck as Storm turned the burgers. Smoke rose as meat juices dropped onto the burning embers. Kristin said, "How did you recognize the girls from the warehouse, Dakota?"

"I've asked myself that several times since I saw them on the computer screen. The only explanation I can come up with is their situation shocked me so bad, their images burned into my memory."

She sipped a beer. "That makes sense." Her gaze never wavered from the deputy. She watched him take a long pull on his beer and concentrate on cooking their dinner. "Dakota?"

He turned. "Yeah?"

"Do you think they will find us out here?"

The deputy turned his attention to her and contemplated the question for several moments. He then took a long breath. "I don't know. The FBI has a leak. I can guarantee that. But I wouldn't think they would suspect me being here. When was the last time you trained FBI K9 units?"

"It's been a couple of years. As you know, most of my business now comes from police and sheriff's departments. The only government agencies I work with now are the Marshals Service and the military."

Staring at the glow of the charcoal, Storm sipped his beer. He then turned back to her. "Let's not take anything for granted. You've currently got five security cameras installed. Tomorrow we'll go to Home Depot. They have numerous systems we can get to beef up the number."

With a nod, she took another swig of her beer. "Plus, we've got Bruno and Apollo."

"Yes, but there's nothing wrong with giving them a little assistance."

By evening the next day, eight additional cameras were installed to survey the activities around the academy. A large standalone monitor provided the ability to see anything within each camera's angle of view in real time. Three of them were in plain sight. The other five were well hidden and would give the occupants of the house at least a few minutes warning of possible threats.

"Where did you learn to set up security systems, Dakota?"

"While I worked at the St. Louis County sheriff's department, we offered a service to local businesses on how to keep their buildings secure. I picked up a lot of good ideas there."

Kristin sat in front of the monitor. "This helps me feel like the place is more protected."

"Good. Let's hope we never have to use them."

"Yeah, let's hope."

"I've got another idea to give us an edge."

"What is it?"

"It will entail cutting a hole in the floor somewhere."

She chuckled. "And you feel the need to ask my permission?"

"It is your house, Kristin."

"I've been meaning to talk to you about that."

He folded his arms. "Uh-oh."

"No, it's a good thing. Why don't we refinance this place and put it in both our names?"

"I don't know. What if things don't work out between us?"

"What's the chance of that?"

A grin came to Storm's lips. "Unlikely."

"See? There you go."

Two Weeks Later

A low throat growl from Apollo startled Storm to full alertness. As he reached for his Sig Sauer in the nightstand drawer, he glanced at the digital clock: 3:14 a.m. Touching Kristin on the back, he said, "Something's wrong. Get your shotgun."

She pushed the covers aside and reached under the bed. Withdrawing a Remington 870 Tactical shotgun, she asked, "What's going on?"

Storm now stood in front of the camera monitor studying several of the video feeds. "Apollo senses something. We have movement on the access road, and it's not a vehicle."

Dressed only in boxer shorts and a sleeveless T-shirt,

Kristin slipped on black track pants and matching top. At the same time, Storm pulled on a pair of jeans as he kept his attention on the video monitor.

"I see two individuals approaching on the access road and two others checking the kennels."

"We don't have any dogs there at the moment." She whistled and Bruno ran into the room. "Good boy. Stay." The Belgian Malinois sat and kept his eyes focused on her. Turning to Storm, she asked, "Are they armed?"

"Can't tell, but we have to assume they are. Call 911, and get the sheriff's department on the way."

Picking up her cell phone, she made the call. When answered, she said, "This is Wakarusa K9 Academy. We have multiple intruders on our property." She paused for a moment. "Yes, we think they're armed." More silence. "We are a half mile east of the junction at CR 1900 and CR 1275. Your K9 officers know how to get here." Another pause. "Yes, thank you." She ended the call, her attention returning to Storm. "Ten minutes."

"Might as well be an eternity. We're on our own for now." He looked at Apollo and displayed an open palm then made a circling motion with his index finger. The border collie padded out of the room to make a silent search of the house. Bruno whimpered but stayed put, his eyes still locked on Kristin.

Referring to the video monitor, Storm pointed to the one covering the back door. "Looks like they are going to breach that entrance first. Take Bruno and guard it. I'll barricade the front door and then join you."

The seconds passed slowly as Storm secured the front door by scooting a sofa against it. If someone pushed the door in, the couch would be wedged against a wall and prevent the door from opening more than two inches. He then rushed back to the kitchen where Kristin stood behind the refrigerator, her shotgun pointed at the back door.

Due to the kitchen's layout, an open space with a dining area next to the door, barricading it presented a more difficult challenge. Bruno and Apollo crouched on the floor. Their attention focused on the entrance.

Placing himself against a wall, the deputy viewed the back deck and saw two figures step onto the wooden planks. He looked at Kristin and held up two fingers. Both of them heard a commotion at the front door, a loud crash, and then muffled cursing.

Checking on the two men in the back, he noticed one of them take a large pry tool off his back and insert it into the door. Turning to the two dogs, Storm said, "Guard and alert."

Both Apollo and Bruno began to bark ferociously. Keeping his eye on the two men, he noticed the one with the pry bar stop and look at his companion. That man raised a pistol and aimed it at the door. Storm yelled, "Break." Both dogs separated just seconds before the man fired at the entrance.

Kristin aimed the shotgun at the door and pulled the trigger. She pumped the weapon and repeated the process. Storm aimed his Sig Sauer out the window and emptied the magazine as fast as possible.

Sheriff's deputies scurried around the academy grounds collecting evidence as EMTs tended to the wounded man on the deck. His dead companion lay next to him, the body covered with a blanket.

Sergeant Ramirez, the supervisory county deputy, took

notes as Kristin explained what had occurred. When she finished, he looked at Storm. "Anything to add, Dakota?"

With a shake of his head, he said, "No."

The sergeant turned to Kristin. "We found an abandoned F-150 behind the kennels. Plates indicate it is one of two pickups reported stolen last night in Kansas City. Got any idea who these guys are?"

Kristin glanced at Storm. He said, "We think they are tied to an investigation I've been conducting."

The sergeant frowned. "Do I need to call somebody?"

Storm shook his head. "I've called my supervisor. He's sending a team out."

"Got it. Since this is a crime scene, is there somewhere you two can stay for a few days?"

With her arms folded, Kristin shrugged. "We'll figure it out."

"Okay." He walked out of the room.

Turning to Storm, she placed her head on his shoulder and wrapped her arms around him. "Thank you."

He returned the embrace. "For what?"

"For being here with me. Not sure I could have handled this by myself."

"You're stronger than you think you are. You did good."

Her only response was to hold him tighter.

He continued, "We need to find somewhere to go that nobody knows about."

"I know. Got any ideas?"

"Yes."

Chapter Thirty-Five

Somewhere On I-70

Storm handed Kristin his cell phone. "I need you to send a text message to the number I have displayed."

Accepting the phone, she turned to him. "I'm ready, what do you want me to type?"

He said, "*There's been an incident. Call me.*"

She finished by hitting the send icon. Returning her attention to Storm, she said, "Now what?"

"He'll call within five minutes if he can."

His phone rang almost immediately. The caller ID read *Unknown*. He answered. "Thanks for calling."

"Is it serious?" The voice of Frank Cole came through the speakers on the SUV's hands-free function.

"Possibly. Your buddy at the bureau. Do you trust him?"

"Trust can have a variety of levels."

"Reach out to him and see what he has to say. My companion and I are in the wind and heading your way."

"Expect a call."

Glancing at the dogs in the back, Kristin saw both lying down, heads up, and eyeing her, their tongues out and panting. She turned to Storm. "Now what?"

"We've only been driving for an hour. We still have three to go. He'll call before we get there."

She stared out the front windshield. "I wonder if it's safe for us to take the highway all the way to St. Louis?"

Storm did not answer immediately. "A good question. I don't see how they found us as fast as they did."

"Dakota, I've had hundreds of law enforcement personnel on my property over the years. Who's to say one of them didn't get paid off and talk."

Shaking his head, Storm said, "Why last night? Why not weeks ago? Something has changed since I got back from Omaha."

"Are they tracking you?"

"Shit. I didn't think of that." He slowed the vehicle as they approached the exit for Highway 7. Taking it, he drove a quarter of a mile and pulled into the parking lot of a local café with a robust breakfast business. He parked in the back of the lot. "The dogs need a bathroom break, and we need to search this vehicle."

Storm opened the back door, and the two canines scampered out. They did their business and then sat waiting for playtime or work. The deputy pointed to the Ford and said, "Search."

Apollo immediately started sniffing and looking over the car. Bruno did the same. After five minutes, Bruno crouched next to the rear passenger side wheel well and stared up. Kristin lay prone next to him and examined the area within the wheel well. "Dakota, you need to see this."

Lying next to her, he saw the object she pointed at. He shone a flashlight from his glove compartment on the disc.

"That's how they found us." He reached up and removed the magnetized GPS tracking device placed directly above the tire.

He stood and studied the object. "You know these things don't cost that much anymore. You can get them on Amazon for around twenty-nine bucks."

"You're kidding."

"Wish I was."

She congratulated Bruno for his find and stood. "Now what?"

Looking around, he searched the parking lot. An idea suddenly came to him. He casually walked over to an SUV with an out-of-state license plate. Bending over, he attached the GPS tracker to the driver's side rear wheel well. Straightening, he looked around and then walked back to his Ford and got in. The dogs and Kristin followed.

Storm said, "We'll head south until we hit US-50 east. It will take us longer, but we won't be on I-70 anymore. They might have different chase cars stationed in various spots along the route."

She nodded but remained quiet.

Fifteen minutes later, he turned east on US-50 and put the Ford back on cruise control.

Kristin asked, "These people have an awful lot of resources at their disposal. Plus, they apparently know what is going on within the bureau. How are you and Frank by yourselves going to defeat them?"

"Haven't got a clue. I just know that if we don't do something, you and I won't have a future together."

Directing her gaze back to the road ahead, Kristin grinned. "Well, we can't have that, now, can we?"

Near the eastern city limits of Sedalia on US-50, a call came in on the hands-free option. He pressed a button on the steering wheel. "Yes?"

"I will meet you at the same place where we met the second time."

"Got it. Two and a half out."

"See you there."

With a chuckle, Kristin said, "Glad you two understand each other."

"If, by chance, someone is listening, they won't." Storm checked the rearview mirror, an action he repeated every few minutes since turning onto US-50 earlier in the day. "I'm going to stop and get gas at the next chance. We can let the dogs do their thing." He said this as he glanced in the rearview mirror.

She said, "You keep checking the mirror. What's wrong?"

"Probably nothing. But there's been an Audi SUV two cars behind for the past thirty miles. It hasn't gotten closer or farther behind, always two vehicles between us. I need to make sure it's not following."

Exiting the highway, he parked the Ford next to a fuel pump at an Eagle Stop convenience store. He watched the Audi pass the station without its brake lights flaring. While Kristin attended to the dogs, he engaged the pump and watched the highway for any signs the vehicle had stopped and might be circling back. After filling the Ford's tank with gas, he walked inside the store and purchased a pay-as-you-go Tracfone with sixty minutes of time.

Back in the SUV, he turned his regular phone off. "Change of plans. We can circle back to US-65, head north and hit I-70 at Marshall Junction."

"Does it save us any time?"

"No, but if the Audi was following and is waiting ahead to get behind us again, we won't provide him the opportunity."

"You act like you've done this before?"

Shaking his head, he said, "Misspent youth reading spy novels."

———

The rest of the drive went without incident. Storm and Kristin arrived at Frank Cole's house a little before 5 p.m. He noticed the garage door open, so he pulled into the empty side and the two adults and two dogs got out. As soon as they were out of the garage, the door started to close. Kristin turned to Storm. "I thought he said to meet him at the second place you met."

"We did. The second time I was with Frank, I stayed here for a week. I got to know him better."

The back door opened and Frank Cole greeted his guests with a smile. "Have you had dinner?"

"No."

"Good. We'll make something here, and I can fill you in on what I've found out."

After the dogs were fed and exercised, they sat around a small bistro table. Frank served iced tea.

Storm asked, "What did your friend at the bureau say?"

"The conversation felt a little strained this time. Like I wasn't supposed to know about their dirty laundry. Anyway, apparently, Adam Lowe is claiming he had no idea Leah Sutton would break into your house. There are those within the ranks of bureau management who believe him, and a far more who don't. His meteoric rise within the FBI seems to have hit an obstacle. If he survives, he'll be transferred to a small field office, and that will be it."

Twisting his iced tea glass clockwise, Storm nodded. "The truth is probably somewhere in the middle. He might not have precisely told her to break in, but I imagine he told her to make sure she obtained Judy's journal."

Cole took a sip of iced tea. "You're probably right."

Kristin stirred her glass with a teaspoon. "How do we stop these guys?"

With raised eyebrows, Cole said, "We?"

"Yes, Frank, we. Dakota and I are in this together."

A slight grin appeared. "We it is." He paused. "To answer your question, we'll have to do something totally illegal in the United States."

Storm looked at his late-wife's grandfather. "What's that, Frank?"

"Use CIA assets and resources."

"Like Peter Khan?"

"Him and a few others who will remain anonymous, by choice. We have a computer guy examining websites they own. He's making progress."

"By shutting them down?"

"Not yet. He's learning who owns them and the billing information."

"You're kidding."

Cole shook his head. "He's in the process of following the money generated by the websites and tracing it to where it is being deposited. Once he knows the bank, he can learn who the owners of the account are. Once we know more about their finances, it will be a matter of following the money."

Storm stood and went to the back door. He clasped his hands behind him as he stared out over the backyard of

Cole's house. "Once we have suspects, I've been assured the Marshals Service will start making arrests. No bureau, just the Marshals Service."

Cole folded his arms. "Dakota, finding Yankovic or Smirnov is the key. If their finances are exposed, it shouldn't be too hard to determine their location."

Turning to look at his friend, Storm said, "Don't bet on it. My guess is those two are well insulated from the day-to-day workings of Bayou Global. But if we can flush out enough underlings, someone will talk."

Kristin said, "Most everyone you've encountered so far, Dakota, is scared to death of them."

"You're right. But the weaker the organization becomes, the less scared those accountant and midlevel managers will get. In fact, men like Landry might actually start making deals with prosecutors."

Cole nodded. "I've been told by my associates to expect new insights early tomorrow."

Chapter Thirty-Six

Kansas City

Adam Lowe pinched the bridge of his nose with his left hand as he listened to the phone call.

"Sir, they must have spotted us. They ditched us in Sedalia, and we haven't seen them since. Also, the tracker we installed on the deputy's vehicle is compromised." The agent on the phone chose not to tell Lowe the tracking device was located on a Chevy SUV heading north toward Omaha, Nebraska.

"If he was driving east, he's probably heading toward Cole's place. Get eyes and ears on the house."

"Yes, sir."

Ending the call, Lowe stared at his desktop for a few moments. Loose ends concerning the Bayou Global investigation spewed forth like sparks from a Roman candle. Rubbing his eyes with the palms of his hand, he remained quiet for a period. The shrill tone of his desk phone broke the silence.

Looking at the caller ID, he sighed and answered, "Agent Lowe."

"Agent, please hold for the director."

Closing his eyes, he prepared himself for what he suspected would be a contentious conversation.

"What the hell is going on there in Kansas City, Lowe?" The director's tone loud and menacing.

Closing his eyes, Lowe took a breath and kept his tone neutral. "We have a lot of investigations going on, sir. Which specific case are you referring to?"

"You know exactly what I'm talking about. The one where Agent Sutton was executed inside the home of a deputy U.S. Marshal."

"We have our best agents working on it, sir."

There was a long silence. The director's growl intensified. "That's not an answer. Why was she found with lock picks in her hand?"

"Something we are looking into, sir."

"Lowe, choose your next words with caution. They might be your last as a Special Agent in Charge. I just had an extremely uncomfortable discussion with the director of the U.S. Marshals Service and my boss the attorney general. They asked questions I could not answer. Now, why was she breaking into the home of a deputy?"

"Because we suspect Deputy Storm of withholding vital information about Bayou Global and the men who run the company."

"Deputy Storm is the one who uncovered this mess, and you are investigating him? Not the men responsible for the human trafficking? Is that what you're telling me?"

"I'm afraid it is, sir."

A long period of silence ensued. "I hope you have a

good explanation for doing so, Lowe. Because I am starting to question your leadership skills."

"We think Storm's involved."

"On what basis?"

"He's been able to produce more evidence than the FBI. That is way beyond the scope of the U.S. Marshals Service."

The silence on the call this time lasted more than thirty seconds. "Lowe, did it ever occur to you he might be a better investigator than you give him credit for? Be very cautious of how you answer that question."

"The FBI should have been handed this investigation from the beginning. The Marshals Service needs to back down and Storm questioned."

"That's not an answer. Now, back to my question."

"No, sir, it did not occur to me. How can a deputy U.S. Marshal be a better investigator than trained agents with the FBI?"

The director sighed. "So, instead of cooperating with the deputy, you sent someone to investigate him. And you did this because you did not perceive him as a capable investigator. Am I hearing you correctly, Lowe?"

Adam Lowe chose not to answer.

"Very well. Your silence speaks volumes, Agent. Because of your shortsightedness, an FBI agent is dead, the attorney general is questioning our tactics, and a valuable member of the U.S. Marshals Service may be compromised. Consider yourself on suspension pending further investigation by the Justice Department." The director paused. "Make sure you vacate your office immediately. Is that clear?"

"Yes, sir."

The call ended at the exact moment two agents unknown

to Lowe entered his office. The one on the right, a tall fellow wearing a navy suit, with short blond hair and blue eyes said, "Agent Lowe, we are here to escort you out of the building."

"How long have you been outside the door?"

Neither spoke. Both stood at parade rest. Lowe stood and reached for his cell phone on the desk. The other agent, an equally tall woman dressed in a dark-gray pantsuit stepped forward and placed her hand on the phone. "Government property. Please leave it in place."

The other agent spoke again. "Please vacate the premises, sir. You are to leave everything as is. Do not attempt to remove anything."

"Even my personal property?"

"It will be returned to you at a later date."

Lowe nodded, walked to the office door, and exited. The two agents followed him all the way to the parking lot. He removed his car keys from his pocket and pointed the fob toward his car. The male agent grabbed them from his hand. "Government vehicle, sir. You are no longer authorized to drive it."

The two agents folded their arms. Lowe looked at them and then the car. "How am I supposed to get home?"

"Call an Uber."

"You took my cell phone."

"To the contrary, it is a government-issued cell phone."

Lowe glared at the two agents but knew the words spoken by the director about him being under investigation did not fully describe his situation. His ten-year career with the bureau had suddenly and unceremoniously come to an abrupt end. He threw his hands up, turned, and walked briskly toward the location of a convenience store about ten blocks away.

Frank Cole stood on the back deck of his home and listened to the phone call. He did not speak, only nodded on occasion. When the speaker finished, Cole said, "Did they recall the agents headed toward my house?" He listened. "Good. Any word on the identity of the dead man from Duffy's property?" More listening. "I see. I'll let them know. Thanks." He ended the call and walked back into the house.

Storm and Kristin waited in the living room. When Cole returned, Storm asked, "What'd you find out?"

"It seems, my young friend, you and Kristin have stirred up a hornet's nest."

She folded her arms. "Frank, what's that supposed to mean?"

"Special Agent in Charge Adam Lowe has been, for lack of a better term, fired. He is being accused of orchestrating the situation leading to Agent Sutton's breaking into your house, Dakota."

"What about the two guys on Kristin's back deck?"

"Both are from New Orleans, and both have criminal records. The one who survived is talking to deputy U.S. Marshals sent to Lawrence by Jacob Gordon. The FBI has been told to cease and desist any investigation." Cole pointed at Storm. "You, my friend, will be notified by your boss, probably tomorrow, that you are now in charge of the task force being assembled to locate and arrest any and all individuals associated with Bayou Global."

Without making a comment, Storm scowled.

Cole chuckled. "Your expression indicates you don't believe me."

"Who was following us?"

"The FBI. They had agents enroute to this house, but they've been recalled."

"Frank, I can't prove it, but there's a leak within the FBI."

"There are those in Washington who agree with you. In fact, there are those within the bureau who suspect it might be Adam Lowe."

"That doesn't make sense."

"I would agree with you, Dakota. Why send Agent Sutton to the house for the journal if you knew Bayou Global planned to steal it anyway?"

"We need to return to the academy. Maybe if I call Jacob, he can give us an update on the police investigation and tell us when we can get back in the house?"

"He'll probably want you back in KC first. He has two prisoners there with a lot of seniority within the organization."

"Are they talking?"

Cole shrugged. "My source didn't know."

Storm grabbed Kristin's hand and whistled for the dogs. "We'll head back to KC and stay there tonight." He glanced at his watch. "I'd rather be on the road than a sitting duck somewhere."

Cole pointed to their hands. "Is this getting serious?"

Storm glanced at Kristin. She gave him a nod. He turned to Cole. "It's not getting serious, it already is."

The retired CIA station chief smiled. "Good for you two. If you need anything, let me know."

Chapter Thirty-Seven

Kansas City

Victor Landry sat in an interrogation room within the Jackson County sheriff's complex. Storm and Jacob Gordon watched the prisoner through a video feed from the room. The deputy asked, "Has he been talkative?"

"Not particularly." Gordon handed Storm a transcript of the interview with the surviving attacker at Kristin's house. "He, on the other hand, is a chatterbox. This is the information he provided. Some of it might help you with Landry."

Skimming the document, he got to the third page and raised his eyebrows. Pointing to the paragraph, he turned to his boss. "This is new. We didn't know this about Landry."

Gordon kept his eyes on the prisoner. "No, we didn't. I'm interested to see how he reacts when you tell him."

When he finished reading, Storm headed toward the interrogation room door.

After sitting across from Landry, Storm clasped his hands together. "Enjoying your stay, Victor?"

Appraising the deputy, the man shook his head. "Are you going to lie to me like that FBI asshole?"

"He offered you a deal. Why didn't you take it?"

"I changed my mind. I'm going to use the lawyer the company will be providing."

"About that. You've been left out to dry. If you want an attorney, you'll be paying for it yourself, or you'll have to utilize a public defender."

The man's eyes grew wide. "Is that why I haven't heard anything?"

Storm nodded.

"Shit."

"Sucks, doesn't it?"

Landry bowed his head. "I have nothing to say, Storm. You're wasting your time."

"Hector Garcia."

The prisoner's head snapped up, and he glared at Storm.

"So, from that reaction, I'd say you know the guy. He made the mistake of trying a home invasion with another of your friends, Jorge Castillo."

"I don't have a clue who you're talking about."

"Did I mention Jorge didn't survive?"

Landry only stared at the tabletop.

"Hector knows you. In fact, he's given us a timeline of all the assignments you've sent him on over the past year. Some of which are felonies and carry life-in-prison sentences. We're really happy he's in custody. He's making deals left and right to lessen his sentence."

"Whoever this Garcia character is, he's lying."

"Probably on some of it, but we've been able to corroborate most of his testimony. And guess what?"

Landry only glared at Storm.

"He volunteered your name. Nobody prompted him." The deputy folded his arms and smiled. "I love it when shit like that happens. Makes my job easier."

The prisoner tried to lunge at Storm, but his constraints kept him in his seat.

"Victor, you need to calm down. With what we already knew and Hector's testimony, the list of charges against you keep piling up. You're looking at constant court appearances for the next five or six years." After a pause, Storm continued, "Want to hear the new charges being filed against you?"

"No."

Storm leaned forward. "We want Smirnov and Yankovic. Do yourself a favor and tell us."

"You guys can't hide me from them. If I talk, I'm dead."

Storm stood. "Okay, be stubborn. We'll just let it leak through the grapevine you're singing like a bird."

Landry pounded his fists on the table. "Shit—shit— shit." He bowed his head again. "What's in it for me."

"Tell us what we want to know, and the district attorney general will make you a deal."

"What exactly do you want?"

"Where can I find Denzel Cruz aka Alexi Yankovic?"

"Get me a deal, and I'll talk to you."

Moving toward the door, the deputy turned to look at Landry. "Let me see what I can do, Victor."

The first meeting of the task force met two days later. With members scattered across six states, a Zoom video meeting seemed to be the best format for getting everyone on the same page. With information gleaned from the interview with Hector Garcia and Victor Landry, representatives from each state level law enforcement agency, fourteen county sheriff's departments, and twenty deputy U.S. Marshals attended. Two computer techs from the Marshals Service assisted the deputy with coordinating the meeting and sharing PowerPoint slides.

Storm's stomach tightened as the time for the meeting neared. He felt a bit intimidated being the leader of so many seasoned law enforcement officers. The FBI had not been invited. At the appointed time, the meeting started with Storm sitting at a table, a computer camera trained on him, and a large-screen TV displaying the various members of the task force.

"Good morning."

Forty individuals returned the greeting.

"Ladies and gentlemen, you've all been muted. If you have a question, please use the chat function at the bottom of your screen. When this is over, I'll answer the ones I can. If I don't know it, we'll get you the answer as soon as possible."

Everyone on the call nodded.

Storm continued, "From the testimony of two captured members of Bayou Global, we have learned the organization is far more extensive than we originally thought. The goal of our first raids will be to deplete as many active members of this crime organization as possible. You have all been sent an action plan for your specific area and who to target. Over the next five days, we believe we can execute the plan with pinpoint precision. There is a possibility of taking over one hundred and twenty suspects into custody during these raids.

"If successful, we feel we can flush out the leaders." He turned to one of the computer techs. "Can you share the pictures of Smirnov and Yankovic?"

She nodded, and the screen in front of Storm displayed two mug shots side by side.

"The man on your left is Denzel Cruz, also known as Alexi Yankovic. He is originally from Russia and a member of the Russian Mafia. He's been in the United States for about ten years and has operated under the radar of most law enforcement organizations. Articles of Incorporation filed with the Louisiana Secretary of State proclaim him to be the CEO of Bayou Global. Interviews with several employees of the company currently in custody identify Cruz as the individual who makes all the decisions." He paused. "The man on your left is Ivan Smirnov. He is also Russian, but we know very little about the man. If he has an alias, which we think he does, it is unknown at this time."

The computer tech said to Storm, "Deputy Townsend in Little Rock has a question."

"Unmute him, please. Deputy Townsend, you have a question?"

"Yeah, what if we find one of these two during our raid?"

Storm frowned. "Protect your team above all else. These men are considered extremely dangerous. A cache of weapons discovered in Memphis contained numerous high-caliber assault rifles. They are well armed, so do not hesitate to use force if needed."

Townsend smiled. "We're not gonna get our asses chewed if something happens to those two clowns. Right?"

"I'll buy the first round if something does happen to one

or both of them. I won't beat around the bush about these two men. They are murderers and have no remorse when a victim or an associate of theirs is wounded or dies. I can't emphasize that fact enough."

Storm could see the relief on everyone's face after his remark. He continued, "I have personally witnessed the ruthlessness of this group of criminals. The total disregard for life among these people is astonishing. So, protect yourselves and your team above all else."

The meeting lasted another two hours as logistics and command structures were established. When Storm finished going through his agenda and answering questions, he said, "I appreciate all the input today. I believe each of you has a good plan for your assigned areas. Operations will commence two days from now. If you have questions, feel free to contact me via the email address in your briefing and action plan packet. Thank you all for your time."

When the meeting ended, Jacob Gordon, who sat in a far corner of the room, clapped. "Very good, Dakota. You have a solid plan. Let's hope no one gets hurt while executing it."

Lawrence, KS

When Storm arrived home for the evening, Kristin sat on the back deck. When he trudged up the steps to the wooden platform, he noticed she looked distracted.

"What's the matter?"

She looked at him, her eyes red and puffy. "I had the next three weeks booked solid. Every single one of those clients has canceled."

"Did they give a reason?"

She shook her head.

"Who were they?"

"Adams County Oklahoma sheriff's department and police from two cities within the county, Quincy and Cimmaron. They're all in the eastern part of the state."

"Cancel or postponed?"

"Canceled."

Storm kept his gaze on her as he mentally reviewed the attendees of his Zoom meeting. "Where is Adams County?"

"East central Oklahoma."

"Huh. We didn't include the counties that far south."

She stood and went to him. He embraced her and could feel her silent sobs as she buried her head on his chest.

As he stroked her hair, he asked, "Any other cancellations?"

"No," she said in a weak voice.

"I doubt there will be."

She raised her head. "Why do you say that?"

"I can answer that after I google who the sheriff of Adams County Oklahoma might be."

After they were inside, Kristin went to the bathroom to splash water on her face while Storm opened his laptop and did the search for the sheriff. When the results came back, he called out for Kristin. When she entered the room, he turned toward her. "Now I know why Smirnov looked familiar and the sheriff of Adams County Oklahoma canceled on you." He pulled his cell phone out and dialed Jacob Gordon's number.

Chapter Thirty-Eight

Lawrence, KS

"Jacob, I am sending you a picture I want you to look at it and tell me what you think."

"Dakota, I am really not in the mood to play games right now."

"Not a game." He pressed the send button on his email account.

There was a lengthy pause. "Okay, the email's here." He was silent for a few moments. "This person sure resembles the picture of Ivan Smirnoff we have. But a few years older."

"Kind of what I thought."

"Where'd you get it?"

"Straight off the website of Adams County Oklahoma. He's identified as Sheriff Dwayne Butler."

"How did you identify him?"

"The sheriff's department and a couple of cities in the county were scheduled for training here at the academy over the next three weeks. They suddenly canceled. Kristin was extremely upset about it and told me."

"Will the cancellations hurt the academy?"

"While the place is profitable, three weeks in a row without generating revenue could cause a problem."

"Okay, tell her I know a sheriff in north Missouri trying to find a place to send his new K9 teams. I'll fill the vacancies for her. Tomorrow, I want you here early. We need to take a closer look at this Dwayne Butler."

"You got it, Jacob." He ended the call and turned to Kristin. "I filled your vacancies."

She gasped. "How…with who…that fast?"

"Well, I didn't do it, but Jacob knows a sheriff who needs a K9 training site."

She ran to him and wrapped her arms around his neck. "I love you."

He returned the embrace. "I know, I love you, too."

Kansas City

Storm placed the headshot of Dwayne Butler taken from the Adams County Oklahoma website on the left side of his computer monitor and the twenty-year-old mug shot of Ivan Smirnov beside it. There were subtle differences between the two photos. But the eyes, the cold, dark eyes were the same.

He picked up his desk phone and dialed the number of his IT friend located at the Marshals Service headquarters in Washington, DC. She answered on the third ring.

"IT Support, this is Lisa."

"Good morning, Lisa."

"Dakota Storm, how are you this morning?"

"Puzzled."

"Uh-oh. Does that mean you have a job for me?"

"I need a comparison on facial recognition software."

She giggled. "Oh, goody. One of my favorite things to do. Who is it?"

"Before I tell you, I would like for you to compare two photos. How do you want them?"

"JPG files work best."

He attached the two images to an email and clicked on the send icon. "On their way."

"How's Apollo?"

"He's doing good. In fact, he is sitting next to me. I think he hears your voice through the phone."

"Give him a scratch behind the ears for me." She paused. "Just got the email. Let me check the photos." Silence filled the phone call. "Who am I looking at here?"

"I'll tell you after you compare the photos."

"Okay. I have a few things to clean up and then I'll run it through the software."

"I appreciate it, Lisa."

The call ended, and he stood. Looking down at Apollo, he said, "I'm going for coffee. You staying here?" The border collie yawned and lay down. With his head still up, he stared at his handler, panting. With a chuckle, Storm said, "Yeah, getting coffee is boring."

When he returned to his cubicle, he saw an email alert from Lisa. He called her.

"That was fast. What'd you find?"

"The two pictures are the same guy. A couple of metrics were different, kind of like he had plastic surgery, but the key ones, like distance between the eyes all match."

"Thanks for confirming."

"Who is this guy?"

"He claims to be the sheriff of Adams County in Oklahoma. But the younger picture is of a Russian Mafia warlord who came here twenty years ago. See what you can find out about our Sheriff Dwayne Butler."

"Sure. Why the interest?"

"There's a strong possibility he may have been the man who ordered the murder of my wife and son."

———

Sitting in Jacob Gordon's office late morning, Storm summarized his research. "Facial recognition indicates the two photos are the same individual. Dwayne Butler's bio on the Adams County website contains the barest of details before 2010. He claims to have a bachelor's degree in law enforcement administration from Sam Houston State University. I checked with them this morning. They have a record of a Dwayne Butler. He graduated from there in 1998."

"There's a however in there somewhere, isn't there, Dakota?"

"Yes, sir. Lisa in the IT department found a reference to a Dewey Butler being killed in the line of duty in 2001. When she checked with the police department where he worked, she discovered his legal name was Dwayne Butler. That individual possessed a criminology degree from Sam Houston University. He had gone by the name Dewey since childhood, but, on all legal documents, he used the name Dwayne. I don't think Smirnov did his homework very well."

"So, you consider this proof that Dwayne Butler is in reality Ivan Smirnov?"

"Yes, sir."

"Will it hold up in court?"

"According to legal, it will."

"We have an outstanding federal warrant for Smirnov's arrest. Take a team of ten deputy marshals. Do you have a home address for him?"

"Yes."

Gordon took a deep breath and directed his gaze out one of the windows in his office. "Arresting him in Adams County could be problematic. We don't know how many of his deputies are loyal to him. Or, for that matter, being paid by Bayou Global."

"I'm aware of that, sir."

"Okay. Smirnov doesn't know we are aware of his true identity. Do some digging. See if there are any surrounding counties where the local sheriffs don't care for him. If there are, you'll need to lure him out of Adams County."

"Why not just snatch and grab him?"

"I guarantee Bayou Global has high-powered attorneys on staff."

Storm nodded. He tilted his head. "One thing puzzles me, Jacob. Why a county sheriff? Particularly in eastern Oklahoma."

Gordon started typing on his desktop computer keyboard. After several minutes, he smiled and motioned for Storm to come around to view his computer screen. Once the deputy arrived next to his chair, he pointed at a Google Map. "What's that, Dakota?"

"The Arkansas River."

"Exactly. It runs right through Adams County. Guess what the Arkansas River is?"

"Sorry, Jacob, geography was not one of my strong subjects in school."

"That's okay, I had to google it, too. The McClellan-Kerr Arkansas River Navigation System stretches 445 miles from the Mississippi River across Arkansas, terminating at the Port of Catoosa, near Tulsa, Oklahoma. It goes right through Adams County."

Storm stared at the map for a long moment. "They're smuggling illegal immigrants from the Gulf to Oklahoma. Sheriff Butler is there to protect the pipeline."

"Exactly. We're going to need a larger force of marshals to take this one down. I'll have to have a conference call with the Eastern District Oklahoma U.S. Marshal."

"Do you know him?"

A grin appeared on Gordon's lips. "He's a she. Do I know her? Hell yes. She and I were both deputies in Memphis for a number of years."

Abbie Hunt, one of the few female U.S. Marshals, presided over the Eastern District of Oklahoma. She accepted the phone call and said, "Well hello, Jacob. How's the vacation going up there in Kansas City?"

"Ha, ha, Abbie. How's sleepy Eastern Oklahoma?"

"Biggest problem I have is all the drug dealers coming out of Arkansas."

"Got a question for you."

"Sure, what's up?"

"Do you know the sheriff in Adams County?"

There was silence on the call. "Why do you ask?"

"Do you know him?"

"Unfortunately, I do."

"What's he like?"

"Secretive and uncooperative. Why?"

"What would you say if I told you he wasn't who he says he was?"

"Wouldn't surprise me. Who the hell is he?"

"Check your Marshals Service most wanted list and check for the name Ivan Smirnov." He heard the clicking of a computer keyboard and then a low whistle.

"Damn, Jacob. That son of a bitch looks a little like Sheriff Butler."

"That's because Butler is Smirnov."

"Holy shit. How'd you find this out?"

"One of my up-and-coming deputies."

"Dakota Storm?"

"How'd you know?"

"A few of my deputies just got back from training with him and his dog Apollo. They were impressed."

"He's an impressive young man." Gordon paused for a moment. "We want to take Butler down, Abbie. He's part of a human trafficking ring involved with smuggling young girls from Central America, plus guns and drugs. We actually think he is one of the higher-ups in the organization."

"I never have liked the guy. He's always seemed a bit slimy to me."

"We don't want to arrest him in Adams County. Too many things could go wrong."

"I agree with you."

"Does he ever leave the county?"

"Not to my knowledge, but I don't pay that much attention to him." She paused. "Wait a minute. What if we schedule a seminar on human trafficking. He would probably attend just to see what we know."

"How many sheriffs would that entail?"

"We can keep it intimate, let's say invite the ones bordering the Arkansas River."

"How long will it take to plan the seminar and get the sheriffs invited?"

"Couple of days. We can make it a one-day conference. We get more responses when we keep it short."

"Let me know when. We'll be ready to assist in the arrest."

"Sounds good, Jacob. I'll get back with you tomorrow."

Chapter Thirty-Nine

Adams County, Oklahoma

Two Days Later

Sheriff Dwayne Butler read the email from the Oklahoma Eastern District U.S. Marshal's office and frowned. He muttered to himself. "What does the bitch want now?" Butler, whose fluent accent-free English helped him hide in plain sight in the middle of the United States, rubbed his chin. A habit he found hard to break even after twenty years of trying. He stood and walked out of his office and motioned for the undersheriff to join him.

When the two men were alone and the door closed, Butler said, "Did you see the email from the U.S. Marshal?"

"Yeah, what's that all about?"

"Don't know, but I think it would be a good idea for me to go. I hope they can shed some new light on the activities we know are happening on the river. Can you handle things around here for a few days?"

"Sure, Dwayne. No problem." He stood and turned toward the door. "Do you have any county commission appearances scheduled?"

"No."

"Good, then have a good time in Muskogee."

After his assistant left and closed the office door, Butler read the email again and replied he would be attending. Yes, a meeting about smuggling up and down the Arkansas River would be of immense interest to him.

Butler's secret kept him hyper careful about discussing anything but sheriff's department matters around the office. He kept no close friends and concentrated on his job. What appeared to be aloofness to the deputies and civilian workers actually stemmed from his desire to protect his real identity.

He left the office at thirty minutes after five in the evening. When he got behind the steering wheel of his unmarked Ford Police Interceptor, he removed a small cell phone from the console. He typed a four-word text message. *We need to meet.* He sat there until the reply came back.

Three minutes later, he saw, *9-regular place.*

He replied with the letter *K.*

East of Fort Smith, Arkansas

The swirling haze of cigarette smoke and the din of multiple hushed conversations completed the atmosphere of a typical dive bar. To get around the law against smoking in a public place, the establishment charged a five-dollar membership fee, which would be credited back on the clientele's tab. Suddenly, patrons were in a private club, not public, which allowed smoking.

Into this shadowy environment, Ivan Smirnov, in the guise of Dwayne Butler, stepped. After his eyes adjusted to the dim lighting, he scanned the room for the individual he would be joining. In the far corner, away from the majority of tables, he spotted the man staring directly at him.

Making a beeline toward the table, he sat, leaned over, and said, "We may have a problem."

Alexi Yankovic, aka Denzel Cruz, snarled. "Great, what now?"

"The Eastern Oklahoma U.S. Marshal is inviting sheriffs' departments located along the Arkansas River to a meeting on smuggling."

"We need to know what they know."

"Exactly. That's why I'm attending."

"So, what's the problem?"

Smirnov straightened as a thin woman with droopy eyes stopped at the table. "What ya having, hon?"

"Bud draft."

She looked at Yankovic. "You good?"

He nodded.

After she wandered out of earshot, Smirnov continued, "We've had several associates detained by the marshals over the past month. Now, all of a sudden, they're holding this seminar?"

The other man narrowed his eyes and sipped his beer. He remained silent for an extended time. Finally, he nodded. "You think it's a trap?"

"I don't see how they would know about me. But it is possible."

"Then, don't go."

He paused as the waitress placed a mug in front of him. When she disappeared, he continued, "I'd be the only one on the invited list who didn't attend. If they're questioning my identity, doing so might raise additional suspicions."

Yankovic leaned over the table, his brow furrowed. "What did you do to raise doubts?"

The sheriff shook his head. "Nothing..." He paused and then pursed his lips. "With all the scrutiny over Bayou Global, I decided to cancel training for the K9 teams."

"Why?"

"There seemed to be too much attention being paid to the training facility we were scheduled to use."

"My dear Ivan. You don't get it, do you? Canceling your appointments at the facility raised red flags. The deputy who now lives there is the one giving us so much trouble."

"Then I have to go to the seminar. If I don't, it will confirm whatever questions they might have."

"I agree. But make sure you have an escape plan in place."

"Agreed." He took a sip of beer. "What are we going to do about the deputy U.S. Marshal?"

"At the moment, nothing. When things cool down, he'll have an accident, just like his wife and son."

Muskogee, OK

Dressed in his U.S. Marshals tactical gear, including dark-lensed wraparound sunglasses and an official U.S. Marshals cap, Dakota Storm patrolled the Ed Edmondson United States Courthouse parking lot in downtown Muskogee.

Apollo, dressed in his tactical harness, trotted by his side attached to a leash held by Storm.

One of several deputy marshals patrolling the courthouse grounds, he kept watch over the parking lot, searching for a specific vehicle from Adams County, Oklahoma. With his hat pulled low over his brow and shades, he blended in with the other deputies on patrol. Except for his unique black-and-white K9 companion, he did not stand out in the group.

His radio crackled. He heard, "Black unmarked Ford SUV entering parking lot from 5th Street entrance. Driver resembles suspect."

Directing his gaze in the direction indicated, he spotted the vehicle. From his perspective, he could not see the driver. So, he followed the truck's progress and watched it back into an empty parking space next to the Okmulgee Avenue exit.

When the driver stepped out of the vehicle, Storm recognized the man. He keyed his mike. "This is unit 3. Positive ID on driver."

"Copy that, unit 3."

"Unit 1 here. Following suspect into courthouse."

"Copy, unit 1. All units take assigned positions."

Smirnov disappeared inside the U.S. district courthouse. Storm and Apollo casually proceeded along the last row of cars heading toward the exit. Before he reached his destination, he strolled up to the suspect's SUV and attached a GPS tracking device within the passenger side front wheel well. The deputy and his K9 companion resumed their patrol of the parking lot.

He stopped and turned toward Smirnov's vehicle. The image of Judy and his son, Todd, invaded his thoughts. As a deputy sheriff on patrol that fateful night, he became the first emergency responder to arrive at the scene of the accident. He closed his eyes. Images of the horrific crash's aftermath still haunted his dreams.

For a moment, vertigo and the dark despair he experienced that night at the bridge, just before finding Apollo, returned. An image of Kristin laughing and stroking his face broke the spell. His eyes snapped open, and he looked around. No one seemed to notice his lapse in concentrating on the task at hand.

His partner, the ever-alert canine, stared up at him. "It's okay, Apollo, I'm back."

With a whimper, the dog's tongue appeared, and he started panting. The look Storm associated with a smile came to the canine's muzzle.

Three hours dragged by as he patrolled the parking lot, always within easy reach of Smirnov's car. At 2:06 p.m., his earbud crackled, and he stopped walking.

"All units, suspect just left the courthouse. Unit 3, your call. Detain or let him leave?"

Storm made the decision without hesitation. "His vehicle is tagged. Let's see where he goes."

"Roger that. All units hold back and proceed to meet unit 3."

As the deputy watched, Smirnov hurried toward his unmarked sheriff's vehicle in the crowded parking lot. The Adams County sheriff entered his vehicle, started the engine, and drove away.

When the vehicle disappeared west on Okmulgee Ave, Storm headed toward his Ford parked in a lot a block away. While he walked, he keyed his microphone. "Units 1 and 2 follow, units 3 and 4 will back you up."

"Roger, unit 3."

When Storm arrived at his Ford, he detached Apollo's

leash and let him scamper into the front passenger seat. He switched on his GPS monitoring unit and saw Smirnov's tracking device move over the map of Muskogee toward US 64. Not knowing which direction the suspect would go on the major highway, he keyed his mike. "All units, state your position. Starting with 1."

"Units 1 and 2 are a quarter of a mile behind target."

"Unit 4 is directly behind you, 3."

"This is unit 5. I'm at 69 and 169."

"Hold your position, 5. Anyone north?"

"Units 6 and 7 are north at junction of 69 and 62."

Storm replied, "Copy, 6 and 7."

"This is 4. What if he goes west on 62?"

"If he does, units 1 and 2 will follow."

The radio traffic grew silent as the blip on the map approached the north-south route of US 69.

He heard one of the deputies say, "He turned north on 69. Units 1 and 2 are following."

Storm thought, *why is he going north?* He keyed his microphone. "Stand by, units 6 and 7. Suspect is possibly heading your way."

"Copy that, 3."

The radio remained silent as Storm took the exit for North 69. He checked his rearview mirror and saw unit 4 make the turn with him. Several minutes later, he heard, "This is 6, target just passed our position."

Storm keyed the mike. "Units 5 and 6, fall in behind target. Unit 5, head this way for backup."

"Roger that, 3."

Increasing pressure on the SUV's accelerator, Storm asked, "Status, units 1 and 2."

"Target is crossing the Arkansas River and has his turn signal on."

"Repeat, 1?"

"He's turning onto County Road 830."

"What's there?"

"Appears to be a sand dredging company."

Storm realized the significance of Smirnov's destination. He changed the channel on his radio. "This is unit 3."

"Go, 3."

"Suspect has arrived at a sand dredging operation on the north side of the river."

Jacob Gordon did not reply immediately. "Why's that important?"

"They use barges to collect the sand. It's a perfect place to park one, smuggle something on shore, and no one would suspect anything."

"Okay, unit 3, what do you need?"

"This is Wagoner County. I believe we will need county sheriff's deputies to help seal this place off. Looking at it on Google Earth, there are four entry and exit points on the site. I need all of them blocked so the rest of us can do our job."

"Got it. The sheriff of Wagoner County is still here at the meeting. I'll get him aside, as soon as I can, and explain our situation."

"How long?"

"Don't know, I'll get back to you."

Chapter Forty

North of Muskogee, Oklahoma

An hour passed before Wagoner County deputies arrived and Storm explained what was needed. He gathered all the deputy U.S. Marshals around him and said, "We need this guy alive, if possible. But defend yourselves first. Any questions?"

Unit 4, Storm's normal partner, Jimmie Russel, grinned. "Let's go get him."

At exactly 3:33 p.m., the raid on the sand dredging facility took place.

Seven deputy U.S. Marshal units converged on the facility with Wagoner County officers backing them up and sealing off the exits from the facility. No lights or sirens were utilized.

Storm's Ford Police Interceptor parked behind Dwayne Butler's vehicle, penning it against the wall of a building. Apollo and his handler took the lead as other deputy U.S.

Marshals surrounded the main building on the grounds. All entered at the same time.

Unfortunately, the building appeared empty. It had been abandoned minutes before the deputies arrived. Radio traffic became hectic as numerous reports described men running in all directions.

With Apollo by his side, he went back out to the vehicle Smirnov arrived in. He opened the driver's door and said, "Find and track."

The dog jumped up into the driver's seat, sniffed for a moment, and then leapt back to the ground. Apollo picked up the trail immediately and took off running to the south, his handler and Russel close behind.

As the threesome raced toward the river, Storm noticed other officers guiding men back toward the main building. About a hundred feet in front of them, Apollo broke into a sprint. Glancing toward the river, the deputy saw what the dog chased. A lone figure attempted to scale a large sand pile. His progress slow as he kept slipping in the loose material.

Apollo reached the area and leapt at the man. He nipped at the heels and kept him from trying to scale the pile of sand again. When Storm was in range, he pulled his service weapon out and yelled, "U.S. Marshals, freeze. Hands in the air."

Smirnov ignored Apollo, turned toward Storm, drew his weapon, and brought it to bear on the two deputy marshals approaching his location. In the split second Dakota Storm had to decide, he chose the safety of his partner, Apollo, over keeping the fake sheriff alive. He yelled "Down." The dog dropped like a rock to the sand at the exact time both deputies and Smirnov fired their guns.

U.S. Marshals Jacob Gordon and Abbie Hunt, plus the Wagoner County sheriff took control of the crime scene as soon as they arrived from Muskogee.

EMTs assisted the wounded Jimmie Russel, and the Wagoner County coroner tended to the now dead Adams County Sheriff Dwayne Butler aka Ivan Smirnov. Gordon pulled Storm off to the side and asked, "Did Smirnov say anything before he died?"

The deputy shook his head. "Nope. He was dead before he hit the ground."

"It was a righteous shooting, Dakota."

"I know. I got Jimmie's bleeding stopped while we waited for the EMTs. They said he wasn't in any danger. But looks like I'm without a partner for a while."

"I can assign someone else."

"Not yet." Storm turned his attention to the body of Smirnov being transferred to an ambulance. "Our guys found records of all the barges that've stopped at this place. Since most of the barges haul sand. We think the ones labeled as *Import from the Gulf* may have contained the smuggled females."

Folding his arms, Gordon said, "The owner claims he knew nothing about Smirnov or the girls, claims he can prove he's innocent."

"Jacob, it really doesn't matter, unless some of these workers here start talking. This was a dead end. We didn't get to question Smirnov. We basically gained nothing."

"On the contrary, Dakota. This operation exposed one of the main routes used to transport sex trafficking in the Western United States." He patted Storm on the shoulder. "You did good, Deputy. You did good."

Gordon walked off to take care of other business, and Storm looked at Apollo sitting next to him. He knelt next to him and scratched his ears. "Well, buddy, guess we get to keep our jobs for another day." He stood. "Come on. Let's see what else we can learn about this place."

The two entered the main building where other deputy U.S. Marshals were searching through filing cabinets. Storm went to where one of the Eastern District deputies worked. "Hey, Bob, have you guys found anything yet referring to Bayou Global?"

"Funny you should ask, Dakota." He closed the drawer he had been searching and moved left two cabinets. He pointed to one drawer labeled Bayou Global. "We saw this one a few minutes ago. You weren't around, so I moved on. We felt you might want a crack at it."

"Thanks, I will."

Storm opened the drawer and started to flip through the folders. Apollo sat patiently by his side. About a third of the way through the drawer, he found a file labeled, *Pending Schedule*. He pulled it out and thumbed through the papers. Skimming the contents, he stopped on one particular page. He raised an eyebrow and said, "Holy shit."

Law enforcement activity at the sand dredging facility intensified twofold after Storm discovered the contents of the drawer. An intense behind-closed-door phone call between U.S. Marshal Jacob Gordon and the United States Attorney General resulted in the FBI field office in Tulsa being dispatched to take over the investigation.

A frustrated Gordon spoke to Storm outside the building, away from other investigators.

"Sorry, Dakota, the powers that be are transferring everything we've discovered here over to the bureau. We're basically done here. But I made sure the Marshals Service will be involved in any subsequent search warrants. Of which there will be many."

After a nod, Storm said, "Hopefully, the FBI Special Agent in Charge of the Tulsa office isn't compromised like Adam Lowe was."

"Abbie Hunt told me he's strictly by the book, but an excellent investigator."

The deputy folded his arms. "What's next for Apollo and me?"

"The file you found outlined the schedule for Bayou Global's deliveries for the next six months. You're still the lead on our task force. But the Justice Department will have to decide on which warrants to issue. That will take some time."

"Jacob, you and I both know once Bayou Global learns this place has been raided, they'll shut down the operation."

"I'm aware of that, as is our director, Calvin Fox. From the preliminary information we have, U.S. Marshals will be executing a number of raids in Louisiana tonight."

"Good."

Gordon looked over his glasses at the deputy. "How long have you been up?"

A shrug from Storm.

"Kind of what I thought." He checked his watch. "Grab a hotel room and then go home in the morning. Get some rest for a few days. We're done here. I need you fresh next week because I have a feeling, we're going to get busy."

"Yes, sir."

Storm found himself on the road before the sun peeked over the horizon the next morning. Apollo slept on the seat next to him. Coffee in a Styrofoam cup from the hotel lobby sat in the holder on the console.

He glanced over at Apollo. "Glad someone can sleep."

The dog raised its head and yawned.

"What are we missing here, buddy?"

No answer came from the canine.

"Denzel Cruz is the key to this group. Why is finding him so elusive?" The question hung in the air without an answer, and silence returned to the interior of the Ford.

An hour and a half later, as Storm crossed the Kansas state border, his cell phone chirped. "Storm."

"It's Gordon."

"Yes, sir."

"Where are you?"

"Kansas state line."

"They found a cell phone in Smirnov's car with one number called repeatedly. Text messages and physical calls."

Storm raised an eyebrow. "Alexi Yankovic?"

"That's the assumption. The number belonged to a phone bought at a Walmart in northeast Arkansas. The FBI tech guys believe that phone has been destroyed, or at least the battery removed."

"Where was its last known location?"

"East of Fort Smith, Arkansas. That fact, plus where the phone was purchased, implies Yankovic may be hiding in Arkansas."

"What city?"

"Jonesboro."

"That's actually close to Memphis."

"Huh." Gordon remained quiet for a few moments. "What do you think, Dakota?"

"I think it's a start, Jacob. Jonesboro is large enough for him to stay anonymous but small enough not to have a lot of federal agents running around."

"Want to take a shot at finding him?"

Storm did not answer right away. Finally, he said, "I didn't do a good job taking Smirnov alive. Maybe other deputy U.S. Marshals will have better luck with Yankovic."

"You sure?"

"For now, yes."

"Okay, I'll keep you abreast of the plans."

Chapter Forty-One

Lawrence, KS

Early Saturday Morning

Sipping coffee on the back deck, Dakota Storm used his other hand to scratch the neck of his constant companion, Apollo. The dog watched over the Kansas flatland with contentment.

Kristin emerged from the house dressed in a robe and holding her coffee cup. "Good morning." Before she sat next to Storm, she bent over and kissed him on the forehead. She peered over at the dog. "Good morning, Apollo."

The canine looked up at her, panting, his eyes bright.

After she sat, Storm asked, "Did you sleep okay?"

"Finally. I didn't sleep well while you were gone."

Placing his coffee mug on the arm of the deck chair, he reached over and patted her partially exposed thigh. "I didn't sleep much either this past week." He paused for a few moments and glanced over at her. The robe gaped open slightly at the top. He could see she wore nothing under the garment. The memory of their lovemaking the previous night made him smile. "I've been thinking."

She opened the robe a little wider. "I have, too."

He glanced at her again and took a deep breath. "I've been thinking about resigning as a deputy U.S. Marshal."

Closing the robe with one hand, she frowned. "Why?"

"A lot of reasons. Mainly, I don't like being away from home."

Her frown disappeared, replaced with a smile. "Glad you think of here as your home."

"Well, I do. But I think it's more about being away from you."

She let the robe gape open again.

He continued, "While I feel I'm part of something larger than myself as a marshal, I don't like how much time it steals. Time I could be with you and helping with the academy. I'm proud of my ability to train service dogs. Maybe that's a higher calling."

Reaching over, she took his hand. "Dakota, any decision to resign has to be yours and yours alone. While I would love to have you here full-time, you have a mission to complete before you will ever find peace within yourself."

The deputy remained silent. His eyes locked on hers.

"I don't want anything I do or say to prevent you from finishing your quest. Because if I did say anything, someday it might drive a wedge between us. Something I do not want to risk." She smiled and squeezed his hand. "You have to complete what you started, Dakota. I will be here when you finish, and I will help you with your journey to find peace within yourself."

Squeezing her hand back, he said, "Close your robe. You're giving me ideas."

"That's why it's open, silly."

He stood, pulled her to her feet, and led her inside the house.

Sunday Afternoon

In the middle of cleaning paintbrushes, Storm's cell phone chirped. He answered it on the third ring. "Storm."

"Where are you?" The voice was Jacob Gordon's.

"At home, why?"

"Be in my office first thing in the morning." The call ended.

Closing his eyes, he shook his head. "Geez, what now?"

Monday

At seven thirty in the morning, Storm sat in Gordon's office watching him pace while talking on the telephone.

"What's the final casualty report?" He kept his eyes locked on the carpet as he walked and talked. "That many. Shit." More listening. "Okay, keep me in the loop." He replaced the handheld set back in its cradle on his desk. "Guess you heard."

"How many?"

"We lost four deputy U.S. Marshals and five Craighead County deputies."

Storm frowned. "How?"

"They were ambushed. The burner phone we found in Smirnov's SUV only had one number on it. That number went active in Jonesboro on Friday. They located the signal at an old warehouse outside the city limits and staked it out. During the night, and well into Saturday, deputies observed a lot of traffic in and out of the building. So, they raided it early Sunday morning. It was booby trapped. The explosion brought down the roof. The collapse and the resulting fire resulted in the death of the nine deputies."

Storm remained quiet as he kept his gaze on Gordon. Finally, he asked, "Any bad guys?"

Gordon sat behind his desk and shook his head. "Three girls in their mid-teens were injured. They're being inter-viewed as soon as the doctors will allow. One of them has been able to talk so far. She told investigators they were brought to the place on Thursday from Memphis."

Storm pursed his lips. "Memphis, again. Why is Memphis at the center of most of this activity?"

"Good question, Dakota. I want you there by tomorrow night. But first, I want you to stop in Jonesboro on the way and learn more about the explosion. Today, you need to have a chat with Landry."

With a nod, Storm asked, "Will this incident intensify the FBI's involvement?"

"Yes. We can't keep them out now. Washington is freaking out. With Smirnov's death, and now the explosion, it's become too big for only one agency. The Coast Guard is involved as is ATF."

"Why the Coast Guard?"

"That file you found in the Oklahoma sand dredging company."

"Yeah, what about it?"

"It identified five ships used to transport girls to the Port of New Orleans. They are then transferred to barges, moved up the river to Memphis via the Mississippi or on the Arkansas River to Tulsa. Since the 8th District of the Coast Guard has jurisdiction over the heartland, they're the ones confiscating the ships and barges."

"How many rescues?"

Gordon smiled for the first time since Storm's arrival. "We've been fortunate. All five ships have been intercepted. They've confiscated ten barges containing evidence of human cargo. You'll be happy to know thirty underaged girls from Central America have been rescued."

Storm offered Gordon a slight grin. "Maybe what we did in Oklahoma actually did some good."

"It did a lot of good. By current count, we have fifty members of Bayou Global under arrest with five dead. Along with the seized ships and barges. I suspect, with Smirnov's death, Yankovic has got to be feeling pressure."

Standing, Storm asked, "Yeah, all it cost were the lives of nine law officers. Where's Landry?"

"Same place: Jackson County Jail. They're expecting you by ten this morning."

"Good. Has he made a deal yet?"

"No, he's been wanting to talk to you again. It appears he only trusts you."

"Somehow, I doubt that. He's waiting to make sure he gets the best deal he can."

"Let me know what you find out. I can have the district attorney general there within an hour."

The orange jumpsuit Victor Landry wore contrasted with

the pallor of his complexion. He sat across from Storm in an interview room.

"What do you want this time, Storm?"

"To update you on what's transpired since we last talked."

"Save your breath. I don't care."

"You should."

Rolling his eyes, the prisoner tilted his head. "Well, I don't."

With a grin, Storm extracted a photo from his shirt pocket. "Recognize this man?" It was a copy of the official portrait from the Adams County Oklahoma website showing the late Dwayne Butler.

"Never seen him before."

"Take a closer look."

Landry hesitated but studied the photograph a little closer. "It's a picture of a sheriff. Big deal."

"You're right." Storm tapped the image with his finger. "That is the late Dwayne Butler, you probably knew him as Ivan Smirnov."

"What do you mean, late?"

"The term normally refers to someone who is deceased. Smirnov's dead, Victor."

"Let me see that."

Storm handed the prisoner the picture. After careful study, he handed it back. "Yeah, it looks like Smirnov."

"That's because it is. He's no longer a problem for you. Time to make a deal with the district attorney."

"Yankovic is still out there, Storm. He's more dangerous than Smirnov."

"Yeah, well, Alexi Yankovic's little empire is shrinking at an alarming rate. His ships have been confiscated and, including you, forty-nine Bayou Global employees are under arrest. His fleet of barges has been depleted by ten. He's also being charged with the death of nine law enforcement officers."

Landry remained silent, a slow smile developing on his face.

"We don't know exactly how many men work for Yankovic, but the loss of forty-nine has to hurt."

The prisoner continued to stare at the image of Smirnov. "That's about two thirds of them."

"So, you see, Victor, making a deal with us might save you from being included in charges in the death of nine law enforcement officers." Storm leaned over the table. "I don't have to remind you of how pissed off that makes us."

"I have an alibi."

"You were a top lieutenant. You're guilty by association with this bunch. Sucks for you."

The prisoner blinked. "What if I decide to make a deal?"

"You said that last time we met."

"I changed my mind. But, since you've brought news, I think I'll take you up on a deal."

"You might actually see the sun again. You're looking quite pale."

The man studied the tabletop, his hands clasped in front of him. "Make the call, Storm. I'm ready to talk."

"Wise decision, Victor."

Lawrence, Kansas

Storm packed his duffle bag as Kristin leaned against the bedroom doorframe. He turned his attention to her. "I stopped by the sheriff's department before I got back this afternoon."

"Why?"

He walked over and took her into his arms. She returned the embrace. "I asked him to keep an eye on the place while I'm gone."

After she placed her head on his shoulder, he felt her nod. "Bruno won't leave my side while you and Apollo are gone. He's perceptive."

"Good."

"I also called Frank Cole."

She raised her head. "Why?"

"I asked him if he knew anyone who could help watch over the place."

"That's not necessary, Dakota. I'll be fine."

"Peter Khan volunteered. You won't even know he's around."

She stared at the deputy.

"Apparently, when Peter was in the CIA, he was pretty good at that sort of thing."

A tear trickled down her cheek. "How did I ever get along without you?"

"Same way I got along—one day at a time." He felt her shudder with a sob.

Chapter Forty-Two

Jonesboro

Monday

Alexi Yankovic listened, without comment, to the phone call from one of his associates. When the briefing finished, Yankovic ended the call abruptly. He turned his attention to the other person in the room. "Nine deputies. Only nine."

The guest shrugged. "Nine less federales to deal with, Alexi."

"My dear Javier, making light of this turn of events does not become you."

Javier Perez, a capo in one of the more violent Central American cartels, sat on a sofa with his arm stretched over the top, his demeanor unreadable. "I am not making light of recent events, my friend. But, if you wish, I can explain how unhappy some of my compadres are with your recent failures. The fact you eliminated nine policemen will set well with them."

"What do you mean failures?"

Perez jumped to his feet, his nostrils flared, and he clenched his jaw. In a low growl, he said, "What about the loss of the five ships and many of the barges we loaned you? Your top lieutenants are either dead or in prison. These events do not give my associates what you Americans call, a warm and fuzzy feeling about your abilities. In fact, there is talk of breaking our alliance with your organization."

Yankovic folded his arms and narrowed his eyes. "I am not an American. I'm Russian."

"Whatever, Alexi. You have experienced a lot of failures lately. My associates do not like failure."

Pointing his finger at Perez, Yankovic growled, "My organization has paid you millions of dollars for your so-called assistance. We were successful without you. If you don't wish to participate, fine. We can be successful without you." He pointed toward the hotel room door. "There's the exit. All you have to do is walk out, and our arrangement is canceled."

Placing his hands on his hips, Perez chuckled. "That's the trouble with you Russians. Your overinflated egos resulted in the breaking up of the Soviet Union, and now your country is isolated from the world. All because of egos."

"Spare me your insults, Perez. I have more important matters to attend to than listening to you tell me how great the Central American cartels are. So far, all you have assisted with is supplying ships and the merchandise. All of which cost me money. This so-called partnership has bene-fitted only one side, yours."

The El Salvadorian threw his head back and laughed.

"Now that we have insulted each other, how can I help you?"

Yankovic took a deep breath and let it out slowly. "For now, I need soldiers. Men who are more interested in making money than climbing ladders to power."

"In other words, men who are more brawn than brain."

"That's one way to put it."

"I can supply those men. My country and the surrounding ones seem to have ample numbers of those types."

"How long?"

"Do they need to speak English?"

"Yes."

"Give me a month to recruit. How do I get in touch with you?"

Yankovic gave him a phone number. "It's a burner."

Perez walked to the room's door. "How many do you need?"

"Twenty." He paused. "Do you have any of your specialty merchandise with you?"

"Always."

"How much?"

"I will put it on your bill."

The two men met again in the parking lot, and a gun case was transferred to Yankovic's trunk. When the lid closed, he turned to Perez. "When will you know about the men?"

"I will be in touch." He got in his car and pulled out of the parking lot.

After returning to his room, Yankovic made ready to leave the motel. His next stop would be Lawrence, Kansas. Time to finally take care of the source of all his problems, Deputy U.S. Marshal Dakota Storm.

Unbeknownst to Storm, he and Yankovic passed each other on US 63 about halfway between Thayer, Missouri and Hardy, Arkansas. Storm's trek took him southeast while the Russian drove northwest. Arriving an hour and a half later, in Jonesboro, he met with a team of deputy U.S. Marshals at the site of the collapsed warehouse. ATF personnel were there investigating the explosion.

Nathan Parker, a deputy U.S. Marshal from Memphis shook Storm's hand. "Heard you were coming. How've you been, Dakota?"

"Good, Nathan. How 'bout yourself?"

"Not so good. Lost two fellow deputies out of Memphis."

"That's why I'm here. Sorry for your loss." He paused and studied the collapsed building. "Do you know anything about the explosive?"

Parker nodded. "Ammonium nitrate and diesel oil. A lot of it."

"How the hell did they obtain that much ammonium nitrate?"

The fellow deputy smiled. "You're in the Arkansas Delta, Dakota. It is considered some of the most fertile land in the world. Rice, cotton, and soybean farms are one of the main industries around here."

"Forgot the Mississippi River isn't that far from here."

"You got it. There's a farm supply company in practically every small community in this area. They all sell it. It's legal to buy, but not in the quantities we believe they used in the bomb. Probably bought it from numerous store locations. ATF has someone checking on it."

"Nathan, how did the girls survive?"

"They almost didn't. They managed to break out a window when the fire started. While they did escape, most of them have severe burns."

Storm turned his attention to the deputy. "Do you know a bar called Blues on Beale in Memphis?"

"Yeah, why?"

"We know it's owned by Bayou Global. Any word on what's going on there?"

"Burned about a week ago. Police found a body in the back. It was identified as Robert Trent."

"They're tying up loose ends, Nathan."

"Didn't think of that, but yeah, it sounds like it."

Folding his arms, Storm returned his gaze to the burned rubble of the warehouse. "I had planned to drive on down, but there's no point if Trent's dead." He paused. "When this warehouse was being watched, how many men were seen coming and going?"

"I was on the team. We determined there were at least four different individuals."

Pulling a photo out of his shirt pocket, he handed it to Parker. "Was this guy one of them?"

Putting on glasses, Parker studied the picture for several moments. "Possibly. I'd have to check the photos we took. Who is he?"

"He's goes by Denzel Cruz. His real name is Alexi Yankovic, ex-Russian Mafia. It's the first official sighting of him we've had."

Parker held the photo and raised an eyebrow. "So, this is Cruz." He paused for a moment. "Wait a minute. Now I remember. This guy resembles a suspect captured by a security camera across the street from the Blues on Beale bar the night of the fire. We weren't able to ID him due to the poor quality of the image."

"That tells me Yankovic has lost so many men in our raids, he's having to do some of the grunt work himself."

"Is that good?"

"Yes, it is. The more involved with operations he is, the easier it will be for us to find him. I'll update the most wanted list notation on where he was last seen."

Parker nodded.

"Unfortunately, Nathan, it might mean he's shutting down the operation and getting ready to leave the country. If he does, we've lost him."

"I'll have our guys hit the hotels in the area and see if anyone's seen him."

"I'll help."

Tuesday - Early Afternoon

It took most of the morning for the six deputy U.S. Marshals to canvas the Jonesboro hotels with only one hit. Parker found the motel and had Storm join him.

"Deputy Storm, this is hotel owner, Nader Patel."

The two shook hands.

"Mr. Patel identified the picture of Yankovic as his guest registered under the name Denzel Cruz. He checked out yesterday morning after staying four days."

Storm asked, "Mr. Patel, did Mr. Cruz have any guests you were aware of during his stay?"

"Yes." Patel answered without the accent Storm anticipated. "A Hispanic man inquired about him on Monday morning. Three hours later, Mr. Cruz checks out."

"Did the Hispanic man leave a name?"

"No." The man looked at both the deputy marshals and blinked rapidly. "Am I in trouble?"

Parker tilted his head. "Should you be?"

"No. No, no, no, no. But this is not the first time police have questioned me about a guest. I run a very clean motel, my rates are less than the national chains, and sometimes people of questionable backgrounds stay here. Sometimes I feel like I am being profiled because I'm from Pakistan."

Storm smiled. "Sir, I can assure you, we've had a team of deputies with the U.S. Marshals Service fanned out across Jonesboro looking for Mr. Cruz. He just happened to stay at your hotel. You weren't targeted. Can I see a copy of his registration?"

"Of course. Let me print it out for you."

Studying the registration, the two deputies zeroed in on the license plate number. Parker said, "Tennessee plates."

"It confirms our suspicions he was staying in this area."

"I'll call them in, Dakota." He turned to the hotel owner. "Mr. Patel, Deputy Storm has a few more questions for you."

After Parker stepped out of the office, Storm turned back to the owner. "Mr. Patel, did you get a security camera video of the man who asked about Cruz?"

"Yes, of course. Let me show you."

A half hour later, Storm had a still shot of Cruz's guest. He emailed the photo to Liz in Washington.

While the two deputies waited in the motel's parking lot for her to reply, Parker filled in Storm about the license plate.

"It's a 2018 Chevy Equinox registered to Bayou Global."

"These guys don't put anything in their own name."

"Apparently not."

"Okay, Nathan, we know the make, model, and license plate. Why don't you request a nationwide BOLO on the SUV and identify him as Denzel Cruz. Make sure he's labeled extremely dangerous."

"You got it, Dakota."

While Parker called in the BOLO, Storm answered a call on his cell phone. "Storm."

"Dakota, it's Liz. I've got an ID on the picture."

"That was fast."

"Yeah, seems the FBI and DEA want this guy as well. He's Javier Perez, a top lieutenant in an El Salvadorian drug cartel. He's on the FBI's most wanted list."

"Shit." He paused for a moment. "For what?"

"Racketeering conspiracy, cocaine importation conspiracy, possession of machine guns, and conspiracy to commit securitiesS fraud."

"Machine guns?"

"Yes."

"Damn."

"What's the matter, Dakota?"

"This clown just met with Alexi Yankovic."

"Oh dear."

"Yeah, oh dear."

Chapter Forty-Three

Eastern Kansas

Having stayed in a motel outside Harrisonville, Missouri. Yankovic drove north on US 59 heading toward Lawrence. A few miles north of Ottawa, Kansas, he noticed a sheriff's car following him. Keeping his eye on the road with occasional checks of his rearview mirror, he kept his speed right at seventy. The sheriff's car gradually caught up and passed him on the left of the divided highway. As it drove past, the deputy glanced at Yankovic with a disinterested expression. The sheriff's car then accelerated and drove ahead.

When it was several hundred feet farther ahead, the sheriff's car flipped on its emergency lights, accelerated, and disappeared into the distance. Breathing a sigh of relief, the fugitive kept his Equinox at the speed limit, trying not to be noticed.

Four miles later, he exited US 59 when it intersected US 56 and drove east. This part of Kansas contained fields of corn, silos, the occasional farmhouse, and not much else.

Slowing the vehicle on the sparsely traveled highway several miles later, he made a K-turn to reverse the SUV's direction. Now facing west, he parked and studied the sky. The sheriff's car passing him and then running with emergency lights gave him pause. Had it been a coincidence, or did they know what type of vehicle he drove? The latter concerned him.

The few clouds visible were cirrus, high, wispy, and scattered. After sitting and observing for a few minutes, he exited the vehicle and stretched his legs. He scanned the skyline to the west looking for any signs of surveillance.

Ten minutes later, he observed a single engine plane flying high above the US 59 intersection with US 56. The plane continued to fly south. He kept his gaze on it until it shrank into a dark speck.

Turning his attention back to his current location, he consulted Google Maps on his cell phone. According to the map, he could continue east and use back roads to travel north. These roads would lead him to the area of Kansas where the dog-training academy was located. Returning to the driver's seat, he drove the Equinox farther east, searching for a particular road.

Kansas State Highway Patrolman Bob Mercer flew the Cessna 206 out of Topeka for the patrol's air service. When he reached Ottawa, KS, he turned the aircraft back toward the north and radioed in.

"Negative contact on suspect SUV. He might have turned off on 56."

"Copy Air 1, fly east on 56 and get back to us."

"Roger, base. Air 1 out."

Yankovic turned north onto Douglas County Road 1055 when he got to Baldwin City. This route would take him to the southeast corner of Lawrence, Kansas. According to the Google Map function on his phone, he could find an out-of-the-way hotel and then figure out how to get to the dog-training facility. He maintained the speed limit while he drove.

In his driver's side mirror, he noticed the white plane flying perpendicular to the road he was on. This confirmed his suspicions they knew what kind of a car he drove. Keeping as calm as possible, he exited the county highway onto a small dirt road lined with trees.

Securing the Equinox under a canopy of branches, he stepped out and watched the plane continue its path to the east. After the plane disappeared from view, he walked back to the rear of the Chevy SUV and lifted the tailgate. A briefcase lay under his duffle bag. Moving it to an open space of the cargo area, he opened the latches and removed the Heckler & Koch MP5K. He attached a magazine and then closed the tailgate. When he got back in the driver's seat, he laid the H&K on the passenger seat.

Things were going to get serious from here on out.

Jonesboro, AR

Storm answered his cell phone on the third ring. "Storm."

"It's Gordon. Where are you?"

"Jonesboro."

"Get your ass back to Lawrence, ASAP."

"What's happened?"

"A Douglas County sheriff's deputy ID'd Yankovic's car on US 59 going north. They sent a plane out and couldn't find it. My guess is he turned off the main highway and is now using back roads to get to the academy."

Storm listened as he walked to his vehicle. He made a hand signal, and Apollo jumped into the car the second the door swung open. Getting behind the wheel, he drove the SUV back toward north US 63.

When Gordon finished talking, Storm said, "I'm seven hours away. I'll call Kristin and tell her to drive to KC."

"They don't know where he is, Dakota. You sure you want her driving?"

Storm remained silent. "No, you're right, I don't. Can you get sheriff deputies out there?"

"Already made the call."

"Okay. I'll be there as soon as I can."

The call ended as the deputy merged onto north US 63. The temptation to light up his hidden emergency lights came to him, but he needed the time to think. Concentrating on dodging civilian traffic would not allow him to plan his next steps.

He pressed the speed dial for Frank Cole.

"Any news, Dakota?"

"Where's Peter?"

"In Lawrence. Why?"

The deputy thought for a moment. "Can you contact him?"

"Yes."

"Alexi Yankovic was spotted driving north toward Lawrence in eastern Kansas. He might already be there."

"Do you know what he's driving?"

"Yes, a Chevy Equinox." Storm recited the license plate number. "Tennessee plates."

"He's panicking. This is the first mistake he's made."

"I thought the same thing. Tell Peter he may have possession of a submachine gun."

Cole did not speak for a moment. "How?"

"We have evidence he met with an El Salvadorian who specializes in supplying such weapons."

"I'll tell him."

"Also, let him know I'll be there in seven hours."

"Got it."

The call ended, and the deputy looked over at his companion. "You good?"

The dog raised his head and started panting, his eyes almost closed.

"You're good." He concentrated on the road, once again lost in thought.

Five minutes later, he glanced at the dog again. "Apollo, I am struggling why Yankovic is still driving a vehicle that belongs to him. He makes very few mistakes, and this seems to be a doozy."

Apollo only yawned, which produced a slight whine. He closed his eyes.

Storm continued, "I think you're right. He's been having others do things for him for so long, he's gotten a little lazy. Do we assume he'll continue this trend, or is it to throw us off?"

The dog's eyes opened and his panting grew more rapid.

"Yeah, I think we need to assume he'll steal something and abandon the Chevy." He paused. "You are a creature of few words, my friend, but what you do say is wise."

Checking the GPS function on his phone, he muttered, "This is going to be a long drive."

He pressed the icon to call Kristin using the hands-free function on his Ford and waited for her to answer. The phone went to voice mail. "Wakarusa K9 Academy, sorry I missed your call. Please leave a message and a number. I'll get right back to you."

"It's me. Call when you can."

Checking the time, he realized she would be out cleaning the dog kennels after the day's activities. The fluttering sensation in his stomach intensified.

Twenty intense minutes passed without a call. At exactly 7:34 p.m., his phone vibrated. He answered it immediately. "Kristin?"

"Hey, Dakota. Are you on your way home?"

"Yes." He hesitated. "Are you in the house right now?"

"Yes, why?"

"Where's Bruno?"

"Lying at my feet. Again, why?"

"I want you to lock all the doors, turn on the alarms, and take Bruno with you to our bedroom. Do not answer the door, and do not leave the room. I will be there in, uh… five hours."

"What's going on?"

"Get your Sig Sauer from the nightstand drawer. I want you to keep it with you until I get home."

"You're scaring me, Dakota."

"I hope so. Someone is in Lawrence who may want to harm me. I don't want him finding you instead. Bruno will raise an alarm if something odd happens. Pay attention to him."

"When will you be home?"

"Five hours, max."

"That's midnight, Dakota."

"I know. Can you stay awake?"

"I can now."

He pursed his lips and pressed harder on the accelerator. "Kristin, I love you. I have sheriff's deputies in route to help guard the house. I also have backup in position. You will be fine. Bruno will be there to assist. You know how to use the Sig. Do not hesitate to use it if someone gets close to you. Understand?"

She did not answer right away. "Yes." There was silence on the phone for several moments. Finally, she said, "I love you, too, Dakota. I'll be fine. Hurry home."

"That's the plan."

Chapter Forty-Four

Lawrence

Twenty Minutes Before Midnight

Dakota Storm held his badge out the window as he pulled up to two Douglas County sheriff deputies blocking the road to the academy. "Deputy U.S. Marshal Dakota Storm, Deputies."

The one closest to his window shined his flashlight on the badge and then on Dakota's face.

"Hey, Dakota. It's Josh and Darren. Glad you're back."

"Thanks, guys. Seen anything?"

Both men shook their heads. "Other than a couple of false alarms, nothing."

Handing them a business card, Storm said, "This is my cell phone. If you see or hear anything weird, could you send a text or give me a call?"

Josh put the card in a pocket on his uniform shirt. The

thickness of his chest enhanced by the bulk from his body armor gave the sheriff's deputy a menacing appearance. "Sounds good, Dakota."

As Storm pulled away from the roadblock, Apollo sprang to his feet on the passenger seat and pressed his nose against the side window. A low growl rumbled deep in his throat.

"What's the matter, boy?"

The dog barked once, its concentration out the window. Slowing, Storm pulled his cell phone out and started to make a call. A text message appeared from an unknown number. *Glad you're back. All clear so far on the Kansas plains. Pete.*

Reaching over, Storm touched Apollo on the back. "It's okay, buddy. He's one of the good guys."

Looking over his shoulder back at Storm, Apollo started panting and relaxed.

Storm entered the dark kitchen through the doorway. Movement ahead startled him as arms wrapped around his neck.

"Gawd, I'm glad you're home." The kiss he received from Kristin became long and passionate.

"Glad I'm home, too." He returned the embrace.

Kristin buried her head against his neck.

He said, "Did you miss me?"

With a wide grin, she said, "Of course, I did. Silly question."

Returning the embrace, he sighed. "I missed you, too. That was the longest drive of my life. Are you, okay?"

"I am now that you're home."

His cell phone interrupted the welcome-home party. Breaking from her embrace, he checked the ID and answered immediately. "Storm."

"Hey, Dakota. This is Josh with the sheriff's department.

Just got a call. KC cops found a Chevy Equinox with Tennessee plates burned out in the Northeast Industrial District near the Missouri River. There's a body in it."

"When?"

"About an hour ago. No ID on the victim."

"It won't be Yankovic."

"Why?"

"He figured out we knew about his car. Whoever is in the vehicle will be the owner of the car he's stolen."

"Okay, I'll pass along your theory."

"Thanks, Josh."

At the same time, he ended the call, another notification appeared on the screen. This time, it was Jacob Gordon. He answered, "I'm back, Jacob."

"Good. They found Yankovic's SUV."

"I just heard. It's not him."

"I'm at the scene. You're correct. Fire marshal determined it's a female."

"He'll have her car."

"They haven't found an ID on the victim. Plus, it is burned so bad, identifying the body could take a while."

"Bad enough to make bone DNA questionable?"

"That's what I'm being told."

Storm remained silent as he stared at Kristin who listened with a frown.

"Jacob, you know he did this on purpose to slow down discovering what type of vehicle he's driving."

"Hadn't thought of that. But it makes sense."

"I hope everyone on the task force has been told to shoot to kill. Yankovic will not hesitate to kill a police officer."

"I'll re-emphasize those instructions." Gordon paused.

"Now that you're back, don't leave the premises until we get this guy, Dakota."

"I have no plans to."

When the call ended, Kristin hugged herself and asked in a voice just above a whisper. "What's happened?"

"You sure you want to know? It'll make you worry even more."

She tilted her head. "Dakota, don't start treating me like a child. What happened?"

"Yankovic's Chevy was found burned out near the river in KC. There was a body inside. A female body. Identifying her will take time, which means, the police won't know what he's driving for at least a day or two."

"I'm not running from this SOB."

"Neither am I." Storm put his arms around her again and kissed her forehead. "Are the cameras in the kennel on?"

"Yes."

"Let's give the dogs a chance to relieve themselves and then we'll get busy in here."

By four in the morning, Storm held Kristin as they reclined on a sofa in the living room. Both slept fitfully but would be ready if the dogs alerted them to any danger.

Bruno woke them first. He stood still near the front door and barked once. Both dog trainers woke at the sound. Kristin rushed to her dog and kneeled next to him. Apollo trotted up to Storm and whimpered.

He turned to his partner. "Talk to me, buddy."

Apollo stared at his handler for a split second and then

tore out for the back of the house. Storm turned to Kristin. "Get behind something solid."

She positioned herself behind the bricks of the free-standing fireplace separating the kitchen from the front room. Holding her Sig Sauer P229 with both hands, she whistled for Bruno. He dashed to her side as a low growl emerged from his throat. She patted him on the head. "Good, boy." Her attention, and the dog's, trained on the front door.

Storm and Apollo dashed toward the back of the house.

Positioning himself between the refrigerator and the rear entrance, Storm felt his cell phone vibrate with an incoming text message. He checked it. *Someone is here. P.*

Removing his Sig Sauer P226 from its holster, he touched the top of Apollo's head then gave him the hand signal to follow. He moved silently to a small bedroom where they kept the laptop controlling the security system. He activated the computer and clicked on the academy security program. An image from six cameras on the property appeared.

Each image covered a strategic section of the academy. Three monitored the kennel area, which for the moment was unpopulated. The remaining three were trained on the house. All six HD units gave him a detailed real-time depiction of events.

On the upper left image, a man with a weapon larger than a pistol in his hand crept around the kennels. With his thumb, he typed a reply to the text message still showing on his phone. *Man with gun near kennel. Do you copy?*

Seconds dragged like minutes as he waited for the reply. He kept an eye on the shadow, which had now shifted to the upper middle camera image.

Checking on Apollo, he saw the dog staring at him. An idea came to him. He said, "Alarm."

The border collie gave a series of sharp barks. The deputy rubbed the dog's head, smiled, and said, "Good, boy." He turned his attention back to the monitor.

Peter Khan, retired CIA operator, maneuvered in the lush prairie grass surrounding the academy for a better view of the kennels. Wearing a hunter's ghillie suit, he would have been difficult to see in the daylight. At night, he was invisible.

In this part of the state, the land could only be described as flat. Trees and brush existed, but not around the academy, making the intruder's entry into the area difficult. Somehow, the shadowy figure managed to sneak past numerous county sheriff deputies. But now he drew the attention of the ex-CIA field agent.

He moved his suppressed Remington 700 outfitted with a Sightmark HD Night Vision scope to get a better view of the kennel area. The man carried what Khan suspected was an H&K MP5K. The cell phone in the ghillie suit pocket vibrated, but he ignored it. Diverting his attention from the shadowy figure making progress toward the house would be a strategic blunder.

The figure, dressed in black, stood out in the greenish-hue of the night-vision scope. He made slow progress, inching his way toward the rear of the residence.

Khan heard a series of sharp barks coming from the interior of the dwelling. This caused the intruder to freeze. Placing the crosshairs of the scope on the man's head, he squeezed the trigger. Just before it broke, the man jerked backward. The muffled sound of the shot and the loud crack of a bullet hitting a brick-and-mortar column between kennel sections broke the night's silence. The black-clad man hesitated only a second before reversing course and running toward the open flatland.

Khan mumbled under his breath, "Shit."

The black-clad figure froze. Storm was sure a debate waged within the intruder's mind on how to proceed. Apparently with his decision made, he took a few steps back. As soon as this occurred, the deputy saw a head-high spark on a concrete wall directly where the trespasser previously stood. The mysterious shadow reversed course and took off in a full run.

"Huh." His cell phone vibrated. "Storm."

"Didn't know the guy could run that fast."

"Was that you, Peter?"

"Yeah, not as good of a shot as I used to be."

"Think he's still running?"

"Let's wait until first light. I want to track him and see where he parked."

"Apollo's an excellent tracker. He can help."

"Perfect."

Chapter Forty-Five

The Plains of Kansas

Apollo trudged through prairie grass in front of Storm and Peter Khan as the sun popped over the eastern horizon. Two Douglas County sheriff's deputies followed close behind. The dog kept his nose close to the ground. Occasionally he would stop, raise his head, and sniff the air. He would then either keep going straight or change direction. His last turn took him left.

Khan asked, "Where's this leading to?"

"We're getting close to a county road that passes to the north and west of the academy. This is probably where he parked."

"Didn't know border collies could track."

"If trained properly, they make excellent trackers."

"I take it he's been properly trained."

Storm gave the ex-CIA man a mischievous smile. "He has a few other tricks up his sleeve as well."

The group came to a gravel road. Apollo once again sniffed and promptly sat.

"This is where he parked." Turning to the deputies, Storm said, "Not sure what they can find, but could you get the forensic van out here?"

One of the deputies nodded, walked a few paces to the south, and spoke into his shoulder mic.

Returning his attention to the country road, Storm pointed at tire tracks in the dirt. "My guess is those are his."

Khan stayed in the grass beside the road and studied the area to the west and to the east. "It gets dark as hell out here, doesn't it?"

"If it's cloudy, you can barely see your hand in front of your face."

"Then how did he locate your house?"

Storm stared at the older man for several moments. He turned to the deputy not on the radio. "Hey, Josh."

"Yeah, Dakota."

"Did you have men patrolling this area last night?"

"Most of the time, unless they were needed elsewhere."

"I take it they didn't see anything."

"As far as we know, they didn't."

"Check with them, just to make sure."

"You got it." He joined his partner out of earshot.

Returning to studying the tire tracks, Storm noticed a series of dark reddish-brown drops. He turned to Khan. "Peter, take a look at this." He pointed to the trail.

The ex-CIA man studied the closest droplet to the grass. "Appears to be blood."

"Kind of what I thought." Violating all of his crime scene training, the deputy carefully followed the drips until they stopped in the middle of the road. Looking at the tire tracks, Storm knelt for a closer look. "He was bleeding and got into the vehicle here." He pointed to the spot.

One of the county deputies returned and said, "Dakota, they were called to a multi-vehicle accident on 59 at 3:14 a.m."

Storm nodded. "We saw Yankovic around four. So, he was watching them and took advantage of them being gone. Tell the forensic team we have a blood trail."

"Got it. I'll let Darren know." He walked back to where the other deputy continued his discussion with the sheriff's dispatcher.

Storm studied the pool of drying blood in the middle of the road. "This one is larger, like he stood here for a length of time and more blood dripped." Looking up at Khan, he asked, "I thought you said you missed him?"

"I did miss him."

"By how much?"

Khan spread his hands apart. "Oh, about a foot or less, why?"

"What'd you hit."

"One of the brick columns separating the kennel sections."

"What kind of ammo?"

"308 Winchester, why?"

Storm nodded. "If you hit a brick wall a foot from him, he probably caught pieces of the shattered bullet and shards of brick and mortar."

"I was aiming for a head shot."

"I believe our Mr. Yankovic might be wounded, Peter."

"Then we'd better check out the kennel."

"Yeah, I think we should. Let me mark this area." When he finished, Storm patted his hand against his leg. Apollo fell into step next to him, leaving the deputies to wait for the forensic van as they headed back to the academy.

Lunchtime found Dakota Storm meeting with other deputies of the U.S. Marshals Service in their district courthouse offices in downtown Kansas City. The deputy faced a map projected on the wall of the area from KC all the way to Lawrence. Storm stood pointing at various spots on the map.

"Each of these dots represent either a hospital or an urgent care facility. We know Yankovic was injured last night during a failed invasion of the Wakarusa K9 Academy. We need to canvas these facilities to see if anyone matching the Russian's description was treated for injuries to the face."

Murmurs rose from the group of deputies sitting in the conference room, and a few hands shot up.

Storm pointed to a female deputy in the back. "Yeah, Marcie."

"Do we know what kind of injuries he might have suffered?"

Shaking his head, Storm answered, "Only speculation. We believe he wore NVG goggles. There wasn't a moon last night, so it was extremely dark. His movement indicated he didn't have difficulty navigating. If he did, the bullet fragments might have shattered the device, and he'd have injuries to his eyes. Injuries that would require the assistance of medical personnel."

Another deputy spoke. "Are we sure the intruder was Yankovic?"

"Yes. Blood samples collected at the scene, and a rapid

DNA test this morning, confirmed the suspect's identity. It was Yankovic."

No other hands rose. Storm continued, "We'll work in pairs. You each have a list of clinics or hospitals to cover, plus, you have a booking photo of Yankovic circa 2015 from New York City."

A hand shot up. "What was he booked on, Dakota?"

"Extortion and sex trafficking."

"Huh. At least he's consistent."

Storm smiled. "That he is." He paused and looked around the room. "If there are no other questions, let's go find this guy."

Mingled conversations and the metallic scrape of chairs scooting on tile flooring filled the room. Jacob Gordon appeared beside Storm. "I don't believe I have ever seen you without Apollo by your side."

"It's a rare occasion. Questioning doctors or nurses with a dog on a leash would be distracting. Besides, it's too time-consuming to get permission for him to enter a clinic or hospital."

Gordon said, "Didn't think of that." He paused. "Since Jimmie Russel is still on sick leave, who's your partner today?"

Storm shrugged. "Thought I'd do it solo."

"Not on my watch. I'm going with you."

"Aren't you needed here?"

"You forget, Dakota, before I was a U.S. Marshal, I worked for a living as a deputy. And I was pretty damn good at this sort of activity. Besides, I'm the boss here, and you don't have a say in it."

With a chuckle, Storm said, "Happy to have you on board, Jacob."

The call came just as Storm and Gordon finished interviewing several nurses at a CareNow urgent care facility on State Line Road. Storm answered. "Deputy Storm."

"Hey, Dakota, this is Marcie. We found an intern who said he treated Yankovic this morning."

"Where are you?"

"University of Kansas Medical Center emergency room on 39th."

"I know where it is. We'll be right there."

Running with emergency lights only, Storm and Gordon arrived at the facility thirty minutes later. Marcie introduced them to the soon-to-be doctor.

Storm asked, "What time was he here?"

"I came on duty at six, and he was in the waiting room. I was told he'd arrived about fifteen minutes till."

"What did you treat him for?"

"Lacerations of the face. Mostly from glass. I had to wash his eyes. His vision will be blurred for a few days."

Marcie walked up to Gordon and Storm and handed a sheet of paper to her boss. "He gave his name as Jefferey Santiago. We checked the address on Google Earth. It's a vacant lot."

Gordon scanned the page and then raised his eyebrow. "He presented a Louisiana driver's license as an ID?"

The female deputy nodded. "The admission nurse said the picture didn't really look like him, but she gave him the benefit of a doubt due to the swollen eye and all the cuts."

Handing the page to Storm, the U.S. Marshal said, "Marcie, get this information to the police and sheriff's departments in the area. Let them know this guy is considered armed and extremely dangerous."

"Yes, sir." She turned and headed out of the emergency room.

Storm read the page and turned his attention to Gordon. "Why this location? How many emergency room facilities are in Kansas City, but he chose this one?"

"Maybe he's staying around here?"

"That's what I'm thinking."

"Okay, I'll pull everyone into this location, and we'll start canvasing the neighborhood."

"While you're doing that, I'll look at the parking lot security videos and see if I can spot the car he arrived in."

"Good idea, Dakota."

Chapter Forty-Six

East of 39th Street and Stateline Road - Kansas City, MO

The basement apartment occupied by the man claiming to be Jeffrey Santiago smelled of stale cigarettes, musty carpet, and fried onions. Alexi Yankovic stared at the bandage covering his left eye and noted the swelling and puffiness of his cheek below the gauze. The sound of a bullet slamming into bricks and mortar less than six inches from his head had left him partially deaf in his left ear. The shrapnel from the shattered bullet digging into his face caused heavy bleeding and immediate help from a doctor.

Instructions about the care of his wounds from a young intern at the ER earlier that morning had been simple. In a *who really cares* attitude, the almost doctor told him to change the bandage daily and to leave it covered for two weeks. Impatience and the urgency of getting Dakota Storm eliminated would accelerate Yankovic's healing timeline.

Returning to the main room of the apartment, he

prepared to use one of his burner phones. Time to contact the other members of Bayou Global. Six attempts later, none of his calls had received an answer. Not a good sign.

Finally, on his seventh try, he heard a tentative, "Hello?"

"It's me."

"Hope you're not in Louisiana."

"I'm not. What's wrong?"

"Not the best place to be right now. I left six days ago and, from what I understand, everyone who stayed there is either dead or under arrest."

Yankovic's breathing rate increased, but he remained silent.

"Cash flow doesn't exist anymore."

"All accounts?"

"Of the ones I checked, all had been seized by the feds."

"Okay, lie low for a while. I'll be in touch." He ended the call. Without hesitation, he dressed, gathered his few possessions, and left the apartment for the last time.

———

With help from the hospital security team, Storm managed to find an image of a heavily bleeding Alexi Yankovic entering the emergency room. The time stamp read 5:46 a.m. Backtracking on other camera feeds trained on the parking lot, they found a shot of him exiting a dark-colored Ford Fusion in a far corner of the designated area.

Zooming in on the car's license plate, Storm used his cell phone to call his friend in Washington.

"Forensics, this is Lisa."

"How're your computer skills this afternoon?"

"Well, what do you know? If it isn't Deputy Dakota

Storm. I've talked to you more in the past few weeks than almost anyone else."

"Got a plate for you to run."

"Which state?"

"Missouri."

"Go."

He told her the make, model, and plate number of the car. He heard the clicking of a computer keyboard and then silence. Finally, she said, "Uh-oh."

"That doesn't sound good, Lisa."

"Well, it's not catastrophic, but it's inconvenient for you."

"What's wrong."

"The plate belongs to a 2002 Chrysler Sebring. Carfax is claiming the vehicle was totaled four months ago."

"Huh." Storm grew silent.

"You still there, Dakota?"

"Yeah, just thinking. Can you cross reference personal property tax records if I give you a name?"

"Sure, but so can you."

"I'm in a hospital security office at the moment."

"Just kidding, Dakota. What's the name?"

"Rolanda Smith."

"Who is she?"

"She was identified as the victim found burned in a Chevy Equinox registered to Bayou Global and driven by Yankovic."

"Oh dear. Give me a moment." The technician remained quiet as Storm again heard a keyboard clicking. Two minutes later she said, "Black 2010 Ford Fusion."

"Bingo. What's the VIN number?"

She gave it to him.

"Lisa, you earned your pay today."

"Always glad to help, Dakota."

The call ended and he returned to where Jacob Gordon stood huddled with four other deputy U.S. Marshals. He handed Gordon his notes and said, "The victim who died in Yankovic's burned-out Equinox was identified, and I just found out she owned a 2010 black Ford Fusion." He showed the screenshot of the parking lot video. "That's Yankovic getting out of a similar vehicle. The license plate on the car belongs to a Chrysler totaled four months ago. Since we have the Fusion's VIN number, we know what to look for and how to identify it."

Gordon nodded. "I'll have all the teams converge on this area, and we'll start searching for the Ford. My bet is it will be around here somewhere."

Most residents were just curious. More than a few panicked and crept out of the neighborhood. The reason being a total of twenty deputy U.S. Marshals converged on the neighborhood. They began the task of inspecting cars and VIN numbers on vehicles parked on the street. Whenever they encountered one of the residents, they showed Yankovic's picture.

A shake of the head sent the deputies on to the next witness. An hour later, Storm walked up to a black Ford Fusion and looked in the driver's window. Blood soaked the seat. He checked the VIN number and then radioed his discovery. He noted the time, 6:16 p.m.

By seven, a small basement apartment revealed fingerprints confirming who the resident had been. According to the woman who owned the house, the tenant had paid for a month's rent less than a week prior. She identified the man from a picture of Alexi Yankovic.

An FBI forensics team showed up and scrutinized the

small area as more and more federal law enforcement types arrived and became involved.

During this circus, Storm walked up to Gordon and asked, "Who invited the FBI?"

"Unfortunately, I was overruled by the Department of Justice."

"Figures."

"Where do you think he is?"

"Jacob, I wish I knew. He's been two steps ahead of us for weeks now, and I'm tired of it."

At the same time Dakota Storm met with Jacob Gordon, the man known at the emergency room as Jefferey Santiago sat on the rear seat of a Kansas City Area Transportation Authority bus heading north. His destination: KCI airport. Not to catch a plane but to steal a car from the long-term parking facility.

When he exited the bus at the terminal, he waited for it to drive away before heading to the long-term parking shuttle bus. Fifteen minutes later, he wandered the lot looking for a specific model of car with the parking ticket stuck in the sun visor. He found one on the last row of the facility. Utilizing a tool purchased at an auto parts store designed for cutting seat belts and breaking safety glass, he broke the window on the side of the car hidden from security cameras. He gained entry in five seconds and had it hot-wired two minutes later.

As he neared the exit, he checked when the car had been parked. Three days prior. He had as little as a day or as many as three or four before the car would be reported stolen.

With the broken window on the other side of the car, he paid the parking fee and headed for the airport exit.

Traveling north on I-29, he pulled off the highway in St. Joseph, Missouri and found a Motel 6 for fifty-eight dollars. The attendant never looked at him; he just took his money. He entered his room a little after ten, and at ten thirty a pizza arrived from a nearby Dominos.

Taking the burner out, he munched on the pizza and dialed the phone number of the associate who had answered the other day.

"Yeah."

"It's me."

"We're more or less out of business, boss."

Closing his eyes for a moment, Yankovic asked. "What now?"

"Feds raided our place in St. Louis. Two dead and four arrested. The last batch of merchandise was confiscated."

"What about funds?"

"Using the records they found in Oklahoma, they've seized the rest of the bank accounts."

Yankovic remained silent for a long time. Finally, he said, "All right. Make sure you disappear. I won't be calling you back."

The call ended, and he threw the small phone at the hotel door.

The next morning, he covered the broken car window with a plastic trash bag he found in his room. At a convenience store not far from the hotel, he filled the car with gas and bought a Kansas state map.

Sitting in the car, eating a breakfast burrito from a McDonalds, he plotted his way back to Lawrence, Kansas.

Chapter Forty-Seven

U.S. Western District of Missouri Courthouse

Apollo, back on duty with his handler, sat quietly next to Storm. The deputy used his computer to search multiple websites for updates on car thefts possibly involving Alexi Yankovic. Gordon walked up to his cubicle and dropped a file on his desk.

"All your hard work paid off, Dakota."

Picking up the folder, he skimmed through a few of the pages. Looking up, he smiled. "Really. All the bank accounts?"

"All of the ones we know about. The records from the sand barge company were critical."

"So, Bayou Global is basically out of business."

"Correct. Only two individuals are unaccounted for: Yankovic and some guy named Erik Maris."

"Never heard of him."

"According to two of the men arrested in St. Louis, he's an accountant."

Storm thumbed through more pages. He closed the folder and looked at Gordon. "I can't find a trace of Yankovic. He's disappeared off the face of the earth. The guy doesn't use social media, and I'm not finding any stolen car reports that might be him."

Gordon folded his arms. "Figures. He hasn't made many mistakes so far."

"So, now what?"

"Until we have something concrete on him, back to business as usual."

Storm placed the file back on his desk. "Understood. But I won't relax until the Russian is behind bars or dead."

"Don't blame you." He patted his deputy on the shoulder. "Excellent work on this, Dakota. The director sends his congratulations as well." His boss walked away.

Storm did not quite share the man's enthusiasm. He stood and walked to the elevator. Apollo followed, and the two rode it to the ground floor.

When outside near the parking lot, he pulled out his cell phone and dialed Frank Cole's number. The call was answered on the second ring. "Good morning, Dakota. I understand congratulations are in order."

The deputy raised an eyebrow. "For what, Frank?"

"Closing down Bayou Global."

"How…" He paused, chuckled, and said, "I forget you have contacts everywhere. It's not over. I don't care what the suits say."

"Oh? What do you know that they don't?"

"Frank, it's the road of least resistance. They want it to be over. So, it's time to mark this off as a major victory for federal law enforcement."

"That's a bit of a negative attitude, Dakota."

"Yeah, well, Alexi Yankovic is still out there, and I don't think he's done."

"What do you mean he's still out there. I thought…"

"They don't have him in custody. He walked away from his apartment in central Kansas City yesterday, right under the noses of the task force. He's not been seen or heard from since."

The ex-CIA operative did not respond immediately. Finally, he said, "As a rule, his type doesn't run and hide."

"Nope, not in my experience."

"What can I do to help?"

"I can't think of anything. I'm going to have to keep my guard up."

"Want me to come over and help with security?"

His feelings about Frank Cole intensified when he heard this. "Thanks, Frank, I appreciate your concern. But there's not much else to do. We put the cameras where you suggested. The kennels are secure and we've installed stronger locks."

"Why don't I take a trip over there tomorrow? I might be able to see something you don't."

"I'd appreciate it, Frank. Thanks."

───────

On the trip back to the academy later in the day, Storm kept going over what other security options he could install to protect the place. On the approach road, he slowed when he saw a silver-gray Kia parked at the entrance to the academy grounds.

After he stopped behind the vehicle, he remembered a memo circulated several weeks ago about certain models of Kia's and Hyundais. The memo explained how thieves could gain access to one of these cars by breaking a window. Once inside, all it took to start the car was to yank down the bottom half of the steering column and use a flathead screwdriver and a USB-A cable. The whole process took less than a minute then the car could be driven off.

He exited his Ford with Apollo hot on his heels. He made a circling motion with his index finger and the dog circled the car several times and then sat behind the trunk. With his Sig Sauer P226 held with both hands pointed down, he circled the car, moving around to the passenger side. The tightness in his stomach increased when he saw the right rear window covered by a trash bag.

Pressing his lips together, he bent down and looked inside the vehicle. The bottom half of the steering column was exposed.

"Shit."

He finished circling the automobile. When he verified it was empty, he holstered his gun and went back to his Ford to use his cell phone.

"Gordon."

"Jacob, I have an abandoned vehicle at the entrance to the academy. Rear window out, and there's evidence the car was hot-wired."

"Stay where you are, Dakota, I'll contact the Douglas County sheriff's department and send backup."

"Sorry, Jacob, I can't do that. Kristin could be in trouble." He ended the call without listening to his boss's response. He unholstered his pistol as he and Apollo headed toward the house.

Storm knew where the motion sensitive security cameras were hidden. He used an app on his phone to switch off the ones he would encounter on his path to the house. If anyone was watching the security monitor, they would not suspect anything.

The sun hung low on the western horizon as he came within sight of the house. He lay low in the prairie grass as he observed the place. Nothing appeared out of the ordinary from this distance. Apollo lay quietly beside him, his eye trained on the house.

A flurry of motion occurred to his left. Apollo looked in that direction and then whimpered. "What is it, buddy?"

Without a sound, Bruno appeared next to him and snuggled against his body. Placing a hand on the dog's head, he whispered, "Good boy." The appearance of the Belgian Malinois confirmed Kristin was in trouble.

Time to move.

Alexi Yankovic concentrated on the video monitor and the different camera angles displayed. Turning to the individual tied to a chair in the room, he growled, "Why aren't the cameras facing the entrance on?"

"Don't know. I didn't set the system up."

Glancing at the woman, he narrowed his eyes. "I think you're lying to me."

Kristin shrugged. "Believe what you wish. It doesn't change the fact I don't know anything about the security system."

"Who does?"

"Who do you think?"

Yankovic stood and walked over to his captive. He swung his hand and slapped her with an open palm. "Don't lose sight of the fact your life is in my hands, bitch."

She glared back at him as a trickle of blood oozed from her nose.

Returning to the video monitor, he used the mouse to try to change cameras but to no avail. The camera on the lower right of the screen picked up a flash of black and white at the very bottom of the view. "Which camera is this?" He turned toward her.

"Northwest corner of the house."

While he glared at her, she kept her eyes on the camera view and saw the black-and-brown coat of Bruno follow the black-and-white streak. She wanted to smile but chose not to.

He returned his attention to the monitor.

Storm checked to make sure the camera trained on his current position remained off. He then made a quick dash for the house. Using his index finger, he made a twirling motion. The two dogs ran hard to get behind the dwelling. With his back against the front wall, he crawled toward the west side. From there, he would stay below the camera angle until he reached the backyard. Removing a panel of wood lattice blocking the underside of the deck, he crawled under the structure at the back of the house. Now in the shadows, he got on his hands and knees and turned. Retrieving the removed section, he propped it against the opening to hide the access point.

After crawling to the middle of the back wall of the house, he located and carefully removed a metal panel leading to the crawl space. Once under the house, he was able to crawl toward the area under the room with the security monitor.

After he arrived, he could hear the conversation between Yankovic and Kristin. He did not like what he heard.

Kristin watched her tormentor turn to stare at her, his eyes narrow and cold.

"Where is he?"

"Who?"

"Your boyfriend."

"I have no idea."

Yankovic stood again and stomped over to where Kristin sat. "I will ask you one more time. Where is Dakota Storm?"

"Probably in Kansas City."

This slap stung worse than the first one. But Kristin refused to let her captor know how much it hurt. Coppery blood pooled in her mouth from a cracked lip.

Bending down to glare at her, Yankovic screamed, "You know exactly where he is. He's out there waiting for me. Isn't he?"

"How would I know that? I've been inside all day."

Yankovic pulled the gun out of his belt and placed the barrel on her forehead. "One last time. Where is he?"

She closed her eyes as the cold steel of the Heckler & Koch VP9 pressed into her forehead. A tear leaked and ran down her cheek. "I don't know. He left early this morning, and I haven't seen him since."

Yankovic withdrew the gun from her forehead. "Lucky for you, I need you alive for a while." He returned to sitting in front of the monitor.

The escape hatch in the laundry room leading to the crawl space, originally designed to allow them to hide if the house was compromised, rose quietly as he pushed it up. He eased himself up and sat on the edge, trying not to make a sound. When Storm stood, he listened. The muffled voices from the room with the monitor told him Kristin was at least still talking. But time was running out.

Walking softly, he reached the kitchen and opened the back door. Both Apollo and Bruno silently entered and looked up at him. He bent down and whispered, "Seek and contain."

Both dogs headed into the interior of the house, followed by Storm.

Chapter Forty-Eight

Southeast of Lawrence, Kansas

Sirens in the distance attracted the attention of Yankovic. "What the hell?" He stood and walked to the room's closed door. Once it opened, two dogs immediately attacked him. The Belgian Malinois went for the wrist of the hand holding the gun. The border collie bit hard on the Achilles tendon of the opposite leg.

Panic seized Yankovic, and he reacted by dropping the H&K before he could pull the trigger. With the searing pain caused by the 1400 pounds-per-square-inch pressure from Bruno's bite, he screamed in agony. At the same time, Apollo managed to do severe damage to the man's lower left leg. He toppled over just as Storm appeared and kicked the H&K out of Yankovic's reach.

"Release."

Both dogs broke off their attack but did not move. They kept their attention on the prone man.

Storm called out, "Are you okay, Kristin?"

"Never better," she lied.

"Bruno." The dog's attention sprang to Storm's face. "Kristin, call Bruno."

She whistled, and the Belgian Malinois rushed inside the room. He heard her cheerfully say, "You're such a good boy."

Blood from Yankovic's leg wound oozed onto the carpet. He stared up at Storm while he cradled the arm Bruno had clamped down on. Yankovic's nostrils flared with his rapid breaths.

Storm held the Sig Sauer pointed at the man's head. Both glared at each other as the deputy's finger grew tighter on the trigger.

When sirens approached the house, Storm took a deep breath and said, "Guard." Apollo growled at the captive. The deputy withdrew his finger from the trigger guard. He holstered his gun and rushed in to check on Kristin. He cut the tape securing her hands and feet with a utility knife. She immediately sprang up and grabbed him around the neck. "Thank you for being you."

Apollo produced a deep growl. Storm returned to the hall and saw the dog staring at Yankovic, teeth bared. The Russian remained silent and did not move.

Douglas County Deputies took control of the scene. The arrival, a few minutes later, of an ambulance allowed one of the EMTs to address Kristin's bleeding lip. Another one attended to Yankovic's wounds. The deputy U.S. Marshal's eyes never left Yankovic as he sat with his back against a wall and glared back.

The Russian's eyes flicked to the weapon on one of the

335

sheriff's deputy's utility belt and then back to Storm. "Don't even think about it, Yankovic," he growled.

The deputy turned to Storm then to the Russian. "What's he doing, Dakota?"

"Eyeballing your service weapon, Steve."

The deputy smiled and yanked the prisoner to his feet. "Hope you bleed to death, dude." The deputy placed cuffs on his wrists. Yankovic wrenched as his injured arm received the pressure of the metal. "Okay, let's go. We'll let the county patch you up. Then you'll get a free ride to the county jail."

The siren on the ambulance with Yankovic inside spooled up. Storm watched the vehicle head out toward the northwest. Kristin, standing beside him, placed her arm around his waist. "How much did you hear?"

"Not a lot. I did hear him slap you." He turned and examined the butterfly bandage on her lip. "How many times did he hit you?"

She closed her eyes as he touched her face. "Twice."

"Glad the deputies got there when they did."

"You had the situation under control."

He shook his head. "No. I had my gun pointed at the man's head and was squeezing the trigger when I heard the sirens."

She gazed into his eyes.

"While it would have felt good at the time, I would probably regret it later."

Placing her hand on his cheek, she asked, "Are your demons gone?"

"Not yet, but they're packing their bags."

She smiled.

Lawrence Memorial Hospital

Yankovic watched carefully as the emergency room doctor stitched up the gash in his leg from Apollo's fangs.

"This is a dog bite. You're gonna need a tetanus shot, and a couple of antibiotics, sir." The doctor looked at the deputy. "Is that okay?"

The deputy standing guard said, "Fine."

The physician stood and walked out of the treatment room. Yankovic looked at the man and said, "They need to put those two damn dogs down. They're vicious."

The sheriff deputy chuckled. "You got off lucky. I saw military dogs rip a man's arm off when I was overseas. That's barely a scratch, Yankovic. Now, shut up and quit your bitching."

The Russian closed his eyes and lay back on the bed. Mentally, he practiced the move he would need to rid the deputy of his service weapon and make his escape. Timing would be critical, and he would have to do it before they put the handcuffs back on him.

He opened his eyes to check on the deputy who had turned his back on the prisoner and was looking out the curtain covering the examination room. Yankovic knew where the scalpel was on the exam table, and he knew how many steps he would need to reach the deputy.

Taking a deep breath, he grabbed the knife and was at the deputy's back in less than a second. He shoved the scalpel with his left hand upward into the base of the man's neck at the same time he reached for the Glock 22 in his belt holster. The deputy was dead before he hit the floor. Yankovic ran down the hallway brandishing the gun and yelling at people to get out of the way.

Twenty deputy U.S. Marshals gathered in the parking lot of the Lawrence Memorial Hospital. The majority were from Kansas, with the rest from Missouri. Jacob Gordon joined Kansas District U.S. Marshal Adrian North in coordinating the search for Alexi Yankovic. Dakota Storm and Apollo were there, along with two other dog handlers from Kansas.

North, a burly barrel-chested man in his fifties, addressed the group first.

"Okay, Deputies, we have a dead Douglas County sheriff's deputy and a stolen ambulance. You each have pictures of Yankovic for ID purposes. Why the hell this clown thought it'd be a good idea to take an ambulance is beyond me. This situation reminds me of a scene in the movie *The Fugitive* when Harrison Ford's character stole one from a hospital.

"They didn't have GPS back then. We do now. Apparently, he discovered how bad an idea this was, since the ambulance was found abandoned on US 59 a little north of Ottawa. He's on foot, as far as we can tell. He's injured and didn't have shoes on when he stormed out of the emergency room.

"We have helicopters enroute to take the dog handlers to the ambulance's location. Each of you will be accompanied by another deputy." He turned to Jacob. "Marshal Gordon, do you have anything to add?"

"Yes. I don't need to explain to you how dangerous this man is. He is now desperate and even more dangerous than before. He is in possession of a Glock 22. Do not, I repeat, do not hesitate to shoot first. Is that clear?"

A chorus of "Yes, sir," filled the air.

The thumb, thumb, thumb of incoming helicopters approached the empty section of the parking lot.

Gordon pulled Storm off to the side. "Dakota, time to put this rabid skunk down."

"Yes, sir."

"You and Apollo know him better than anyone. Let's make this the last time we have to discuss Alexi Yankovic."

"I do hope so, Jacob."

The two men shook hands, and Storm and Apollo ran to one of the waiting helicopters and scrambled aboard. Storm found his partner, Jimmie Russel, already strapped into a seat.

"About damn time you got busy, Deputy Storm."

The two men shook hands. "Where'd you come from?"

"Couldn't get here in time, so I hitched a ride on this chopper."

The aircraft took off and headed toward the south.

Chapter Forty-Nine

Along US 59 Eastern Kansas

On the way to the site of the abandoned ambulance, Storm and newly returned-to-duty Jimmie Russel worked out a plan. Storm, with the assistance of Apollo, would pick up the fugitive's trail and track him on the ground. Russel would stay with the chopper and scout ahead.

"Think we can find him, Dakota?"

"If he can be found, Apollo will."

Russel stared out as Kansas passed below the helicopter. "Had a lot of time to think while I was off."

"Was that a good thing?"

"Not sure. The wife's worried, plus she's expecting."

Storm smiled and patted his partner on the shoulder. "Congratulations, Jimmie. You're finally getting domesticated?"

"Not hardly. But I'm not sure I can concentrate on the job if I'm gone with her taking care of a new baby. You know how this job is. We're here one day then somewhere else the next."

"Couples have been doing it for centuries, Jimmie. It's part of growing up and being an adult."

His partner smiled. "Yeah, I know. My dad always said you have to pick yourself up by your bootstraps and get the job done. What the hell are bootstraps?"

With a chuckle, Storm said, "It's a saying, Jimmie."

The pilot interrupted the conversation over the headsets. "Ambulance coming up on your right, guys. Do you want me to set you and Apollo down, Dakota?"

"Yeah. That's the plan."

When the chopper settled on the highway, Storm and his canine partner jumped to the ground, and the aircraft lifted off again.

A Douglas County deputy Storm knew greeted him with a handshake. "We think he took off to the west, Dakota."

"I need Apollo to sniff around the driver's seat first."

"Sure."

The dog jumped up into the ambulance and sniffed the seat and back of the driver's side section. He then put his muzzle on the floormat for a few moments. Finished, he jumped back down to the highway. Sticking his nose in the air, he looked to the east and then the west. Glancing at his handler, he barked once and started trotting to the east.

Storm turned to the deputy. "I guess the nose knows." He took off after Apollo.

Yankovic watched the helicopter circle the area where he had abandoned the ambulance. He guessed the distance to be at least a mile from his present location. He was barefoot, his leg was bleeding again, and walking on the furrowed land made him stumble on occasion. His destination was an old farmhouse to his right. He held the sheriff's deputy's Glock in his left hand, the right one useless from the attack by the brown-and-black dog.

The helicopter circled closer to his location. He glanced back at the farmhouse and hurried toward an outbuilding he thought he could reach in less than a minute.

———

Storm heard in his earbud, "Dakota, we have movement due east of you about half a klick."

"Copy." He jogged after Apollo who kept his nose to the ground. The dog would stop and occasionally test the air. He would then return his muzzle to the land and continue. Stopping to check his Sig Sauer, the deputy charged it then took off after his partner.

Off to his left, an old outbuilding with chickens wandering around it could be seen. Apollo stopped and sat. Storm knelt beside him and put a hand on his partner. "What is it, boy?"

The border collie's attention remained glued to the outbuilding. Storm stood and moved cautiously, both hands gripping the Sig Sauer as he approached the building.

"That's far enough, Storm. Drop the gun."

The deputy could hear the helicopter approach from his right.

A figure emerged from the darkness of an overhang. "Tell them to back off, or the dog is dead."

"Congratulations on getting this far, Yankovic. How's the leg? It appears to be bleeding again."

"Fuck you, Storm. Tell the helicopter to back off."

"Can't do that."

"Why not?"

"Taking you down is far more important than myself or the dog. You are a fucking maniac, and I'm here to make sure you go back to Lawrence in a body bag."

"Not if you're dead first. Tell the helicopter to back off. The gun's pointed at the dog. I will once again take something precious from you."

Dakota Storm made his decision with that statement. "Left, fast."

Apollo broke out into a sprint to his left. Yankovic mumbled something and brought the Glock to bare on Storm. The deputy already had a bead on the Russian. The Glock fired at the exact moment the Sig Sauer discharged a bullet.

EMTs attended to the shoulder of Dakota Storm as he sat in the back of an ambulance from the hospital in Lawrence. The .40 caliber bullet had passed through muscle without breaking bones or severing any major blood vessels. Apollo sat next to his handler, patient, panting with his tongue out, his concentration totally on Storm. The deputy smiled at the dog and scratched him behind the ears. "It's okay, buddy. You did what you were supposed to do."

Russel stepped up. "Glad your aim was true, partner."

Looking up, Storm asked, "Why?"

"He'd taken an elderly lady hostage in the shed."

"What was she doing out there?"

"Gathering eggs. Wrong place, wrong time."

"What about Yankovic."

"He's got a new hole in his forehead just above his left eye. Righteous shot, my friend."

"Good."

"Kind of what everybody around here is saying as well."

Storm placed his hand on Apollo's head and scratched. "Good boy. You earned your pay tonight."

The rate of panting increased, and the dog rewarded Storm the look the deputy associated with a smile.

Russel said, "Uh-oh, here come the suits." He turned and wandered back toward the outbuilding.

The Western District of Missouri U.S. Marshal smiled as he stood next to his deputy. "Glad you can take orders, Deputy Storm."

"It's over, Jacob."

"Yes, it is, Dakota." He paused and surveyed the area. "Let me guess, Apollo led you to him."

With a nod, Storm said, "Yes, he did."

"Effective immediately, you're on leave to take care of that shoulder. I don't want to see you at the office until your doctor releases you for duty. Is that clear?"

"Yes, sir."

"When you get back, we'll discuss your future with the U.S. Marshals Service."

Storm frowned.

"Don't worry, I've got plans for you. Enjoy your time off. It might be the last you have for a while."

Gordon turned and headed toward a group of reporters gathered around a helicopter.

Taking a deep breath, Storm patted Apollo on the head and said, "Well, shit, buddy. I may have screwed up in reverse here."

Chapter Fifty

Lawrence, KS

Frank Cole sat in a chair on the back deck and appraised the wounded Dakota Storm. "You know, Dakota, staying out of the path of a bullet is one of the first things they teach you in basic training."

"I remember that. Thanks for coming over, Frank."

"My pleasure. I assume we don't need to go over your security system now."

"No. Bayou Global is no more. They even captured the accountant. He was boarding a flight to South America in Miami when a couple of deputy U.S. Marshals walked up behind him and put him in handcuffs."

"I heard about that." He paused for a moment. "How long do you have to wear the sling?"

"Couple of weeks."

Cole nodded. They were alone, Kristin giving them some privacy.

Storm cleared his throat. "Uh, Frank?"

"Yes."

"I'd like to stay in touch."

"I would like that as well. I don't have any other family and, well, I've come to think of you like a grandson."

"I thought you had a son?"

Shaking his head, Cole said, "He died of an overdose a few years after he abandoned Summer."

"I'm sorry."

"It's just the way it is."

"You never told me what happened to your wife."

"Not much to tell. She left me not long after I joined the CIA. She remarried, and that was the last I saw of her. I don't even know where she is now, or if she's still alive."

"So, Summer was your only family."

"Yes." The older man turned his head away from Storm toward the Kansas landscape behind the house. He remained quiet for a while. He finally asked, "Are you and Kristin making plans?"

"Yes. Nothing right now, but someday."

"Good."

"Uh…"

"Go on."

"I haven't filled out my final report yet. I wanted to ask you how much credit you would like on bringing Bayou Global down."

Closing his eyes, Cole laughed. "Absolutely none. In fact, I would appreciate it if you would not even mention my or Peter Khan's involvement."

"I hate taking all the credit."

The older man pointed to Apollo, lounging next to Storm. "Give him all the credit. He deserves it."

"Oh, he'll be a prominent feature in my final report."

"Seriously, Dakota. I would prefer no one know about my involvement."

"Kind of what I thought you'd say."

The two men fell into a silence that lasted five minutes. Finally, Cole said, "You might want to know one of the bank accounts owned by Bayou Global kind of got misplaced by one of my old associates."

The deputy raised an eyebrow.

"Nothing like that. We set up a trust fund for some of Bayou Global's victims. We have their names and are reaching out to the ones we can locate. There should be enough in the fund to help them get their feet on the ground."

"Thank you."

"My pleasure."

The silence fell over the two again.

Turning to the grandfather of his lost wife, Storm said, "I'd like for you to be a part of Kristin's and my life. If we have kids, I'd like to introduce you as their grandfather."

Returning his gaze to the younger man, Cole eyes moistened. "I'd like that very much."

Two Weeks Later

Kristin sat on the bed next to Storm and watched him sleep. She brushed the hair off his forehead.

His eyes fluttered open and squinted in the bright sunlight shining through the bedroom window. "What the hell? What time is it?"

"A little before ten. You slept in."

"Why didn't you wake me?"

"I enjoyed watching you sleep. You seemed so relaxed."

He smiled and scooted into a sitting position. She offered him a mug of coffee.

"Thanks."

"You're welcome. It's Sunday, our official day off. How's the shoulder?"

"It didn't hurt last night. So, I'm guessing it's getting better."

"That's good." She folded her arms. "What do you want to do today?"

"Why don't you get naked and slip in beside me."

"I did that last night. Besides, I had something a little less physical in mind."

"Like what?"

She kissed him on the lips, stood, and let her robe fall. "I'm taking a shower. You can join me, if you wish, or you can finish your coffee. I'll tell you what we're doing when I'm done."

He followed her into the bathroom.

The large home sat on the northwestern corner of a two-thousand-acre cattle ranch. White PVC fencing encircled the land and lined the driveway to the palatial two-story colonial house. Still restricted from driving, Storm sat in the passenger seat of Kristin's Ford F-150 Crew Cab pickup. Apollo and Bruno were in the back, their noses pressed against the glass in anticipation of running on open land.

As they neared the home, Storm said, "This guy's spent more money on the fencing than I did on my first house."

"Raising cattle is a hobby for him. He's a retired lawyer, and his wife was a good friend of my mother's. I've kept in touch with her since Mom died, mainly because she's one of the best dog breeders in the state. Bruno is from one of her litters."

Storm looked back at the Belgian Malinois. His respect for the breed had only intensified since the incident at the academy less than a month ago. "I'm impressed. So, why are we here?"

She glanced over at him and smiled. "It's a surprise."

As they pulled up to an enormous white barn with the appropriate red roof, an elderly lady stood outside and waved.

Kristin said, "That's Delores. When I asked her if we could visit, she jumped at the opportunity to meet you."

With a furrowed brow, Storm trained his attention on her. "She's heard of me, how?"

"Did you know you have a reputation within the dog-breeding community?"

"No."

"Well, you do. I didn't know about it myself until I talked to her and told her what I was searching for. When I mentioned your name, she insisted we visit."

"I still don't understand how she knew about me."

"Dog breeders are a tight-knit community. Word gets around about trainers. You are a legend within the halls of the working-breed group."

Storm stared at her like she had a third eye growing out of her forehead. "You're blowing smoke up my ass."

Her smile told him she wasn't.

She opened the driver's side door. "We're here. I'm anxious for you to meet her."

When Kristin and Storm let the dogs out of the truck, Bruno ran to the woman. She knelt and rubbed his neck. "Oh, it's so good to see you, Bruno." She stood as her guest stepped up. She and Kristin hugged and then she offered her hand to Storm.

"You must be Dakota Storm."

"Yes, ma'am."

Kristin said, "Dakota, this is Delores Flounders."

"It's nice to meet you, Ms. Flounders."

"Call me Delores." She tilted her head and appraised him. "I understand you are on leave from the U.S. Marshals Service."

"I am." He pointed to the restricted movement sling encumbering his left arm. "I had a little incident a few weeks ago. I got in the way of a bullet."

"That's what Kristin told me. She worries about you, Dakota."

He nodded and studied the asphalt driveway where he stood.

"Delores, Dakota doesn't know anything about our surprise. Want to show him?"

"Of course. Follow me."

They entered the barn, and she led them to an area of the interior where Storm saw a border collie in a sectioned-off space. Delores said, "This is Mollie." She turned to Storm. "Mollie is in heat and being kept from other male dogs at the moment. She is waiting to meet Apollo."

Kristin hugged Storm's good arm. "Delores shares my dream of providing service dogs to police departments that struggle to afford a K9 team."

Storm glanced at Kristin and then Delores. His attention returned to Mollie. "If the department can't afford a K9 officer, how do you know they'll take care of the dogs?"

"My husband has volunteered to work out the legal issues. The departments will be highly vetted before a dog is granted to them."

"Who's gonna train them?"

Squeezing his arm tighter, Kristin looked at him. "You."

His breathing stayed steady. But he realized his dream of becoming a full-time trainer might be at hand. Patting Kristin's hand, he said, "Let's see what Apollo thinks of the idea."

Epilogue

Two Days Later

With the sling off, Storm could drive again. Apollo remained at Delores' farm and would be there for another day. Kristin had a full schedule at the academy for the week. As the sun rose, he sat on the back deck drinking coffee and stared off into the distance.

She joined him, dressed in her work clothes. "What are your plans for the day?"

He didn't answer right away.

"Hello, are you with me, Deputy Storm?"

Smiling he turned and nodded. "Thinking."

"About?"

"Since I don't pick up Apollo until tomorrow, I need to make a trip to St. Louis."

She tilted her head. "You need closure, don't you?"

"Yeah, I believe I do."

"Are you sure?"

"Yes. While I will always love Judy and Todd, I need to

say goodbye." He sipped his coffee. "I'd never really accepted the fact they were gone. Until now. A part of me always thought I would wake up one morning and they'd walk through the door."

"Why now?"

"The death of Alexi Yankovic and the demise of Bayou Global brought that chapter of my life to a close." He looked at her and smiled. "I have you and could be on the verge of doing what I've always dreamed about doing."

"What's that?"

"Stepping away from law enforcement to start training dogs full-time."

She reached over and patted his arm. "I'll support you no matter what you decide."

"Thanks."

Chesterfield, MO

The drive from Lawrence, Kansas to Chesterfield, Missouri took four hours. Storm kept the radio off as he drove, his mind finalizing what he needed to do when he got to the cemetery. He parked his Ford SUV on a path in view of the headstone. Draping his arms over the top of the steering wheel, he rested his chin there. He remained in this position for a long time. Memories of Judy and their brief life together flooded over him. A tear leaked from his eye as he thought about Todd. How old would he be now? Was it eight or nine? Would he have played baseball, soccer, or been a studious young man? More tears flowed as he realized he would never know.

He lifted his head and wiped his cheeks with the palms

of his hands. Opening the door, he stepped out and walked to the grave, holding two roses. He placed both of them on the ground above where the casket lay buried.

"The men who did this are no more, Judy. You and Todd can rest peacefully now. They will never victimize young girls again." He paused and looked up at the bright sky above. "I know you can hear me."

Taking a deep breath, he put his hand on the granite stone. "I will always keep you in my heart, but I have to move on for my own sanity." Another pause. "I've met someone who is precious to me, and I plan to marry her, someday. I hope you are okay with it and understand."

The only sounds he heard were birds chirping in the surrounding trees.

"I wish you could give me a sign letting me know you understand." He did not expect one, but the hope she would send a message remained. Staring at the grave, he stayed silent for over twenty minutes. Finally, he said, "Rest in peace, my love." Turning, he walked back to his vehicle.

As he started the Ford, two doves landed on Judy and Todd's headstone.

Understanding flooded over him. The weight of his guilt lifted and he felt free for the first time in years. "I got your message, Judy. Thank you."

More by J.C. Fields

vinci-books.com/seankruger1

A murder with no witnesses. A suspect with no identity. A truth worth killing for.

FBI Special Agent Sean Kruger is hunting a ghost. The suspect in a high-profile Wall Street murder doesn't exist, and every witness account is suspiciously identical. As Kruger digs deeper, he realizes he's not the only one searching—someone else wants the truth buried for good.

Turn the page for a free preview…

The Fugitive's Trail: Chapter One

After descending from the thirty-fourth floor, the elevator doors opened revealing an expansive deserted lobby. Glass and steel comprised the front wall from floor to the top of the atrium four stories above. Crystal chandeliers hung from the ceiling, adding a note of elegance to the otherwise industrial look of the lobby. A firm hand on the man's back pushed him out of the elevator toward the building's entrance.

Two security guards escorted the man. Both were big and muscular, biceps stretching the material of their dark gray suits. One was slightly taller and on the right of the man. The other guard was shorter, to his left and slightly in front. The only other occupant of the lobby, besides the three men walking toward the front door, was at the security desk. He was a tall young black man dressed in a dark blue blazer, white shirt, and tie. He nodded at the guards as they escorted the guest toward the front door.

The man being escorted could see through the front glass a black Suburban waiting at the curb—the same vehicle he had been pushed into earlier in the morning. As the guard in front reached to open one of the building's front doors, he was turned slightly toward the guest, exposing his weapon.

While the guard's attention was trained on opening the door, the guest's left hand extracted the Glock from the belt holster on the man's right hip. At the same time he was reaching for the gun, his right leg lifted. With as much force as he could, he kicked at the leg of the taller guard behind him. His shoe slammed into the kneecap of the man's left leg, which bent in the wrong direction and the guard collapsed screaming in pain.

His left hand, which now held the Glock, rose and the trigger was pulled twice. The shorter guard was forced back against the adjacent glass door and collapsed. The now unescorted man rushed through the door in front of him, turned to his right, and ran.

Before the guard at the front desk could get out of his chair, the entire incident was over. The man had disappeared into the crowd on the street.

The lobby guard hurried over to the two men on the floor, saw a pool of blood spreading under the shorter guard. The taller guard was writhing on the floor, trying to straighten his now ruined left leg. Hurrying back to his desk, he picked up a phone and dialed 911.

The driver of the black Suburban sat stunned as he watched the man rush out of the building, turn right, and disappear into the midday crowd. He slammed the Suburban into park, opened the door, and rushed into the building. As soon as he was through the front doors, he stopped.

His first sight was the carnage of the dead man slumped against the glass and the shattered leg of the other. At the same time, his cell phone rang. Glancing at the caller ID, he sighed. The pending conversation would not be pleasant.

Staring out the window of his thirty-fourth floor office, Abel Plymel realized he had made a hasty decision, a decision made in anger. He needed the man alive.

Turning back to his desk, Plymel picked up his cordless phone and dialed the cell phone of one of his security guards. It went unanswered, totally unacceptable. He paid them to answer their phones twenty-four seven.

He dialed the cell phone of the second guard, no answer. Finally he called his driver, who answered on the fourth ring. His eyes grew wide as he listened then suddenly threw the handset at his office door.

The Fugitive's Trail: Chapter Two

Standing in the front room of the now empty house, it seemed alien to him. Not the place where he'd raised his son. Looking around the room, he smiled, opened the front door, and stepped out. He twisted the knob to make sure it was locked, closed it, and walked to his new car parked in the driveway, a Ford Mustang. Sitting in the driver's seat, he stared at the house for several minutes before making a call on his cell phone. It was answered on the second ring. He said, "Sandra, this is Sean Kruger."

"Sean, I was just about to call you. Did the cleaning service do a nice job?"

"Yes, they did. They left about ten minutes ago. Thank you for recommending them. Please let the Carsons know I'm out of the house a day early."

"They'll be thrilled. Have I told you how much they love the house?"

"Several times, Sandra."

"And the neighborhood, their little girl is already planning sleepovers—"

"Sorry, Sandra, I don't have a lot of time. I just wanted to tell you my keys are on the breakfast bar in the kitchen."

Sandra was quiet for a second and then said, "I'll give the Carsons a call and let them know."

"Thank you for all your help these past few months. I wish I could talk longer, but I'm late for an appointment."

"You're more than welcome. Why don't you call me after you settle into your new condo. We can have dinner." She paused for half a second. "My treat."

Hesitating for a few seconds, he finally said, "I'll do that." Although he knew he never would. He ended the call and smiled. Sandra O'Dell was a nice person and a very good real estate agent. But, if he had not cut her off, she would still be chattering about sleepovers. As for the dinner, the thought of listening to her for several hours made him shiver.

He sat in the car for a few seconds, then opened the door and stood up to look at the house one last time. It had been his home for seventeen years. A lot of good memories were here: his parents moving in to help raise his then one-year-old son, the joy of watching them interact with their grandson on a daily basis, watching a little boy turn into a bright and talented young man. There were also sad memories.

Finally, after staring at the house for several minutes, he sat back down in the car, started the engine, backed out of the driveway, and accelerated the Mustang toward his new home. It was the first day of a new chapter in his life.

The condo was a newly renovated two-bedroom unit on the west side of the Kansas City Plaza. The extra bedroom would serve as his office and a place for his son Brian to sleep when home from college. One of the reasons he had chosen this particular unit was the open living space. The living, kitchen, and dining area were all one room separated only by a breakfast bar in the kitchen. But the main reason he liked the place was the balcony. It had a clear view of the Plaza, which was spectacular at night.

Fifteen minutes later, the Mustang was parked in his designated parking slot. It was approaching dusk and the shadows from adjacent buildings were growing long. He sat quietly in the car and thought about the hectic and emotional four months since his mother's death. The doctors had told Kruger it was a heart attack, but he disagreed. He had a Ph.D. in psychology and knew the mind was far more complicated than most people imagined. His father and mother had been married for sixty years, marrying right after high school. Something died inside his mother when his father passed away two years ago. She would put on a happy face and say nothing was wrong. But Kruger could tell she was hurting. Finally, after Brian moved away for college, she quietly passed away one night in her sleep.

Even as a non-practicing Catholic, Kruger believed in a hereafter. He was comforted with the concept of his mother and father together again. But occasionally doubt crept into his faith. As one of the FBI's premiere profilers, he had seen the darkest recesses of the human psyche. And sometimes he wondered how a benevolent God would allow such terrors to occur. But that was for religious philosophers to debate, not him.

As he opened the car door, he heard a woman scream, "Let go of me, you bastard."

His first reaction was to draw his service pistol, a Glock 19, and run in the direction of the voice. As he rounded the northwest corner of the building, he saw two muscular, tattooed young men: one white and the other black. The black guy was holding a woman by the arms as the white guy dug through her purse. Kruger was fifteen yards away when he stopped. Taking a Weaver stance, he yelled, "FBI, on the ground *now*."

The black guy was startled and released the woman, who quickly ran toward Kruger. The white guy turned around, stared at Kruger, and said, "Shiiiittttt, you ain't no FBI. Show me a badge, mutafukr."

Kruger yelled again, *"On the ground now!"*

The black guy looked at Kruger and then at his partner. He appeared to be choosing whether to get on the ground or run. The white guy threw the purse on the ground. Reached behind his back and pulled out a snub-nosed revolver. As the guy raised the revolver in his direction, Kruger didn't hesitate and fired the Glock twice. Both shots hit their target. The white guy dropped the revolver and grabbed his chest. Two circles of red appeared high on his chest and shoulder. He dropped to his knees and then fell back. The black guy bolted in the opposite direction as fast as he could. Kruger quickly moved to the fallen gun and kicked it aside, still pointing his Glock at the man on the ground.

He looked back at the woman, saw she was okay, and reached for his cell phone. He punched in 911 as he trained the Glock on the prone assailant. He said to the operator, "My name is Sean Kruger; I'm a special agent with the FBI. I have shots fired and a man down. I need an ambulance and a squad car." He was asked for the address, which he gave and ended the call.

The white kid stared up at him with wide eyes. The blood loss was moderate. Kruger did not offer assistance and kept the Glock pointed at the man. Within five minutes, a patrol car arrived and one of the two officers told Kruger to drop his weapon and stand aside. Kruger complied, laying the Glock on the ground. He put his hands above his head and backed up ten steps. One patrolman checked the wounded man, and the other officer cuffed Kruger and led him to their squad car.

Within ten minutes, five patrol cars and two ambulances occupied the parking lot of Kruger's new condo. He watched from the back seat of the patrol car as the wounded man was placed on a gurney and loaded into one of the ambulances. As it sped away, a Kansas City police sergeant opened the squad car's back door and leaned in.

"You want to tell me how you got involved."

Kruger stared at the police officer and said, "The lady was in trouble, I helped her out."

"You live around here?"

"Yes, second floor, apartment A."

The sergeant continued to stare at Kruger. "Lady lives on the second floor also and she's never seen you before."

"Because I just moved in today, *sergeant*." Kruger spat out the police officer's title with as much sarcasm as he could muster. "Are you going to take these cuffs off?"

"Not yet, just cool your heels." The sergeant shut the door and walked away.

Sitting back in the seat with his hands cuffed behind him was difficult and uncomfortable, but he managed. Dusk had turned to night and the area was bathed in the artificial glow of street lamps, police car headlights and the rotating blues and reds of their emergency light bars. Finally after another fifteen minutes elapsed, a man in a suit opened the door.

"You Kruger?"

Nodding, "Yes, who are you?"

"Detective McAdams. Get out."

Swinging his legs out of the squad car, Kruger leaned forward and stood. McAdams reached around and unlocked the cuffs. "Sorry about the cuffs, Agent Kruger. Your story checks out."

Kruger rubbed his wrists, trying to get the feeling back. He said, "May I talk to the victim?"

The detective shrugged and nodded his head in her direction. "Suit yourself, you're free to go."

As he was walking toward the woman, she rushed to him, hugged him, and said, "Thank you. I'm not sure what would have happened if you hadn't come along."

Surprised by her embrace, he limply returned the hug and said, "Glad you weren't hurt. My name's Sean Kruger."

The woman backed away, smiled, and said, "I'm Stephanie. I really don't know how to thank you, Sean. I've never been in a situation like this."

"Well, to be honest with you, it's a first for me too."

Stephanie smiled and said, "One of the officers asked me if you lived around here. I've never seen you before. Do you?"

Nodding, Kruger said, "I bought 2A and just moved in today."

She stared at him for a few seconds and said, "I moved into 2B a week ago, but I've been out of town on business. I had just gotten home from the airport when those two grabbed me. Hope this isn't a common occurrence around here."

Shaking his head, he said, "This can happen anywhere. It's safe—at least that's what I was told."

She smiled. "Good, I like the area. And with a good-looking FBI agent living next door, I feel even more secure."

Kruger returned the smile. It had been a long time since

he had enjoyed a conversation with a woman. The conversation felt out of place in this situation, but he didn't care. He immediately liked her. She was a petite woman in her late thirties or early forties, several years younger than he was. She was strikingly beautiful, with naturally curly brown hair she wore touching her shoulders. Her pale blue eyes sparkled in the streetlights of the parking lot, and her smile was infectious. Realizing he was staring, he said, "I'm glad you feel safer." He chuckled. "Hell of a way to meet your new neighbor."

She brushed the hair off her forehead, tucked her newly returned purse under her arm, looked up at him and smiled. She said, "It will be a great story to tell our grandchildren." She walked over to the police sergeant, thanked him, and headed toward the building's rear entrance door.

Kruger watched as she opened the door, walked through it, and disappeared into the building. Not really sure how to take her last comment, he decided it was going to be fun trying to find out.

Stephanie Harris climbed the one flight of stairs to her condo. She was intrigued by this man who had just prevented something very unpleasant from happening. The ability to assess individuals quickly had allowed her to rise to the level of senior vice president of sales at a large greeting card corporation. Her assessment of Sean Kruger was very positive. Maybe it was an infatuation with the white knight coming to her rescue, or a high school–type crush, she didn't know. Her experience tonight should have left her shaking and concerned about the safety of her new residence. But it didn't. Knowing he was next door gave her comfort. The decision was made; she wanted to get to know this tall, good-looking FBI agent.

She unlocked her front door, walked to her bedroom and threw her purse on the bed. Exhausted from her business trip and the parking lot incident, she changed into jeans and a baggy sweatshirt. After checking her messages on the phone, she had an idea. Since he wasn't wearing a ring on his left hand, she assumed he wasn't married. But she wanted to find out for sure. She grabbed her apartment keys and walked to his front door.

Kruger was unlocking his door when Stephanie walked up to him and said, "Hi, I didn't properly introduce myself when we met in the parking lot earlier. Too many distractions, I guess."

He smiled and said, "You could say that."

She offered her hand and said, "Stephanie Harris, Mr. Kruger."

Shaking her hand, he said, "My dad was Mr. Kruger. I'm Sean. It's nice to meet you, Stephanie Harris."

"I really appreciated what you did in the parking lot. Do you think that young man will be okay?"

He nodded. "Probably. One of the patrol officers told me before I came up, both the white guy and his partner were well known to the local cops. In fact, they already had the black guy in custody. Both were out on parole. I imagine this little incident will change that status."

"Good. But, I would really like to thank you properly. Can I buy you dinner tomorrow night at a place of your choosing?"

He shook his head. "No, I'm afraid that won't work."

"Oh... I'm sorry, I mean..." She paused for a few moments, looking disappointed, "I didn't realize you were married."

Kruger laughed. "No, I'm not married, that's not what I meant. I'm a little old-fashioned. I'd love to have dinner with you tomorrow night. But you can't pay for it. I will. Since you've lived here a week longer than I have, you get to pick the restaurant."

Smiling, she said. "Houston's. It's my favorite place. Knock on my door at seven."

The Fugitive's Trail: Chapter Three

NEW YORK CITY

NYPD Police Detective Preston Alvarez was approaching his mid-forties and had over twenty years in the department. During those twenty years, his blue-gray eyes had seen a lot. This morning he saw barely controlled chaos as he pulled up to the crime scene. At least ten patrol cars sat parked around the office building. Their light bars were rotating and reflecting off the building's glass façade.

An EMT vehicle was just pulling away from the scene, its light flashing and siren screaming. He pulled in behind a patrol car and put his unmarked detective car in park. Pushing his rimless glasses up to the bridge of his nose, he stepped out and stared up at the building, forty stories of glass reflecting the midmorning sun. He ducked under the crime-scene tape, gave his badge number to a patrolman with a clipboard, and walked through the unblocked side of the glass front entrance.

A crime scene tech was taking pictures of a body on the floor to his right, just inside the front entrance. A patrolman stood next to him, watching. Alvarez said, "Any witnesses?"

The patrolman nodded and pointed to a black man dressed in a dark blue blazer standing next to the large reception desk. The desk was situated in front of a bank of elevators. The witness was talking to another patrol officer with three stripes on his sleeve. Alvarez walked over to the two men, showed his badge, and said, "I'm Detective Alvarez. What's the story here, Sergeant?"

The sergeant turned to Alvarez and said, "This is David Leonard. He mans the security booth for the building. He was here when the incident occurred." The sergeant turned to Leonard. "Tell him what you just told me."

Leonard stared at the sergeant and then at Alvarez, his eyes wide. "Man, the guy moved like lightning. One second he's walking between these two big guys and the next, the big guys are on the ground and he's running out of the building."

"Whoa, slow down," said Alvarez. "Who did what to whom?"

"Well, see, the two big guys, they work for P&G Global on the thirty-fourth floor. They brought this guy in thirty minutes before all this happened. That's when, see, they pushed him out of the elevator and walked toward the front door. The shorter guy—I don't know his name, but I see him and the taller guy all the time with Mr. Plymel. See, the smaller guy was in front; the taller guy behind. Anyway, see, the guy in the middle is looking scared, man, real scared. Just as they're going out the front door, the guy in the middle does this karate thing, and man, just like that"—Leonard snapped his fingers—"the guy kicks the guy in back in the knee. He grabs the gun off the hip of the guy in front and shoots him. He did all of that in one fluid motion, man—one fluid motion. Man, he was fast." He paused and shook his head. "I never seen anything like it. It looked more like a movie stunt, but it was real. He then pushed the front door open and ran that way." Leonard pointed to the right side of the building.

Alvarez said, "So they brought him in thirty minutes before all this started. Is that what you're telling me?"

Leonard nodded. "Yeah, man, thirty minutes. I checked my computer log. I'm supposed to keep track of who comes and goes."

Alvarez wrote in a small notebook and said, "Do you know why he was brought here?"

Leonard shook his head. "Nah, I don't ask questions man, I just watch the lobby."

Alvarez nodded. "Okay, Mr. Leonard, don't go anywhere. I'm going to the thirty-fourth floor and see what they say." He pointed at the sergeant and said, "Would you come with me?"

The scene on the thirty-fourth floor was the same as the lobby: police officers talking to various individuals, and crime-scene investigators taking pictures. As soon as Alvarez walked out of the elevator, a man several inches shorter and in a very expensive suit walked up to him.

"Are you in charge of this investigation?" the man asked.

Alvarez stared at the man. "Who are you?"

The shorter man snorted. "I'm Abel Plymel, CEO of P&G Global. Have you caught the man responsible for this mess?"

Alvarez shook his head. "Not at the moment. We're trying to find out what happened."

Plymel's face reddened. "Isn't it obvious? A man stormed in here and started threatening my employees. My security guards subdued him and escorted him out of the building. Now one of them is dead and the other severely injured. What are you doing about it?"

Alvarez frowned. "He stormed in here?"

"That's what I just said. Are you deaf?"

Ignoring the last comment, Alvarez turned to the sergeant standing next to him. "Go back down and see if you can find any more witnesses. I'll stay here and try to straighten out the conflicting stories."

The sergeant nodded and headed back to the elevator.

Plymel continued to glare at Alvarez.

Alvarez said, "When you say 'stormed in,' what do you mean? We have a witness that said he was escorted by two men into the building."

Plymel turned and looked at a taller man standing a few feet away and then looked back at Alvarez. Alvarez watched as the taller man turned, walked to a hallway, and quickly vanished out of sight. Plymel said, "Just that. The elevator opened and this crazed man steps out and starts threatening our associates. He was very belligerent and knocked a vase of flowers off the receptionist's desk. Then he started yelling. When we confronted him, he threatened everyone with bodily harm."

Alvarez nodded and wrote in his notebook. "Who saw the man?"

"I and several staff members tried to reason with him. He wouldn't settle down. That's when our two security guards forced him back into the elevator."

Nodding again, Alvarez said, "Okay, I'll need to talk to each of the individuals who were involved. Is there an office I can use?"